SIX

D0381378

Books by Charles W. Sasser

Nonfiction

The Walking Dead (w/Craig Roberts)
Homicide!
Always a Warrior
In Cold Blood: Oklahoma's Most Notorious Murders
First SEAL (w/Roy Boehm)
Fire Cops (w/Michael Sasser)
Doc: Platoon Medic (w/Daniel E. Evans)
Raider
Magic Steps to Writing Success
Crosshairs on the Kill Zone (w/Craig Roberts)
Going Bonkers: The Wacky World of Cultural Madness
The Shoebox: Letters for the Seasons (w/Nancy Shoemaker)
Devoted to Fishing: Devotionals for Fishermen
The Sniper Anthology
Back in the Fight (w/Joe Kapacziewski)
The Night Fighter (w/Captain William Hamilton)
One Shot/One Kill (w/Craig Roberts)
Shoot to Kill
Last American Heroes (w/Michael Sasser)
Smoke Jumpers
At Large
Arctic Homestead (w/Norma Cobb)
Taking Fire (w/Ron Alexander)
Encyclopedia of Navy SEALs
Hill 488 (w/Ray Hildreth)
Patton's Panthers
God in the Foxhole
None Left Behind
Predator (w/Matt Martin)
Two Fronts, One War
Blood in The Hills (w/Bob Maras)

Fiction

No Gentle Streets
Operation No Man's Land (as Mike Martell)
Detachment Delta: Punitive Strike
Detachment Delta: Operation Iron Weed
Detachment Delta: Operation Cold Dawn
OSS Commando: Final Option
No Longer Lost
The Return
Sanctuary
Shadow Mountain
The 100th Kill
Liberty City
Detachment Delta: Operation Deep Steel
Detachment Delta: Operation Aces Wild
Dark Planet
OSS Commando: Hitler's A-Bomb
War Chaser
A Thousand Years of Darkness
The Foreworld Saga: Bloodaxe
Six: Blood Brothers
Six: End Game

SIX™

END GAME

CHARLES W. SASSER

Based on the New HISTORY TV Series

Skyhorse Publishing

SIX: End Game (an A+E Studios™ production) was adapted from the teleplays written by:
Episode 105: Karen Campbell
Episode 106: William Broyles & Bruce C. McKenna
Episode 107: David Broyles & Bruce C. McKenna
Episode 108: David Broyles & Alfredo Barrios Jr.

Visit our website at www.skyhorsepublishing.com.

10 9 8 7 6 5 4 3 2 1

Library of Congress Cataloging-in-Publication Data has been applied for.

Cover design by Erin Seaward-Hiatt
Cover image courtesy of A&E Television Networks, LLC

Print ISBN: 978-1-5107-2726-7
Ebook ISBN: 978-1-5107-2727-4

Printed in the United States of America

To the brave men and women of US Special Operations

Introduction

***Previously in* SIX: Blood Brothers**

A US Navy SEAL Team Six operation into Afghanistan's Kunar Province to capture or kill high value target Hatim al-Muttaqi went bad when team leader, Senior Chief Richard "Rip" Taggart, shot and killed a wounded American jihadist under questionable circumstances. Taggart resigned from the SEALs, a bitter and beaten man, and sold himself out as an international security specialist to SyncoPetro, a US oil company operating in Nigeria.

During the opening ceremony for a new grade school sponsored by SyncoPetro near Benin City in Nigeria, Boko Haram terrorists kidnapped Taggart, oil executive Terry McAlwain, his PR man Nick Rogers, Nigerian driver Hakeem, and a young African schoolteacher named Na'omi along with several of her preteen female students. After Boko Haram warlord Aabid discovered Taggart's identity, he released a video in which he threatened to decapitate Taggart at the end of one week unless he received a ransom of ten million dollars.

The abduction created an international news blitz. Michael Nasry, a terrorist leader under Hatim al-Muttaqi's Umayyad Caliphate, a loose affiliate of ISIS and Boko Haram, discovered that the abducted former SEAL, Rip Taggart, was the man who killed his brother in Kunar Province two years previously. Seeking revenge, Nasry plotted to circumvent his boss, al-Muttaqi, and wrest Taggart from Boko Haram using Chechen extremist soldiers.

Since the 1999 Chechen uprising against Russia, Chechen extremist Islamists had allied with ISIS, al-Qaeda, Boko Haram, and other terrorist groups to fight against "infidels" throughout the Middle East and Africa. However, their loyalty to any particular group proved tenuous at best. Through another minor terrorist leader, Akmal Barayev, himself a Chechen, Nasry obtained a force of Chechen soldiers to plot with him against Aabid to seize Taggart.

With time running out, Taggart's former SEAL teammates led by Chief Joe "Bear" Graves worked desperately to effect the rescue of a brother SEAL. CIA and Intel ops led Graves and his team to an abandoned village in Nigeria where the hostages were held by Aabid and his jihadist soldiers. They blew through the village only to discover to their astonishment that the Boko Haram terrorists had fallen to treachery and been gunned down by a Chechen force. After a brief bloody firefight with a Chechen stay-behind element, SEALs defeated them and swept through the village to search for Taggart and the other captives.

They were too late. It was a dry hole. Chief Graves and Petty Officer Alex Caulder spotted a blue SUV and a military-style Humvee truck racing out of the village. Nasry, Barayev, and surviving Chechens were carting Taggart and the other captives out of Nigeria and toward neighboring Chad, where they became hostages held by al-Muttaqi and Nasry. The stakes had been raised.

During the firefight, Petty Officer Beauregard "Buck" Buckley, the team's machine gunner, was critically wounded. Even as he was being medevaced from the village, the team faced the prospect of continuing rescue operations against an even stronger and more ruthless foe before Nasry succeeded in a conspiracy to not only revenge himself against Taggart but also to use him as part of an overall terrorism plot.

Chapter One

Abandoned Village, Nigeria

The abandoned village that had been occupied by Boko Haram was once more a ghost village of greasy huts with tar paper or sagging tin roofs, empty goat pens, discarded possessions strewn about, and yawning empty window frames. A village of the damned and the dead. Boko Haram and Chechen soldier bodies lay in various grotesque positions among the huts and rubble.

Team members Joe "Bear" Graves, Ricky "Buddha" Ortiz, Alex Caulder, Armin "Fishbait" Khan, and Robert "Ghetto" Chase Jr. watched the Black Hawk medevac helicopter, their faces uplifted, until it disappeared on its way back to the warehouse staging area near Lagos. Team machine gunner Beauregard Jefferson Davis "Buck" Buckley had lain unconscious on the gurney as the bird winched him and the PJ pararescueman into its belly. The quiet ones died. If they were still talking, there was still hope.

"PJ said Buck was bleeding out," Chase remarked in a distant voice. No one replied. Chase was in his mid-twenties, muscular, clean-shaved, his hair trimmed short. A recent Harvard grad, he gave up academia and the Ivy League to enlist in the SEALs. Next to Buck, he was the youngest and newest member of the team. Buck and he had gotten close.

Buck might have been on the team's minds, but they were still on mission. Team leader Bear Graves drew in a deep breath and raised command on his radio. "Reaper Three Three, this is Foxtrot Delta One. What do you have on vehicles egressing to the north? Over."

"*Delta One, Reaper Three Three. They are under tree cover at this time. Over.*"

Bear, who stood two inches over six feet, big and mean, was the team's core of implacability and inner quiet. This was no time for melancholy over Buck. That would come later.

"Stay on track," he said to the team. "Me, Buddha, and Chase will sweep the huts for any signs of the hostages. Fish, you and Caulder check the bodies and gather intel—cell phones, whatever you can find."

Before he was hit, Buckley and his machine gun had given a good accounting of themselves, knocking out the enemy's heavy weaponry and laying down cover fire to give the rest of the team room to maneuver. Graves picked up several expended 7.62 rounds off the ground from Buck's gun. He looked at them, shook his head, and handed them to Chase.

The team split up to its assigned tasks.

The body of the Chechen leader who died at the beginning of the fight lay sprawled next to a pair of bullet-riddled SUVs he and several of his men had used as cover. Caulder photographed the corpse for the After Action debriefing. Next to the dead fighter lay a pistol and an AK-47 equipped with laser optics attached to an adaptive rail system. Caulder looked it over and summoned Fishbait.

"Ever seen an AK rigged like that?" he asked. All business now, he was normally the team's free spirited bohemian, a sharp and angular man with a sarcastic sense of humor and skepticism verging on pessimism.

"Look at his kit," Khan pointed out. Fishbait was an Afghan immigrant with swarthy skin and black chin whiskers.

"This shitbird isn't Boko Haram, that's for sure," Caulder noted. "How many we got?"

"Eight. These are soldiers, Alex. Not terrorists. Trained and geared up."

Caulder activated his voice mic and passed the information along to Graves. "Delta One, Delta Six, we've got eight unknown kilos. At least one with a comm set and rail system with laser sights on his AK. Over."

"Bag the kilo with the radio," Graves instructed. "We'll take him to the safe house."

"Roger that."

During the earlier sweep-through action when the SUV and Humvee were spotted fleeing the village, Caulder had located an empty hut at the village square that appeared likely to have housed prisoners. Although it seemed likely the hostages had been cleared out with the escaping vehicles, Graves, Ortiz, and Chase would check it out for proof that Taggart had been among them.

The three men eyed a ten-foot-tall wooden cross erected in the square. Crudely constructed of rough-hewn timber, by all appearances it could have been the same one upon which Christ had been crucified at Calvary. Dried blood on the crossbeam and on the upright at foot level spoke of torture and some sort of sacrilegious mockery.

No need to ask what had gone on here. The only question was who. Taggart? Someone else?

The cell-hut was a small dilapidated structure with slatted wooden sides and a rusted tin roof. Graves and his two teammates entered to find the bullet-filled body of a large, long-limbed African male propped against the inner wall by the door. That his pistol remained holstered indicated the man, whoever he was, had apparently trusted his executioners up until he was gunned down. Again, this spoke of major treachery.

Iron rebar divided the hut into two separate cells. On one side, the SEALs discovered in the dust of the earthen floor small bare footprints, one set larger than the others, which apparently belonged to a woman and children. On the male side were large shoe prints, obviously made by men. So far, all signs fit the profile of those Boko Haram that had kidnapped from the schoolhouse near Ebo Village outside Benin City.

"Those poor little girls," Ortiz murmured.

A thick wooden stake had been driven into the dirt floor of the male section. Tethers hanging from it signified someone, a male, had been tied to it. Senior Chief Taggart?

Graves pointed to a bowl left in a corner of the hut. "Bag that," he said. "We need DNA samples to see if Rip was here."

While Ortiz bagged the artifact in a Ziploc bag and Graves squatted at the stake trying to get a feel for what happened in this wretched hut, Chase left to continue a search of the surrounding area. There was little doubt in Bear's mind that Rip had been here. The cross outside, the stake here, with blood smears on both . . . Terrorists throughout the world hated US SEALs, who were apt to show up anywhere, anytime, like avengers out of the shadows. Any Team Six SEAL who ended up in terrorist hands might well wish he had been cast into Dante's Inferno instead.

Chalk marks at the base of the stake attracted Graves's attention. Moving closer, squinting in the hut's dim atmosphere, he made out crude letters scribbled in chalk: *F D 1.* Buddha knelt next to him to look at what appeared to be someone's initials.

"Foxtrot Delta One," Buddha read—Rip's call sign when he was team chief.

"Fuck!" Graves exhaled, and pounded the post with the meaty side of his fist. "We just missed him."

He got on the radio. "All nets. We have confirmation Taggart was here. No evidence of any other hostages. Over."

"*Foxtrot Two Two copies. Be advised, the Nigerian Army is en route. You have ten minutes.*"

While the United States had coordinated with the Nigerian government for a clandestine in-and-out mission, that agreement would not cover for a village full of dead men. This could be political dynamite if troops arrived before the SEALs got the hell out of Dodge.

Things, however, were about to become more complicated. Ghetto Chase, who had been out in the village kicking around, seeing what he could find in the way of evidence or clues, came up on the radio net. "*Delta One, Delta Six. I found a fresh grave on the east side of Building One One. Over.*"

Bear's eyes locked with Ortiz's. *Taggart!* Graves tamped down on rising panic as he and Ortiz shot out of the cell-hut on a dead run to Chase's location at the edge of the village. Caulder and Fishbait had beat them there and were with Chase staring down at a freshly turned grave.

"Do we have a shovel?" Bear wanted to know

"Bear, we got to get out of here," Caulder warned.

Graves turned on him, his jaw set. "I need a fucking shovel."

His eyes burned on the breeching crowbar attached to Chase's pack. He snatched it and dropped to his knees next to the grave and began frantically burrowing into the loose mound of dirt. The others looked at one another uneasily. They had to find Taggart, if he lay in the ground. On the other hand, they likely found themselves in deep doo-doo if the Nigerians arrived before they got out.

The crowbar proved worthless. Bear cast it aside and used both hands to claw out the dirt, like a dog digging for a gopher. After a moment, Caulder fell to his knees to assist. One by one the others joined the effort—first Ortiz, followed by Chase and Fishbait. *The Team*. Even as they dug, each of them dreaded what they might uncover.

Graves struck something first. He probed until he felt a head and hair. He exhaled sharply, his senses stung by the stench of decay. Girding themselves, the SEALs threw out handfuls of soil to reveal the outlines of two corpses, one of which lay face down on top of the other. They gradually exhumed both, a sight so grisly that Ghetto's stomach turned and he had to struggle not to retch in front of the others. Harvard had not prepared him for this.

Holding his breath against the stink of death and his own apprehensions, Graves brushed off the dirt-matted faces in order to make an identity. To the relief of everyone, neither one was Taggart. Caulder was the first to let out a sigh of relief.

They were white men however. One was an older, heavier man, the other quite a bit younger with the heft of a college football player. The faces were hideous with early stages of decay, but enough remained to identify them from photos displayed during mission briefings. They were Terry McAlwain and Nick Rogers, the SyncoPetro oil executive and his PR man abducted with Taggart and the schoolteacher Na'omi and her students. Each had died from a single gunshot wound to the head. Executed.

"Come on. Let's get them out," Graves urged.

Their ten minutes before Nigerian troops arrived had narrowed down to five.

Chapter Two

Nigeria

Earlier, before Michael Nasry and Akmal Barayev arrived in the Boko Haram village with their two Chechen bodyguards to bargain for the SEAL Taggart, warlord Aabid ordered Taggart taken down from the cross in the village square and returned to his cell. The American was barely conscious from the abuse he had suffered over the past several days and looked much older than a man in his early forties. His face was blood-crusted and bruised, his eyes swollen. Lean and wiry to begin with, he had lost considerable weight off his six-foot frame from days of captivity and torture and near-starvation. His face looked sharper even through the swelling, making him appear hollow and gaunt.

Terrorist guards dumped him on the dirt floor of the holding cell-hut where the females were being detained. Only three students of those kidnapped remained behind with their teacher: twelve-year-old Esther, eleven-year-old Kamka, and nine-year-old Abiye, who was small for her age and wept often. Their schoolmates had been trucked off shortly after the kidnapping to be sold as "wives" or sex slaves.

Shortly after Taggart was dumped back into the holding hut, Aabid entered with a tall, skinny man in his twenties in casual European wear. This man had a long, narrow face and bushy eyebrows.

"Your new masters are here," Aabid announced triumphantly.

"So we meet again," said the bushy-browed stranger with open loathing. He sounded American. He looked vaguely familiar, but Rip failed to place him.

Meanwhile in the forest nearby, two SUVs full of Chechen soldiers that had followed the negotiating party received the signal to move in.

Taggart's "new master" nodded at his bodyguard, a man armed with an AK-47 and kitted out in modern military gear down to armor and webbing. This guy didn't look Middle Eastern, and certainly not African. Without question or comment, he tilted the muzzle of his assault rifle and with a burst of fire sent Aabid to Paradise to claim his seventy-two virgins.

Moments later, gunfire erupted all over the village. It didn't last long, a matter of two or three minutes before all went quiet again. The invaders, all of whom were in uniform, had apparently pulled a fast one on Aabid and his motley crew and wiped them all out before they had a chance to fight back.

At first, Na'omi and her girls were ecstatic with joy, thinking they were being rescued. Even Rip was fooled by Aabid's execution. Aabid was a vicious psychopath not worth the price of the lead that blew him to Hell, which was where he would probably end up rather than in Paradise.

The captives were quickly disabused of the notion that they were being freed. Rather, they were merely transferring from one ownership to another. The new owners quickly took possession, bound the captives' wrists, and prepared them for departure. It seemed to Rip that they might have been rescued from the frying pan only to be tossed into the fire.

The invading soldiers were ransacking the village for weapons and other contraband prior to departure when they in turn were surprised by a separate unknown attacking force.

A sense of urgency suddenly infected the Chechen conspirators as firefights raged nearby on the outskirts of the village. Taggart, Na'omi, and the three schoolgirls were tossed into the enclosed cargo area of a

The Seattle Public Library

Southwest Branch

Visit us on the Web: www.spl.org

Checked Out Items 6/26/2019 12:48

XXXXXXXXXX0310

Item Title	Due Date
0010094362703 Six : end game	7/17/2019

# of Items: 1

Renewals: 206-386-4190

TeleCirc: 206-386-9015 / 24 hours a day

Online: myaccount.spl.org

South Park Branch reopens

June 10 at 1 p.m.

military-style Humvee manned by a driver and a soldier. It gunned out of the village amid the nearby crackle of gunfire, speeding recklessly along a dusty road beneath forest canopy behind a blue SUV occupied by the man with the American accent, his coconspirator, and two other Chechen soldiers.

"Who are they?" Na'omi whispered to Rip. The truck's cargo bay was close quarters with Taggart, the teacher, and the three girls all thrown on top of each other.

"I don't know," Rip replied. "But they're pros."

"And that gunfire after—What was that?"

The thumping of helicopter rotors passed low overhead before turning and heading west toward the coast.

"No talking," the soldier in the front passenger's seat snapped, almost as though he feared the chopper would overhear. Taggart tracked the distinctive sound of the Black Hawk helicopter until it faded away.

A short distance ahead of the Humvee, the speeding blue SUV kicked up a plume of dust that all but blinded the Humvee driver. Nasry held the front seat of the SUV with the driver. Akmal Barayev and the other soldier held down the back seat. Barayev was a Chechen who had made his bones fighting with al-Qaeda when he was sixteen years old. He and Nasry worked with the Ummayyad Caliphate, a loose affiliate of ISIS, whose operational head was Emir Hatim al-Muttaqi, Michael's and Akmal's superior. Their successes within previous weeks included the bombing of the American embassy in Tanzania that killed sixty people and destruction of the hotel at the Dubai Film Festival that wiped out another two hundred or so.

Akmal was on the radio desperately attempting to raise the commander of the Chechen soldiers who assisted Nasry and him in seizing the SEAL from Boko Haram in order to avoid paying the ten-million-dollar ransom that Aabid asked. Akmal's voice grew thin and strained when he received no response from the village. He repeatedly called out the commander's name. The commander, Bashir, was his brother-in-law.

"*Bashir . . . Bashir? Bashir, baz you h'un suiyazeh,*" he pleaded in Chechen. "*Bashir . . . Bashir? Bashir, this is base.*"

He waited. Still no response. "*Bashir! Akmal vu h'un iz.*"

"Stay in the forest," Nasry reminded the driver in Arabic. "The trees shield us."

Barayev was persistent on the radio. "*Khu tchoh'isa . . . Any troop, respond.*"

Still nothing except static. Anxiety stretched Akmal's long, full face even longer.

"They were American," he said to Nasry, switching to English. He leaned forward across the back of the front seat. "I know it. If any of our men survived, they will break them. They will talk. Michael, we can't stay in Africa."

Nasry shrugged. So some of the Chechens had been killed, perhaps even all of those left in the stay-behind force. Michael was nonetheless satisfied with the outcome. He had the SEAL who killed his brother some two years ago in Afghanistan, and, for him, that was sufficient for the mission to have been a success.

"We take the hostages to the facility in Chad—as planned," he informed Akmal.

"Muttaqi will have us both shot. We're dead men. Is that stupid SEAL worth it?"

"Yes, he is worth it. Muttaqi will understand, even if you don't."

Chapter Three

Nigeria

After a forced march cross country to avoid the Nigerian Army, Bear Graves led his band of warriors into the forest-surrounded clearing that had served as operational rally point and launch site for his and Master Sergeant Mule's teams against the Boko Haram village. The men were quiet, withdrawn, and concerned over the condition of their wounded comrade. Last they heard, Buck Buckley was in critical condition.

The attempt to rescue Chief Taggart had also failed. SEALS scrubbed and serialized the ORP to erase all signs of their having been here as they prepared to load back onto the nondescript cargo trucks that had transported them from the warehouse staging point near Lagos just that morning. Loaded, the trucks barreled west, driven by local assets and CIA handlers.

The foul odor of death clotted the air in the enclosed cargo bay of the truck occupied by Bear Graves's team. The decomposing corpses of Terry McAlwain and Nick Rogers lay wrapped in a tarp at the back of the truck, along with the freshly killed Chechen leader. Graves and Ortiz rode the bench on one side of the truck with Chief Mule and some of his men. Caulder, Fishbait, and Chase sat across from them in the near-stifling stench and half-light inside the truck. All were filthy from the fight and from having dug up the grave to recover the bodies of the two oil men.

Graves raised command at the warehouse on his radio. "*Foxtrot Two Two, Delta One. Do we have a sitrep on the CASEVAC? Over.*"

Graves waited for the response while the others watched intently through the dusty gloom. Bear was the only one still wearing his comm headset. The others depended upon him for news about Buck.

"*Delta One, Foxtrot Two Two,*" replied a calm, impersonal voice in Bear's ear. *"Your wounded is now KIA."*

Bear slowly removed his headset and stared down at his hands. Buddha nudged him gently, unable to withstand the suspense. "Bear?"

Graves lifted his head and looked across at Caulder, Fishbait, and Chase. They leaned toward him.

"Buck . . ." Bear's voice caught in his throat. "Buck didn't make it."

The rumble of heavy truck tires on the rutted roadbed filled a long silence during which no one moved or spoke. Ortiz held out his hands and squinted to see them in the dim light. Buddha had dragged Buck to cover after he was wounded in the fight, patched him up, and fought off the enemy. Now, his hands were stained with Buck's blood and caked with mud and red dirt from having helped dig up the grave.

Caulder's eyes riveted on Graves as he waited for some reaction, *any* reaction. Instead, Bear sat numb and unmoving with his eyes closed and his expression controlled, quietly suffering with the rest of the team for a loss that hit them hard and deep in their souls.

Chapter Four

Virginia Beach

During World War II when a soldier, Marine, sailor, or airman shipped off to war, it meant he was in for the duration. He kissed mama and the kids good-bye at the wharf and they likely wouldn't see him again until the enemy was defeated—if they saw him again at all. Same thing for the Korean War. Vietnam was somewhat different in that a typical tour of duty was around one year. If a soldier served that year successfully, he went home again.

The War on Terror that began with 9/11 and, shortly thereafter, the deployment of US troops to Afghanistan was the longest-running war in American history. Soldiers who fought in the early days of Afghanistan in 2001 now saw their sons and daughters fighting in Afghanistan. While deployments were assigned for a specified period of time, units could expect multiple future deployments at unspecified times as required.

Special Operations forces, and especially SEAL Team Six, faced a joltingly different type of war than any of the conventional outfits. For them, the war was continuous, year after year. A dozen or more deployments into combat were not unusual.

One day a fighter from Special Operations Command might find himself knee deep in mud, blood, and shit. The next day he was home again dealing with domestic problems like house payments, dental bills for the kids, daughter's homework, leaky plumbing, and his wife's quarrel with the neighbor. It was a schizophrenic way of life, always on the edge of death in Afghanistan, Africa, Iraq, Syria, or some other shithole plagued by the lice of terrorism—and, then, suddenly back to the edge of a PTA meeting.

Before Rip Taggart's wife Gloria split with him and he split with the Navy and the SEALs, she complained to the other wives that the two of them had not actually been on the same continent together much more than a year total during the past five years of their marriage. She finally could take no more of the stress of repeated missions in a strange war that never seemed to end. The war was as hard on wives and families as it was on their men.

No matter the war, however, one thing was a constant: some men never made it back.

The C-17 with Chief Bear Graves's team aboard, including Buckley's body, put wheels down at Naval Air Station Oceana in the predawn of a lovely spring Virginia morning. Graves, Caulder, and Ortiz took their ritual decompression pancakes at the Gulfstream Diner on the beach. Decompression was unusually quiet and sober this morning in dread of the team leader's unpleasant task that had to be done right away. Even Caulder found no enthusiasm for flirting with the blonde waitress he had been banging.

Afterward, with the sun climbing, Graves and Caulder piled into Bear's GMC pickup to carry out the most demanding duty of a military leader—that of informing a comrade's wife that she had become a widow. The two men rode in complete silence, each lost in his own thoughts. Buck's Lone Star flag that he displayed in his equipment cage at Command lay neatly folded on the seat between them. Buck had been a die-hard Texan.

Buck and his wife, Tammi, had purchased a home together before the op into Nigeria. It was a modest little two-bedroomer in Cedar Crest, the off-base housing tract where many SEALs from Command lived with their families. Graves steered his GMC onto Buck's and Tammi's street. He had lost track of time since he was gone, but today must be either Saturday or Sunday since school seemed to be out. Some kids were racing skateboards on the quiet residential streets. Two laughing grade-school boys and a little girl waved heartily at the passing truck. Glancing into his rearview mirror, Bear saw the boys furiously kicking their skateboards along while the little girl chased after them waving her arms. It was a normal day in normal suburbia where normal people lived.

Caulder looked out and up through the windshield at morning sunshine streaming down through Boston pear trees and maples lining the street and dappling their leaves with nuggets of gold. Graves pulled the pickup into the drive of a little sea-green frame house and killed the engine.

Tammi, Buck's petite young wife, must have seen them drive up. Flushed and sweating from her morning routine workout, she burst out the door smiling and waving and wearing a yellow top and blue short-shorts as she removed her earbuds.

"Where's that asshole husband of mine?" she called out, laughing.

Caulder grimaced. "Damn! We beat the chaplain here."

Bear gripped the steering wheel, staring grimly out at the young woman who remained totally unaware of events in Africa a half-globe away that had made her a widow since yesterday. Caulder laid a hand on his team leader's shoulder and squeezed.

"I got this one, Joe."

Graves waited in the truck with poorly contained grief while Caulder got out to meet Tammi on the lawn to inform her of news that would forever change her life. The look on Caulder's face stopped her in her tracks and froze the happy smile on her face. Tears began to form even before Caulder said a word. Her collapse from an ebullient wife joyfully meeting the morning and the return of her husband was immediate and total. She staggered back under the sudden burden with a terrible cry of agony. Caulder caught her before she collapsed.

Bear drew a deep breath to fortify himself and forced himself to get out of the pickup with Buck's folded Texas flag. He walked slowly toward Tammi, delaying things as long as he could. Men like Graves sometimes found it difficult to deal with their emotions.

"Joe. . . ?" Tammi wailed, not wanting it to be true, not wanting the day to have ever dawned.

Bear hesitantly offered her the flag. "From his cage—"

Tammi snapped. She cried out in anger and disbelief and slapped the flag from Bear's hands. She bolted back inside the house, slamming the door. Caulder looked at Bear. The familiar Caulder with his Dennis the Menace smile seemed lost forever, replaced by a much older, more cynical, and immensely sadder man.

He followed Tammi into the house, leaving Bear standing alone on the lawn. Bear heard children laughing from down the block, a mockingbird in the maple tree singing through its repertoire. With great effort, he bent over and picked up the flag, gripping it in his hands from the hurt welling inside his chest that he feared he would never be able to release.

Chapter Five

Virginia Beach

A death in the brotherhood touched surviving teammates in various ways. Not that all weren't affected. It was just that Buck's passing for Fishbait Khan and Ghetto Chase, who were without wives and children, posed a different equation than for Graves, Ortiz, Caulder, and their families. Families were a part of the grieving process and therefore complicated it through a combination of increased tension, sudden relapses, and hidden fears unexpectedly exposed.

It had been Graves's and Caulder's unpleasant duty to inform Tammi Buckley of her husband's death. Afterward, Caulder and Graves met the rest of the team at SEAL Command for required After Action debriefings involving everyone from White Squadron commander Lee Atkins to the CIA and State Department. Atkins advised there would be a further special hearing on the circumstances surrounding Buck's death within the next day or so.

Ricky Ortiz drove home with no stops along the way. It was a Saturday afternoon with the sun's rays slanting through trees lining the streets of his neighborhood in Cedar Crest. Jackie and the kids—Anabel, fifteen, and Ricky Jr., ten—were not yet aware of his return from deployment. They were exiting the family minivan in the driveway when Ricky pulled his Fusion in behind them.

R.J. wore his Little League baseball uniform, Anabel had apparently just finished a lesson at dance school, and Ortiz's wife was collecting a stack of pharmaceutical sales binders from the open hatch. She was dressed for work as though she had attended a sales meeting while the children were occupied. Seeing her like this—classic Latina beauty with her lustrous black hair and long, well-trimmed legs in a business suit—Ricky thought he had never seen any other woman quite as lovely. God, he was happy to be home and, calloused as it sounded, happy that he had not been the one killed in Nigeria. He would never have to leave home again as soon as Rip was rescued and he left the Navy and the SEALs to accept that job at GSS as its head of security.

The kids rushed to greet him, surprising him with their enthusiastic welcome. Usually, he was lucky if he got a "Hey, Dad" upon returning from a mission.

"Dad!" R.J. shouted joyfully.

Followed by Anabel's, "Daddy!"

"Hey, you two. I missed you guys."

He planted kisses on their faces and held them as tightly as they held him while he cast an inquiring look at Jackie. The news about Buck must have already made the dailies and TV. He gasped a long, tired breath.

"I told them about Buck," Jackie explained.

Ortiz nodded.

"Are you okay, Daddy?" Anabel demanded anxiously.

"I don't want it to be you, Dad," R.J. agonized.

Ricky tried to allay their fears with a quick, "Hey! I'm bulletproof, remember?"

Over Anabel's head he caught the desperately yearning look in Jackie's dark eyes. It said she needed to hold him so she could be sure he was really back safe. She smiled at Ricky, gave him a quirky eyebrow lift, and turned to the kids.

"You two run down to the Dairy Queen and get a treat," she invited.

"But Dad just got here," R.J. protested.

Anabel had caught the look between her parents. She got what the offer was really about and laughed. After all, she *was* fifteen and boys were paying attention.

She and R.J. embraced their father once more and set out for the Dairy Queen with a bill Jackie slipped into her daughter's palm. They paused at the edge of the lawn to wave back. Ricky and Jackie promptly headed for their bedroom, laughing and holding each other. They couldn't get their clothing off quickly enough.

Following their bittersweet reconnecting after the shadow of death had passed over, Ricky picked up a change in his wife's mood. Tears filled her eyes and she began to weep deeply and from the heart. In attempting to comfort her, Ricky found himself also emotionally overcome. Tears flowed as they held each other close.

Things were far from normal at Alex Caulder's run-down, Cape Cod–looking fishing shack on the beach; it had an additional fixture—Caulder's fifteen-year-old daughter Dharma whom he had recently rescued from the Virginia Beach police station. His ex-wife Erica had gone to a yoga convention or something and left Dharma with her weenie-necked live-in as the adult in the home. Predictably, Dharma ended up in trouble at school over a protest demonstration. Caulder was just beginning to get reacquainted with the kid and accustomed to her all-in-black aura, including black lipstick and black eyeliner. Everything about her was dark except for the white skunk streak down the middle of her unruly hair.

The shack seemed to match Alex Caulder's bohemian nature as much as black matched his gothic daughter. Gray paint peeled from the exterior like scales from a wound. An upended surfboard on one side of the porched front door balanced an old car seat with exposed rusted springs on the other side. Ricky Ortiz thought the house resembled a poor man's version of the haunted house from the old *Psycho* movie.

The interior of the house was cluttered with climbing and diving gear, books thrown randomly about, posters on the walls of Bob Dylan and *The Grateful Dead*, Tibetan flags strung across the ceiling, a parachute canopy draped over the sofa, a full-mount standing black bear snarling in one corner—and now a prodigal daughter returned.

The last light of day fading into the orange and pink of sunset placed the shack's interior and exterior in a new and better light. Caulder came out of the shower in jeans and T-shirt. He dried his hair with a towel while Dharma examined a snapshot on the fridge door showing Caulder, Buckley, and the rest of the team mugging while on deployment to Afghanistan back when Rip Taggart was still team chief.

"What was he like? Buckley?" she asked.

He didn't want to discuss it with his daughter. "He was an asshole who believed in aliens."

"And you don't?" Dharma shot back.

Caulder almost smiled, but not quite. He didn't want to encourage her; next thing, she'd be trying to move in permanently. After only a few days, the kid was already expanding into his space. He snatched her sweatshirt and a sock off the floor and tossed them at her.

"What did I tell you about unpacking?"

She plopped down on the sofa, opened her laptop, and looked up at him. "You know," she said, "it's okay to open up about what happened."

So now she was playing the shrink?

Caulder shrugged dismissively. "Buck died a Viking's death, doing what he believed in."

"Wow!" she mimicked in the same flippant tone. "That's deep. Really."

Caulder searched around for a clean shirt in a basket of laundry next to the stuffed bear.

"Shouldn't your mom be home by now?" he hinted.

Dharma ignored him. Wearing a pensive look and tone of voice to match, she said, "My best friend, Tyler, he committed suicide a year ago. Did it with a shotgun."

She stuck her finger in her mouth to indicate a gun barrel.

"So it was a closed casket," she went on with her one-shouldered shrug. "I couldn't see his face. But I needed to, you know?"

She took note of how he turned his back to slip on a clean T-shirt. She suspected he didn't want her to see his face.

"I made a video for him, with pictures and music. I could do the same for your friend," she offered. "Maybe show it at the funeral or something?"

Caulder considered it as, dressed in his faded jeans, T-shirt, and black Birkies, he escaped toward the door to pick up the blonde waitress from the Gulfstream Diner. Having a teenage daughter in the house cramped his home love life.

"But I'm going to need some pictures," Dharma added, looking around and sweeping the place with an expansive gesture. "And you don't have very many."

He closed the door on her and fled toward his red-and-purple Bronco with the top chopped off.

Drinking Wild Turkey raw from the bottle, Bear Graves hid himself away in his home garage workshop while he brooded alone. Buck was dead. Rip Taggart was as good as dead in the hands of the Chechens.

He sorted through a box containing Buckley's personal possessions from his cage. He stared for a moment at one of the Texas Lone Star patches Buck wore on his armor vest. He sighed and took another slug from his bottle. Maybe, he conceded, Buddha had the right idea getting out of the SEALs to live a normal life. Guys sitting at a desk were rarely shot by jihadists and rogue Chechen terrorists.

Lena entered the garage workshop from the kitchen door and walked up to him. His wife was blonde with startling blue eyes and a lithe figure from running triathlons.

"How you doing?" she asked, touching his cheek with her fingertips.

"I'm fine."

He didn't sound fine.

"Wives are coming over soon to prep for tomorrow," she said. "We could use a little help."

Buck's memorial was to be held in Joe's and Lena's large living room. Friends, family, and other SEALs from the base were all expected to attend. Instead of Graves responding to Lena's hint, he gestured at the box he was going through.

"I packed up most of his stuff. From his cage. Bunch of crap. I'll get the rest tomorrow. Don't know why he kept it all in there."

"Want me to take it for Tammi?"

Joe wouldn't look at her, wouldn't look at anyone when he was hurting. To restrain his hands from trembling, he clasped the edge of the shop table and braced himself, head lowered and thick shoulders hunched against his arms.

"I'm supposed to protect my men," he lamented in a low, hoarse voice, not much more than the sting of a bad breeze down a dark alley. "I'm supposed to be the good damned shepherd."

Lena attempted to reassure him. "It's not your fault," she said. She reached for him, but he backed off. He didn't want to be touched.

"You don't know that," he snapped.

She took his hand anyhow. "It's not your fault, Joseph."

Joe's body stiffened. He glared at the box of Buck's things. "*You don't know that!*"

He tossed down another slug from the bottle while still refusing to meet her eyes. Lena looked hurt and walked away. He watched her go. *Damn! What was wrong with him that he couldn't let her in? She was the only person in the world who had ever truly loved him.*

Chapter Six

Chad, Africa

The two vehicle convoy led by Michael Nasry and Akmal Barayev escaped Nigeria across a stretch of unguarded border into neighboring Chad in the middle of a moonless night. Chad had won its independence from France in 1960 and had been in almost constant turmoil since then. As one of the poorest and most corrupt nations in the world, and with over half of its population Muslim, Chad afforded fertile ground for radical Islamic groups like ISIS and Boko Haram.

At daybreak, the SUV and the Humvee were out on the more arid Sahelian belt where they soon approached an abandoned and isolated cement plant set on a dry open plain clumped here and there by stunted forest and, along the banks of streams, more tropical canopy. The Soviet Union had constructed the plant during the Cold War and abandoned it following its dissolution. It hadn't been used since, until now.

The plant's main buildings and its various components—the mill, kilns, preheating tanks, and various other support construction, shone a dull gray-white from age and coatings of limestone. Roofs were missing and walls collapsing. A chain-link fence enclosing the plant had fallen into disrepair and was laced with spindly acacia trees and thorn bushes.

The SUV approached ahead of the trailing Humvee and entered a cavernous loading bay area through wide double doors. The SUV cut its engine in the midst of at least fifteen armed Chechen and Middle Eastern soldiers surrounded in this semi-dark shithole by clutter, cement dust, and discarded and broken equipment. It was a place even cockroaches and snakes might avoid.

The driver and guard in the Humvee jumped out among the waiting soldiers. After a flurry of greetings and news sharing about what had happened to fellow soldiers at the Boko Haram village, the Humvee operators swung open the truck's hatch to reveal Rip Taggart, Na'omi, and three small African girls crammed inside with their hands tied behind their backs. Soldiers unloaded the prisoners, rough handling Taggart and the schoolteacher, but surprisingly more accommodating of the frightened and wide-eyed children.

From long training and habit, Rip absorbed his surroundings for future reference—the platoon of soldiers armed with Chinese-made assault rifles and garbed out in combat fatigues, the condition and former purpose of the building in which he found himself, and its isolation. He was not completely surprised at the presence of the Chechens. He had run into Chechen jihadists based in the tribal mountain havens along the Pakistan-Afghan border. They stood out among the Taliban and al-Qaeda–aligned militias for their ferocity and refusal to surrender. Weeks before the Kunar episode, Rip and his team were present at a major battle along the Pakistan border where NATO's International Security Assistance Force killed scores of foreign fighters, including Arabs and Chechens.

The American jihadist stood to one side and watched the unloading of the prisoners. His narrowed eyes bore into the former SEAL with the type of hatred that eroded heart, soul, and mind. It seemed to be all he could do to contain his rage and bitterness as soldiers herded the captives into the darker musty shadows at the back of the massive structure. The SEAL still did not appear to recognize him.

"What's wrong?" Akmal Barayev asked

Michael smiled. "Nothing."

But his eyes told a different story.

Chapter Seven

SEAL Command, Virginia Beach

Alone in Buckley's gear cage at the Cage House, Bear Graves finished packing the last of Buck's personal possessions into a box—his iPad, a few photos, foreign coins, other odds and ends. His go-to-war personal gear had already been duffel-packed. Team items like weapons, parachutes, climbing rope, scuba, and such were returned for recycling or redistribution. Bear sealed the last box with packing tape and straightened to look around at the empty shelves and bare walls of what had previously been Buck's "office." A man never seemed to leave much behind when he checked out. Caulder with his peculiar Zen bent of mind had once quoted a poem called "The Indispensable Man," which Bear recalled whenever he started feeling overly important.

Take a bucket and fill it with water
Put your hand in it up to the wrist.
Pull it out and the hole that's remaining
Is a measure of how much you'll be missed . . .

Point being, there was no such thing as the indispensable man—although at times such as these a man left a hole in your soul that took longer to fill back up than when you stuck your hand in a bucket of water.

In packing Buck's gear, Graves was primarily keeping himself and his mind occupied until White Squadron Commander Lee Atkins summoned him to his office for a special review about what transpired at the Boko Haram village that led to Buck's death. Atkins could not ask any question that Graves had not already asked himself dozens of times before. Had Bear made the right decision in rushing to the village when it appeared possible enemy vehicles were on the way there to endanger Rip and the other hostages? Should he have waited?

The other team members—Caulder, Ortiz, Fishbait, and Chase—were being interrogated first to get their reaction before Commander Atkins got around to the team leader, who was ultimately responsible for decisions made in combat. Decisions such as like those in the case of Buck that could get men killed.

Ortiz entered the cage after having concluded his session in the commander's office.

"You're up," he informed Bear. "We got your back."

Bear nodded and strode off across the team room with its open parachute canopy across the ceiling, a cutout of Osama bin Laden on a wall dart board, and the full-sized nude lamp with a lightbulb shining in her crotch. Like Buddha and the others, Graves wore starched work-aday cammies for the event. He left the team room and walked down the hallway to Commander Atkins's corner office.

Alex Caulder had followed Ortiz on the hot seat and was leaving the office when Bear arrived for his hearing. They exchanged glances and Bear went on in. Commander Atkins sat behind his wide polished desk, elbows on top of the green blotter and hands tented underneath his chin. He was a tall, rugged-looking man in his forties with a crew cut and a scar clip across his chin. Next to his desk stood Captain Pearson, also a big man but whose muscle was starting to turn to fat in his fifties.

"Hi, Joe. How you doing?" Commander Atkins greeted.

"Good to go, sir."

"You remember Captain Pearson?"

Was he Department of Navy? Had the commander's review tuned into an official inquiry?

"He wanted to talk to you about how things went down in Nigeria," Commander Atkins explained.

Graves remained standing at semi-attention in front of the commander's desk.

"Talk us through your decision-making up to Petty Officer Buckley's death," Atkins invited.

"Yes, sir." Bear paused to collect his thoughts. "The ISR drone identified a group of vehicles heading toward the target compound. I used the Rover to track them . . ."

The portable Rover screen shared a direct electronics link with a high-flying overhead Predator drone, a spy in the sky. The screen revealed four vehicles en route to the village—two ahead trailed by two others far enough back not to be noticed by those in front.

"But after we lost the vehicles in the trees I made the call to ingress immediately and proceed with the rescue of the hostages. They might have been at risk. We patrolled toward the target compound and encountered no resistance . . ."

The team first stumbled upon dead Boko Haram bodies that appeared recently executed and not killed in combat. Team members thought they might have heard gunfire at one point during the patrol march, but were too far out to be sure.

"While securing the target, we encountered hostile fire from an organized enemy," Bear continued matter-of-factly, his outward demeanor belying the chaotic intensity of his recollection.

"We engaged and it was at this point that Petty Officer Buckley was wounded."

Ortiz and the PJ pararescueman from Senior Chief Mules's support team tended the wounded SEAL behind one of the huts while the rest of the SEALs put down resistance. At some point during the chaos, some group hustled Rip Taggart and the other hostages out of the village.

Captain Pearson's critical blue eyes raked over Bear. "You could have aborted the mission earlier, when you were notified of unidentified vehicles on-target," he pointed out. "It was clear you did not have tactical advantage."

He followed up that blunt statement with a gotcha question. "Were you being too aggressive?"

"No, sir. No such thing," Graves responded.

Captain Pearson lifted a skeptical eyebrow and darted a glance at Commander Atkins, who remained neutral.

"No such thing?" the captain repeated in what to Bear sounded like mockery. "This command relies on you to exercise restraint where appropriate. Are you saying you can't do that?"

"No, sir," Graves replied too quickly to conceal the fact that he was rattled by Captain Pearson's questioning of his competency.

"It was my call, sir," he added more firmly. "We had good intel and the hostages *were* there."

Captain Pearson nodded noncommittally. "And do you still think it was the right call to make?"

"Yes, sir. I do."

He realized he failed to either look or sound entirely convinced of it. Even worse, Captain Pearson and Commander Atkins also seemed unconvinced.

Chapter Eight

Virginia City

Beauregard Jefferson Davis Buckley's folks were evangelical Christians from Texas. The setting for his funeral service might well have come from a *Saturday Evening Post* cover by Norman Rockwell—a "Little Brown Chapel in the Dale" complete with a bell and steeple in a rural-like scene on the outskirts of Virginia Beach. American flags in ranks snapped in the breeze. The choir sang "Amazing Grace" and "A Closer Walker with Thee." Preacher Seabolt wore a black suit like an old New England circuit riding preacher from the eighteenth century. He took the pulpit behind Buck's flag-draped casket and selected his message from a Bible that looked worn enough to have been carried a thousand miles by horseback. *For them we know what love is: Jesus laid down His life for us, and we ought to lay down our lives for our brothers . . .*

The "Little Brown Chapel" was packed by an attendance that consisted of the team and most of the SEALs from White Squadron and their families, along with friends and acquaintances. The women and girls dressed up appropriately for the occasion, as did the men and boys in suits and ties. All except for Bear Graves, who wore slacks and an open-necked shirt with the tail hanging out. After services, an Honor Guard of SEALs properly folded the flag off the casket four square with only the field of blue showing. Tammi sat in the front row between

Buck's parents, Don and Barbara. She hadn't stirred all during the services; she sat stone-faced throughout glaring at the casket.

Bear solemnly approached her carrying the flag in both palms. He stood before the widow and Buck's parents at attention while the attendance waited.

"I'm dressed like this because it's what Buck wanted," he explained, and swallowed hard from his discomfort. "He always said, 'Boys, I'm just a country boy. Anything happens, don't shave and get all spiffed up for me."

He presented the flag and, afterward, strode briskly to the coffin where he removed from his pocket a Trident, the Special Warfare Badge presented to every SEAL applicant who endured and completed the rigorous training that qualified him to wear one of the most recognizable and coveted badges in the US military. Bear thrust it aloft for all to see.

"Buck wore this Trident on his dress uniform," he said. "All SEALs do. It's supposed to symbolize that we are masters of the sea. You know. All that good stuff they tell us when we get it. But for me, the Trident means—"

He paused to compose himself. The dropping of a feather would have echoed throughout the chambers.

"—for me it stands for what we are willing to pay. All of us. For each other. Today, Buck picked up the tab. Buck, he was—"

That was as far as he could go. Speechless, he stood frozen in place holding the Trident aloft until Buddha Ortiz rescued him. Buddha came forward and nodded at his team leader. He took his own Trident, turned to the coffin and hit it with the heel of his hand so that it stuck to the wood. "Go with God, *hermano.*"

Fishbait stepped up and knelt with both hands splayed on the casket. "*Inna Lillohi inna ilaihi raji'un,*" he said in tribal Pashtu from Afghanistan. "*Indeed we belong to God, and to Him we shall return.*"

He stood and popped his Trident into the casket lid in line with Buddha's.

Alex Caulder came next. "'Till Valhalla," he said and tapped his badge into the wood.

Chase walked up, looked down at the coffin. Tears filled his eyes. He used his thumb to push his badge into the wood until it stuck.

It was Graves's turn. The others of the team waited, watching him. At last, relying on ritual, he placed his Trident on the wood, took a deep breath, and slammed it in.

After the team properly paid respect, the rest of White Squadron, beginning with Commander Atkins, lined up at the casket and each popped his Trident into the wood. The pounding sounded like gunshots—*Bang! Bang! Bang!*

Chapter Nine

Chad, Africa

An advance party of Michael Nasry's recruiters—four young Middle Eastern men and two women wearing *hijabs*—arrived at the abandoned cement plant in Chad and set up shop in a line of dusty offices full of decrepit and broken chairs, file cabinets, and gray metal desks, most of which remained reasonably intact. The recruiters swept out the offices, wiped down the desktops, and stacked various papers, documents, and files written in Russian, Chechen, or Arabic on the various work spaces. Table top computers, laptops, and satellite TV receivers occupied portable worktables situated in each office.

Since the arrival yesterday of Michael Nasry, Barayev, and the few surviving Chechens, Michael and Akmal remained absorbed either in front of their laptops or glued to the TV ready to pick up any news about the raid on the Boko Haram village in which hostages had changed hands from one terrorist group to another. Among the duties in al-Muttaqi's operation, Nasry, as an acknowledged expert on social media, was in charge of the recruiters and "the Game," whose mission was to locate through social media—Facebook, Twitter, and the like—the disaffected of the world, those who were lonely, restless, and searching for meaning in order to recruit them as warriors for Allah and eager martyrs-in-waiting. Thousands of youth from around the world, many from Western nations all over Europe and from the United States, had enlisted to fight and bomb for ISIS and Allah.

Down a hallway filthy with rodent droppings, Rip Taggart awaited his fate as he lay zip-tied hands and ankles alone in a dimly-lighted room. He had been cleaned up and provided a fresh shave and a pair of loose shepherd trousers and a brown tunic. No matter how hard he thought about it, he couldn't figure out why he was being kept alive when it should have been clear to his captors by now that the US government had a policy dating back to President Thomas Jefferson not to ransom hostages. Even more baffling was the question of why had this band of professional-looking soldiers betrayed alliances with Boko Haram for the sole apparent purpose of wresting Taggart and the other hostages from the warlord Aabid?

What made a man like Nasry, who admitted to being an American, run with terrorists—and actually seem to be in charge in some capacity? He seemed to believe that Taggart should recognize him.

None of it made sense.

Surveying his new prison, a small filthy room long unused, he noticed a camera trained on him. Looking directly into the camera lens, his hands bound at the wrists in front, he shot a one-finger salute at whoever might be on the other end watching him. Then he doubled down with a double-finger salute. *Fuck 'em. Fuck 'em all.*

Neither Michael nor Akmal in an office at the other end of the hallway were watching at the moment to witness his tantrum. Michael was engaged in playing a video game, Akmal in front of the satellite TV. Akmal snapped his fingers at Nasry. "Look at this."

Nasry froze his game to look over Akmal's shoulder at the TV screen and a news flash.

"*—have confirmed there was indeed a failed US special operations rescue of several Americans, including former Navy SEAL Richard Taggart, as well as the kidnapped schoolgirls of Benin City—*"

Akmal lowered his voice to prevent the recruiters from overhearing him. "The Americans will keep coming," he predicted in an ominous undertone.

Michael touched a finger to his lips and pointed at the TV. *Listen.* TV footage revealed the abandoned Boko Haram village in Nigeria swarming with uniformed Nigerian soldiers among the corpses of the dead, most of whom were now covered by tarps. The camera zoomed in on the bodies and then on SUV vehicles riddled with bullet holes.

Akmal was clearly stressed. "We shouldn't have brought the American SEAL and the others here. This is our training facility."

Again, Michael placed a finger to his lips as the reporter on TV continued. "*—sources indicate scores were killed in the raid, including a US special operations soldier, although specifics surrounding the death remain under wraps—*"

Michael appeared exuberant rather than anxious. "You see, Akmal? Everything we've worked for. And it's only the beginning."

He clapped a hand on Akmal's shoulder in reassurance, then turned to receive the interruption of one of the recruiters named Kashif.

"How's the recruiting going?" Michael asked him.

"You were right about the Oregon girl. She's online now. Keeps asking when she can talk to you again."

Kashif displayed Marissa Wyatt's Facebook profile photo on the laptop—an unattractive teenage girl with a sorrowful expression, buck teeth, acne, and stringy straw-colored hair. She had been under cultivation for the past three months; her conversion seemed to be working.

"Bring her up," Michael instructed.

When she came up live on an online video, she wore a hijab and a soccer jersey that Michael had had sent to her in the United States.

"There's my girl," Michael greeted warmly, if condescendingly, like speaking to a child. Which was what she actually was—maybe fifteen or sixteen. "How are you Marissa?"

"I can't see you," Marissa complained. "I want to see you."

"Not yet. Hey, that jersey looks great."

"Like it?"

Michael cut straight to the Game. "Kashif says you're ready for more responsibility. Are you studying the Hadith?"

"*Mashallah.* I want to make you happy."

Michael smiled to himself and settled down for a little productive chat. "Tell me about your day . . ."

Chapter Ten

Virginia Beach

Buck Buckley's funeral services at the Normal Rockwell Church was over and the casket loaded into a hearse for transportation. The hearse moved out, followed by friends and families in their private cars bound for the wake to be held at the home of Bear and Lena Graves. Buck's internment was still up in the air, to be decided by a reading of Buck's will. Before the team departed the church, however, White Squadron Commander Lee Atkins summoned them to a corner of the church lawn.

"Bring it in, boys. Patch-wearers only." He flourished a handwritten sheet of paper. "What I've got here is the rest of Buck's will. I'm going to read it to you, and you can decide what you want to do with it."

He put on his reading glasses as Bear Graves and his guys gathered around. He began to read the will.

"I, Beauregard Jefferson Davis Buckley, being of sound mind and superlative body, in the event of getting killed, task my SEAL brothers to shoot my bodily remains from a cannon at Malvern Hill Civil War battlefield . . ."

Amazement mixed with amusement followed the reading. Head shakes and grins rippled through the team.

"Fucking Buckley," Fishbait burst out, partly laughing, partly crying.

Commander Atkins smiled over his glasses and continued reading. "And make sure my daddy comes, too. That son of a bitch."

He folded the paper and removed his glasses.

For a moment, revelations in the will left the team uncertain. Caulder broke the spell. "Well, hell. We're gonna need maps."

That started the planning. "And a cannon," Buddha added.

Chase thrust up his iPhone. He was already checking for an accommodation. "They got a cannon," he announced triumphantly. "Malvern Hill Battlefield Park. They fire it every year."

Graves couldn't be sure if the team was going along with the will, or merely bullshitting. Caulder turned to him. "Mission planning?" he asked. "At the High Tide?"

Bear looked at all of them like they were nuts.

"Bear?" Ortiz prompted.

Graves finally shrugged and went along. They might all be crazy, but, "Yeah. After the wake."

"You heard the man," Ortiz shouted.

The team and other SEALs broke up to proceed to Bear's house for the wake. Graves drew Commander Akins aside. "Sir, any news on Rip and the girls?" he requested.

Atkins shook his head. "When there is, you'll be the first to know."

In for a penny, in for a pound, as Bear's old Granny used to say. "And Captain Pearson, sir? What'd he say? About me?"

The commander regarded Graves for a short beat. Whatever he was going to say, he didn't. Instead, he said, "The best you can do right now is to be there for your team."

Chapter Eleven

Virginia Beach

In spite of Buckley's unusual will request hanging over the team—a request not shared with anyone outside the team, except for Buck's dad—mourners at the home of Joe and Lena Graves circulated quietly at Buck's wake, speaking in low tones and gathering in little withdrawn clumps by the sofa or at the front window or in the kitchen by the fridge and the breakfast bar laden with snacks. For that brief time the world seemed to rotate in slow motion in the aftermath of Buck Buckley's passing.

The afternoon continued to drag. Squadron SEALs and their wives dropped by long enough to express condolences, then departed with nods and murmurs, hurrying away to get into the late sunshine and escape the gloom of approaching darkness. Buck's teammates, however, hung on until the end.

An 8x10 photo of Buck in uniform went on coffee-table display in the living room, illuminated by a candle next to it. Bear stopped and looked at it, then proceeded into the kitchen to latch on to another beer from the fridge.

Caulder wandered in and tossed an empty into the trash. He went through the fridge, looking. "Where are the Jell-O shots when you need them," he asked.

Bear noted on a completely unrelated topic. "I saw your truck at Tammi's."

"You should have come in," Caulder said casually. "Buddha and Jackie were there before me. Lena before that."

Dharma ambled past the kitchen door. She still wore black, but in a more subdued dress that didn't quite look as though it had survived the Salem witch trials. Even her black lipstick and eyeliner had turned a rather pumpkin orange. The skunk stripe through her hair was still a bit jolting for the uninitiated.

Bear took a second look at the strange young woman. He failed to recognize her. "You bring a date with you?" he needled Caulder. "That's a new low, even for you. Looks like she's in high school."

Dharma reappeared and drifted into the kitchen, saying to her father, "Hey, you said there might be some photos I could add? To the video?"

Caulder smirked at Bear over Bear's "date" comment.

"You remember Dharma," he offered pointedly.

Bear hung a double take when the relationship struck him. "Dharma . . . ! You're . . . Wow! I mean, I haven't seen you since—"

"Birth?" Dharma supplied.

"Right. Birth."

"Look, I'm really sorry about your friend," Dharma said.

"Yeah. Well . . ." Bear was still taken aback by his mistake. "We're shooting him out of a cannon."

Dharma blinked, not knowing whether to take him seriously or not. He looked serious though. She opted to take the safe way out and accept him for his word. Although it had to be the weirdest thing she had ever heard of.

"That's so dope," she conceded. "Can I come?"

"Sorry," Graves replied, "but, no."

"No way," Caulder affirmed.

Before Dharma had a chance to challenge the decision, which was the nature she inherited from her father, Lena Graves walked in to bring more snacks to the living room. She smiled at Dharma.

"What do you think?" she asked her husband. "She looks like Alex, doesn't she? "

Okay," Dharma said, drawing it out for lack of a ready response. She decided to jump the tracks this train was headed down and take a sidetrack. "So . . . these pictures?" she reminded her father.

Caulder turned to Bear. "Where's the box with Buck's stuff?"

"Garage."

Lena tossed a companionable hand on Dharma's shoulder. "I'll show her," she volunteered.

They headed off together toward Bear's garage workshop. Bear shook his head in pretended pity and added a *Tsk Tsk* for good measure. "Poor thing does look like you," he said.

Chapter Twelve

Virginia Beach

Lena showed Dharma to her husband's garage workshop and the packed box of Buckley's possessions Bear left on his worktable. She returned to the wake while Dharma sorted through the items, using her cell phone to snag a still of Caulder and Buckley together on the beach. Digging deeper into the box, she came upon an iPad she thought might contain materials for her memorial video about Buckley.

The device contained a number of live-action files, each preceded by a thumbnail. Curious, she selected one and hit *Play.* It brought up a domestic scene of Tammi, Buck, and Buckley's parents around the dinner table. Nothing extraordinary. She selected another.

She heard someone on the video clap hands, followed by a voice she assumed to be Buckley's. She had never met him when he was alive.

"Testing . . . testing . . ." the voice intoned.

It was footage from a nighttime security camera focused on a bedroom. Buckley entered the frame wearing jeans and a sports shirt open down the front. He really did look like a hip *Miami Vice* cop, like her dad said.

He sat down on the edge of the bed. After a moment, he lifted his head and looked directly into the concealed security camera.

"I love you, Tammi," he said into the camera. His voice sounded strained and needy. He rubbed his thigh nervously with both hands.

"I just don't know if I can trust you," he went on, still talking to the camera.

"Awkward," Dharma murmured to herself.

Buckley on the iPad screen continued talking, although to whom or for what purpose Dharma failed to comprehend. The whole thing was just . . . *weird.*

"So . . . uh . . ." Buckley said, staring off-camera, "the camera is noise activated. Any voice, and it'll record automatically. Uploads straight to my tablet."

Weirder and weirder. Why would a dude be putting all that administrative stuff on a security camera? She felt like a perv peeping through somebody's bedroom window. She started to close out and place the iPad back into the box when something on a file caught her eye and she hesitated. It was recent stuff automatically recorded *today* and downloaded onto Buckley's iPad just as he designed it to do.

Okay, pervert . . . She opened the file and pressed *Play.* Tammi appeared on the screen coming out of the bedroom closet carrying the dress she wore at Buck's funeral today. Tiny and dark-haired with legs a glamour model would die for, she wore a sheer underslip that displayed a push-up bra and bikini panties. She flung the dress on the bed next to two others. She stood looking desperately alone in the bedroom.

"I can't decide," said Tammi on the screen in a tearful voice. "Can you? I need your help."

She wasn't alone after all. There was someone else offscreen. Whoever it was approached with heavy footfalls, like those of a man.

"I just . . . can't be alone right now," Tammi said, looking at whoever came in. "I need you to hold me. Will you hold me? Please?"

Her voice faded into a forlorn hungry whisper. "Please?"

A shadow moved into view on the screen. Before Dharma had a chance to identify the shadow, her dad entered the garage.

"What'd you find?" Caulder asked her.

She quickly closed the file on the iPad and stuck it back into the box. "Nothing. I have enough pictures now."

Dharma accompanied him back into the living room where mourners were proceeding with testimonials to the brave deceased SEAL. Ghetto Chase became the center of attention for the moment. He took the head of the room in front of a wide-screen TV with his hands dangling at his sides. He looked like a clumsy kid making his first recital before a class.

Buck's parents, with Tammi between them wearing the same dress Dharma had seen her in on-screen and from the funeral today, listened to Chase together. Ricky Ortiz, Jackie, and their children sat stiffly on the sofa with Bear and Lena leaning over them from behind. The others put down their drinks and snacks as Ghetto continued his personal tribute.

"I do know that Buck had a special affinity for something called NASCAR," he said, "and that somehow his hair was always perfect. And that . . ." His voice broke. He recovered quickly. ". . . and that he was my brother."

SEALs nodded approval. Chase stepped away from the front and stopped before Buck's parents. "Sir, ma'am," he said. To Buck's mother Barbara he said, "I'm sorry for your loss."

"No, son," Barbara responded, tipping up on her toes to embrace him. "I'm sorry for yours."

Buck's father Don shook Chase's hand solemnly.

Bear Graves summoned Mr. Buckley to take the front of the room. "Mr. Buckley, you want to . . . ?"

The older man shook his gray head and deferred to Tammi, who, a little tipsy from too many trips to the fridge for refreshments, weaved her way forward. She hesitated and looked out over the others, fresh tears glistening her eyes.

"I don't know what to say. I've always been glad it wasn't me up here. And now it is . . ."

That was as far as she could go. She bravely attempted to regain her composure and continue, but finally she gave up and stood there with her cheeks wet in lamplight. Jackie Ortiz, Lena Graves, and the other women rushed to her side.

"Dharma, let's play that video now," Lena suggested.

Graves set up a view screen. The video began to play, accompanied by music from the old country hit "It's Hard to Be Humble." Photos flashed across the screen of Buck as a skinny kid with a fishing pole and a big floppy-eared dog grin; wedding photos of Buck and Tammi, she gorgeous in pure white, he with his wavy hair and *Miami Vice* look in a tuxedo; from the day he earned his Trident at Coronado BUD/S; various other photos of Buck and the guys parachuting, scuba diving, shooting, playing grabass in the team room . . . Dharma had done a thorough job scrounging up photos.

The room remained quiet throughout the presentation except for an occasional soft sniffle or muted sob. Don Buckley watched stoically throughout. Barbara Buckley sniffed and wiped her nose with a hankie, but otherwise held her head high and proud in honor of such a strong, brave, and good son. Tammi's pert little face dissolved into a deep well of conflicting emotions, like a cloudy sky turning dark and breaking up. It was a bittersweet time for all present, this farewell tribute from those who loved the young SEAL and those he loved in return.

Alex Caulder lowered his head when a photo showed him and Buck posed together with Tammi between them, her arms around both of them. He looked up and discovered his daughter Dharma watching him with an odd expression on her face.

Chapter Thirteen

Chad, Africa

The open hand containing two white pills trembled. Michael Nasry, wearing clean khakis, sat on his cot. Other than the cot, the Spartan room was furnished only by a battered stand upon which sat a basin, a glass, and a pitcher of water. Clothing hung on a wire strung across one corner. Sunlight through a small window fractured by fly specks and dust provided the room's only illumination.

Michael had his back turned to the open door. Akmal Barayev appeared quietly and stood for a moment looking at Nasry's back. Before he and Michael left Qatar for Africa, Emir al-Muttaqi charged Akmal with keeping Michael off the pills. How had that worked out?

Akmal knocked on the door frame. "He's ready."

Michael's hand closed in a fist around the pills. The fist and his other hand trembled. As soon as Akmal left, the sounds of his footfalls receding down the echo-producing hallway of the forsaken cement plant, Michael opened his fist and stared at the pills. Then, with a deep indrawn breath to fortify himself, he tossed the pills into his mouth and washed them down with a glass of water. He took another deep breath. *Ready.*

He followed the way Akmal had gone down the hallway to a small room guarded by two tough-looking Chechen soldiers at the door. He entered the room and stopped to regard the prisoner lying zip-tied on the dusty floor. Rip Taggart stared back with his cold, pale eyes. Akmal stepped to one side to watch with his hands clasped in front of his belt.

"What I want to know," Michael began, "is how does a man who was in the best special ops team in the world end up as a burned-out security guard in bumfuck Nigeria?"

He waited for a response. None came.

"You don't recognize me?" Michael prompted.

"Should I? Are you famous on YouTube for sucking camel dick?"

Nasry's bushy eyebrows came together in a reflexive scowl of anger. He recovered and smiled. "Didn't expect that," he said. "A sense of humor. Makes sense, though. Comedians, man, are *dark*. Inside, most of them are crying their eyes out."

Rip refused to take the bait. "Those girls you kidnapped," he said instead. "They need clean clothes. Food and water."

"You think I kidnapped them? I think I saved them. It's all semantics, isn't it? But they're taken care of. We're not Boko Haram."

He paced slowly around the bound SEAL, hands clasped behind his back and looking askew at Rip in a reflective manner.

"You know," he mused, "I remember you being this giant—helmet, goggles, the mythical monster. You get an idea like that in your head about something, thinking about it over and over, building it up . . . Now look at you. I got to say, it's a disappointment."

"You got me mixed up with someone else," Taggart shot back.

Michael nodded with a sarcastic twist to his lips. "Yeah. You're right. We never really got around to introducing each other. I'm Michael. That's Akmal, ex-Spetsnaz and straight up OG."

Rip's slitted eyes looked Akmal over—the tight crop of black hair crowned a long swarthy face. He looked tough enough to have been with the Russian Special Forces. But what was Putin and the Russkies doing mixed up with this batch of terrorists in Africa?

"So that's us," Michael concluded. "Now why don't you tell us a little bit about you?"

Rip merely glared back.

"No?" Michael said, his brows lifting. "How about we play famous last words? 'What an artist dies in me.' Anything? Anybody? How about the Emperor Nero?"

Nasry was striving to sound friendly, reasonable, even humorous. But Rip had no illusions that this renegade American was anything but another Aabid. Rip remained silent—except for his eyes, which broadcast what he would do to Nasry given the right opportunity.

"How about this one?" Michael suggested affably, still stuck on famous last words. His voice changed, became younger sounding. "'He's just a raghead driver. Don't speak English.' Remember? Anything? Anybody?"

"Nope."

But he did remember. *Raghead driver . . . don't speak English.* It had been from that night in Afghanistan's Kunar Province. Those were the last words of the wounded terrorist Taggart executed during the chase for Hatim al-Muttaqi. The wounded one did all the talking. The other one—*don't speak English*—never spoke a word. It occurred to Rip that that silent one might be this Michael.

The wounded terrorist had lay squirming in the dirt clutching his gunshot thigh and howling in agony. "*Wait! Wait!* I'm an American. I'm from Michigan, man. Fucking Michigan . . ."

He continued his urgent patter while Graves and Caulder rolled up the two prisoners, patted them down for weapons, shoved both men to their knees in the dirt, and forced them to clasp their hands behind their heads. Tears rolled down the injured man's cheeks as Caulder checked their faces against the photograph of al-Muttaqi.

"Not him. Not this one either."

Taggart arrived and saw the prisoners kneeling. The double tap of his suppressed H&K 416 splattered Graves's face with blood as two holes appeared in the weeping young fighter's forehead. He plunged face down in the road. Taggart's rifle then shifted to the other fighter. The laser beam spotted his forehead. The man glared back at Taggart—the one who supposedly spoke no English. His face twisted with hatred. Caulder jumped between Taggart and the other terrorist, thus saving him from the same fate as his comrade.

"My brother," Michael now said, his voice dropping a threatening octave. "Omar. He was a good kid, from Detroit, remember? But he loved the Lakers. Because of Kobe. That's what he told you."

Michael's face narrowed. "An unarmed kid who'd surrendered. Right before you murdered him."

The two men's eyes clashed in a silent war of wills. The details of that night came back to Rip in a rush. *I'm totally fucked.* But he stubbornly refused to give up an ounce of satisfaction to this terrorist bastard. What he remembered most about that night was the man and his children this pair had murdered in their bed, slit their throats.

"What did you do with his body?" Michael demanded. "Did you even have the decency to bury him or did you just throw him in the trash?"

If it hadn't been for Caulder's intervention, this one, Michael Nasry, would have been dead also instead of lying around in an Afghan police jail cell for a while and then being released to continue his reign of terror. The way Taggart looked at it, every terrorist killed, whatever the circumstances, saved the lives of scores of innocent beings.

"I remember now," Taggart recalled, his eyes still boring into Nasry's. "I made a big mistake. And I'm sorry."

Nasry blinked in surprise and leaned forward, as though to make sure he had heard correctly.

"I'm sorry . . ." Rip repeated, pausing a beat before adding in a cold, unbending tone, "sorry I didn't kill all you motherfuckers. So, do whatever you're going to do, but spare me your bullshit justification."

Michael's face went blank for an instant. He recovered and the sarcastic smile returned. "Good talk," he said. "We'll finish it later."

At a cue from Michael, Akmal yanked Rip to his feet and ushered him roughly out the door and back down the hallway to his room-cell. Nasry's smile faded. His hands began to tremble again.

Chapter Fourteen

Virginia Beach

The High Tide Bar on the beachfront was an elongated, neon-studded shack outside high tide as marked by a line of seaweed. A late sun crowded elongated shadows of the bar toward the lap of the Atlantic. Shadows from the parking lot included Bear Graves's GMC pickup, Buddha's Ford Fusion, Caulder's red-and-purple Bronco, Chase's new Prius, and Fishbait's Toyota.

Inside, the establishment was rustic with a belly-up-to-the-bar that extended along one side overlording a cluster of tables. The High Tide was jumping in late afternoon with construction workers just getting off work, a road crew in colored hard hats, a few bikers, and other blue-collar types. Among them was Bear Graves's SEAL team, along with Buckley's gray-haired old daddy who had put off returning to Texas in order to see the funeral through the wake and be with the team when it planned and executed Buck's last mission. He sat hunched at the little round table with the others, but in a silent world apart. He had been drinking steadily since the wake.

Fishbait swept aside glasses on the table to lay out a map in front of Bear, who squinted his eyes to study it in the flashing neon light of a Coors sign behind the haggard bartender. The team had rendezvoused here in the late afternoon to drink big and plan big. They showed the effects. As Buddha, Chase, and Caulder craned in over the table to get a look at Fishbait's map, Fishbait staggered back and inadvertently bumped into a big guy crowded around the adjoining table with his buddies. The guy wore a Dodgers baseball cap, a Don't Tread On Me jacket, and a Kentucky hillbilly beard. He and his buddies cut dirty looks at the SEALs, who were dressed out in civvies for Buck's wake.

Fishbait stabbed a finger at the map. "That's . . ." A little drunk, he scrunched his eyes and corrected his finger stab. "Here! That's the field there. The cannon is here, by those hills."

His teammates gathered in closer to get a better look. Graves delivered the mission briefing.

"We take a direct approach," he said, tracing his finger past Fishbait's. "Straight through here. Right to the cannon."

As usual, Caulder had a better angle. "Rushing in like that, head on? Better if we go this way, around these buildings." His finger intruded among the other fingers. "Won't have to worry about park rangers."

"'Worry' and 'park rangers,'" Bear growled, "will never be in the same sentence for me."

Ghetto Chase from Harvard was the analytical type. "So why Malvern Hill?"

Buck's Texas daddy stirred for the first time in an hour. "His great, great granddaddy died there," he supplied.

"The General, right?" Chase recalled. "Buck told me about him."

Don Buckley scoffed. "Cullin? A general? No, he was a buck private. Nineteen years old."

"Of course he was," Chase agreed with a reserved chuckle.

Fishbait brought them back on subject. "Okay, we infil to the cannon. Then what?"

Graves hesitated a beat too long, providing an opening for Caulder. "It's a cannon," he said. "We shoot it. And, anyway, Bear's made enough decisions for a while, don't you think?"

Was that a swipe at Bear's leadership decision to prematurely attack the Nigerian village? Annoyed, Graves's reaction swept a beer bottle off the table. It bounced off the floor and skittered across the feet of Don't

Tread on Me and his boys at the next table. They turned their heads in unison to glare more dirty looks.

"You got something to say to me, Alex?" Bear challenged.

Caulder's eyes flashed. "I just did."

"Sitting there, with that shit-eating grin, questioning me, not taking any responsibility for anything, or anyone."

"Naw," Caulder scoffed. "That's your job."

They stared each other down. Things were about to get ugly. Buck's daddy watched, wondering what the hell was going on between these two guys. From the sound of it, it had been going on for quite some time.

A female voice unexpectedly intruded. "Having fun, boys?"

That deflated the tension. Buck's pretty widow entered the bar and sashayed her way unsteadily across to the SEAL table, giving Don't Tread on Me another bump and knocking over his beer glass, splattering his homeboys with its contents. She untangled herself from the collision, playfully tugged the bill of the big man's Dodgers cap down over his eyes, and finally stumbled into position in front of Graves. She extended to him a Ziploc bag, holding it at arm's length.

"I have something for you," she slurred with a tipsy giggle. "My husband. Here's good ol' Buck. Some of him anyway. Fresh from the oven."

Graves gently took the bag containing the cremated remains. Or at least a portion of them.

"We'll take care of him, Tammi," he said. "I promise."

Tammi made a wry face and gave an exaggerated wave of her arms out toward the Atlantic. "Like you did out there! Huh, Joe?"

She glared at him. He hunched down into his broad shoulders. It seemed everyone was trying to get in their licks at him.

"Let's get you some fresh air," Fishbait offered Tammi, getting up from the table to help her.

She fought him off, crying, "*Don't touch me!* I have every right to get shit-faced, same as you." She turned to Caulder. "Right, Alex?"

She snuggled down with him in his chair and threw an arm around his neck. He shrugged her off.

"I'm calling Lena," Bear decided.

Don't Tread on Me and his friends had had enough of their rowdy neighbors. He pushed back from the table and lumbered to his feet, a big guy who looked like he had been pumping iron for breakfast and eating nails for dinner.

"I've been putting up with your bullshit for the past hour," he rumbled. "I don't care who you are, or why you're here, but the lady can do whatever she wants."

"This isn't your business, friend," Caulder flared back in a low growl.

"This makes it my business," the intruder threatened, dragging open his jacket to display a holstered .45 semiauto stuck in his belt.

Caulder's eyes glittered and he released his Dennis the Menace. "Hey, Buddha," he said, never taking his eyes off Don't Tread on Me. "How many people you kill the other day?"

Ortiz went along. "Two."

"What about you, Fish?"

"One. But from two hundred yards out."

"Hell of a shot," Caulder applauded. "Me, I killed three. And for what, Chase—twenty bucks an hour?

"Given the travel time," Chase said, "it's probably closer to eighteen."

"But we don't do it for the money," Caulder said. "And neither did our buddy."

Caulder took Buck's ashes urn from Graves and held it out toward the other table. His eyes twinkled with a mischievous mixture of raw aggression, drunkenness, and temporary insanity.

"He didn't die for the money. Or for you. Or for whatever you GI Joe wannabes do for a living. Or for the flag. Or the stock market. He died for us. And we'd die for him." He paused. His voice lowered dangerously. "Or kill for him, too."

Don't Tread on Me didn't appear to have much between his ears, but whatever was there seemed to be reassessing matters. His eyes flitted from Caulder to Bear, from the big black guy to the swarthy-looking Middle Eastern type, to the Mexican. It came into his eyes that he thought he might have let his alligator mouth overload his hummingbird ass.

"I'll walk you out," Ortiz volunteered, standing up and clapping a friendly had on the giant's shoulder.

The man and his buddies, now much meeker, let Ortiz guide them to the door. Buddha returned with a grin. "Who wants another drink?"

Graves got up without a word and walked outside to the High Tide's wooden deck. Tammi took his place at the table. Ortiz joined Bear outside where Graves leaned against the railing gazing out toward the gray afternoon ocean.

"The slug that got Buck," Ortiz said softly, standing close to Bear and also looking out to sea. "It was a one in a million shot, Bear. An act of God."

"An act of God," Bear repeated, as though to himself.

"Hey, Bear. In this business, the enemy gets a vote, too. Sometimes it goes against us."

After a moment, he took Bear's arm. "Come on. We got a mission to do."

Chapter Fifteen

Virginia Beach

Golf carts seemingly occupied and driven by maniacs, little engines whirring shrilly in the middle of the night, topped a ridge in Malvern Hills Civil War Park at breakneck speed. Shouts and wild laughter accompanied the stampede. Buckley's daddy, Don, hung on in the cart driven by Bear Graves. Chase rode passenger with Caulder, while Fishbait held down the shotgun position with Ortiz driving.

Laughing uproariously, Chase and Fishbait were Zorro fighting using pool cues as swords while their drivers, Caulder and Ortiz, raced full-speed side by side across the Civil War greens. Chase fended off Fish's thrusts and sweeps until Ortiz lost control of his vehicle and executed a sod-slinging wheelie while Caulder whooped and kept going.

"Just like the movies!" Fishbait cheered.

"Enough!" Bear shouted from his and Don Buckley's cart. "Light discipline, assholes."

"Going tactical," Caulder added.

Headlights doused, the three little carts still kept banging into each other as the drunken SEALs jockeyed wildly and loudly for position.

"Delta is at set point," Ortiz reported when the ancient cannon came into view.

Bear counted down: "Three . . . Two . . . One!"

Caulder's blacked-out cart with Chase as passenger cut dangerously close in front of Bear. Bear swerved. Caulder shouted, "Execute!"

Caulder skidded to a halt next to the Civil War cannon on a grassy knoll overlooking a small valley back dropped by a full moon. SEALs, totally drunk and disorganized, piled out.

"Let's blow it!" Fishbait yelled.

"Yeah?" Ortiz queried. "How?"

"Hold on," Chase interjected, pulling up a Civil War reenactor website on his iPhone, which explained how to fire a cannon. "I got it right here."

"Give it to Bear," Ortiz suggested.

Chase did. Bear pored over it, then looked over at the cannon.

"You got to press *Play*," Ghetto instructed.

"No shit. Okay, okay, here it is." Instructions on the screen were in illustrated sequences. Bear started with the first illustration, reading, "Number one man clears the barrel. That's you, Caulder."

The team gathered around the cannon in the moonlight. Caulder jumped to, shining a Maglite down the cannon's barrel to search for birds' nests and the like. "Clearing the barrel . . . Clear!"

Graves moved on to the second sequence. "Number two man attends the lanyard and inserts the firing pin. Fish."

Fishbait looked over Bear's shoulder at the illustration. He nodded. Minutes later, he called out, "Firing pin in."

Things seemed to be functioning smoothly. The team leader had assumed his rightful authority on the team and everything was moving forward.

"Number three man adds the gunpowder. That's you, Chase."

"Roger." He poured black powder into the chamber and tamped it down gently while Caulder held the Maglite for him. "Added!" he called out.

"Number Four man loads the shell. Buddha . . ."

"What?"

"Where's the shell?" Caulder asked.

"Nobody said anything about a shell."

"You're shitting me." Fishbait sounded defeated.

Leave it to Bear to come to the rescue. "Okay, okay . . ." he murmured, thinking.

He was determined to see it through and follow Buck's wishes. He looked at his beer can and that gave him an idea. He chugged the rest of his beer and cut out the top with his knife.

Ortiz was skeptical. "That won't work."

Bear's determination grew. "It'll work."

"The can's too small," Ortiz pointed out. "The projectile has to fill the barrel so the gun can propel it outward."

"So," Chase offered, "we create more surface area."

He ripped off his shirt and stuffed it into the barrel. "Going where no Brooks Brother has gone before," he commented with a laugh as he tamped it down with his multitalented pool cue that had formerly been a sword.

It was time for the guest of honor. "Who's got Buck?" Caulder asked.

Fishbait rushed forward. "Bag of Buck right here."

Buck in a bag passed from Fish to Caulder to Bear, who pressed the Ziploc bag of ashes into his empty beer can. Buddha produced a roll of duct tape. Bear firmly settled the passenger into his car and wrapped him securely. He then held Buck aloft to the heavens full of moon and stars and called for a moment of silence in which the team and Buck's father paid tribute to a departed brother about to get his last wish as requested in his will.

"To Buck, and to every brother who never came home," Graves announced in a sober voice.

"To Buck!" the others responded in unison.

"And," Graves added, "to Rip, who's still out there."

"To Rip!" came the chorus.

They were drunk and trying to hide their pain, but it still came through, and it ran deep. Bear solemnly dropped the beer can down the cannon barrel.

"Number five man pulls the lanyard," Bear said. "That's you, Don."

Buckley's father shook his head. "I don't think so," he said. "We weren't that close."

Bear rested a hand on his shoulder and repeated, "Number five man pulls the lanyard."

"You need to do it, Joe," Mr. Buckley insisted. "You need to. He was your guy."

He thrust the lanyard at Bear. Graves hesitated. After a moment, he accepted. "Okay, here we go!"

He pulled the lanyard. After all the preparation, nothing happened. The SEALs all looked at each other, puzzled.

"Maybe it was a—" Ortiz began, but that was as far as he got.

The cannon suddenly went off with a terrific *Boom!* A huge tongue of flame shot from the muzzle at the stars. Buck's ashes blew back into the faces of his buddies. Stunned, they stared at each other before they burst into tense laughter. Then, one by one, they fell into silence as, covered in the ashes of Beauregard Jefferson Davis Buckley, they honored their fallen comrade.

A gentle ocean breeze from the Atlantic stirred after the successful firing of Buckley's ashes from the Civil War cannon. The taste of his ashes lingered in the air, a sign of Buck's presence as the sun rose over Virginia's Malvern Hill Park. The sun could always be counted on to come up and shine equally on the living and the dead.

Buck's gray-haired old daddy watched sunrise from behind the wheel of a golf cart parked on a rolling hill overlooking manicured grounds and stands of maple and oak. Shafts of morning sunshine exploded gentle golden rays through the trees and touched Don Buckley's face, revealing nothing in it other than a quiet stoic silence. In his background, a pair of golf cars raced each other up another hill, their occupants—Caulder, Buddha, Fishbait, Chase—letting off steam and blowing a hangover from last night's all-nighter. None of them had slept.

Bear Graves, appearing haggard and tormented, approached the elder Buckley and slipped into the passenger's seat of the golf cart. For a long while, the two men sat together silently looking out over the park at the sunrise. Don seemed not to have noticed Bear until he finally spoke.

"My son would have loved this," he said.

Graves nodded. After another long silence, Bear said, "I keep playing it over in my head. Wondering if there was something I could have done to save him."

How would he have classified this? *Regret? Guilt? An apology?*

They still did not look at each other. After a while, Don began speaking in a tired voice that seemed to have been worn down to a whisper over years of wrestling with his conscience. He spoke as though to the sunrise, or perhaps to the universe.

"I was in the 101st Airborne, Vietnam," he said, pausing to take a deep breath. A shudder earthquaked through his aging body. "I lost seven men. Fifty years ago. Not a day goes by I don't think about them."

Bear looked at him then. He understood.

"These decisions, most men never have to face," the old man resumed. "Hell, most soldiers don't. But when you make them, you got to live with them. You've got to make peace with them—here. Now. You hold onto them like I did, they're gonna tear you apart. They're gonna tear apart you family. It's too late for me and Beauregard. But it doesn't have to be too late for you."

Graves took it in, knowing the old man was wise and right. But *how* did you do it? How did you rid yourself of the hurt and guilt of knowing it was your decision that got a comrade, a brother, killed? Even more, how could you ever place yourself back into a situation that required such decisions again?

They sat together in the golf cart and in silence watched sunshine slowly spread over the rolling hills.

Chapter Sixteen

Chad, Africa

Hands zip-tied behind his back, Rip Taggart caught a good look at the large interior space of the cement plant as Akmal ushered him roughly along a second-deck open passageway overlooking the cavernous main docking area of the building. A company of at least twenty-five Chechen soldiers engaged in the first of five daily prayers were lined up in ranks, kneeling on prayer rugs and facing the direction of Mecca, their heads bowed to the concrete floor, butts in the air, their voices lifted in droning ripples of supplication. What, Rip wondered, did men dedicated to the eradication of half the world's population pray for, except for more death?

Akmal hurried Taggart down a dim hallway to where Michael Nasry waited at a closed door. White shepherd trousers and a loose black tunic clad his skinny form. Why was it, Taggart again wondered, that, if Michael was an American convert to Islam as he purported to be, he wasn't down on his prayer rug with the others obeying the *salat* obligation to pray five times a day, one of the five pillars of Islam? Could it be that his devotion lay more toward terrorism and revenge against supposed wrongs of his own country than any commitment to Allah and Islam?

Michael stepped aside to allow Akmal to open the door and shove Rip inside. Akmal sliced Rip's zip-ties to free his hands. Rip froze in the doorway in astonishment. Na'omi and her three schoolgirls were drawing with crayons at a long table. Their faces lit up with surprise and delight when they saw Rip. They scurried to him with cries of relief at seeing him again when they thought he had been taken away or killed. Little Esther flung herself into Rip's arms.

"Mister Rip!"

He knelt and gathered all three children into his arms. They rained smacking kisses all over his hands and arms and face. Na'omi remained seated at the table, a smile radiating her face. All of them, including Na'omi, had showered and changed from their filthy and ragged school uniforms of white blouses and short plaid skirts into baggy gray linen trousers and short tunics of the same color and material.

Rip's eyes drank in the image of Na'omi as she sat at the table with her clean skin, her gentle poet's soul but fighter's spirit, her almond-shaped eyes he had feared he'd never look into again.

Nasry stood at the doorway a moment and with ruthless satisfaction watched the emotional display between the American SEAL and the African females. Then he closed and locked the door behind him, leaving the captives alone together.

"Is everyone okay?" Rip asked.

"Look!" Esther cried. "We have beds! And cookies!"

Though Esther was only twelve, and even small for her age, it was she who had had the courage to cut Rip's bindings while Na'omi distracted the guard during their failed escape attempt from Boko Haram to reach a nearby oil refinery.

At Esther's urging, Rip looked around the room in which Na'omi and her girls were imprisoned. It was reasonably clean, with scrubbed bedrolls spread on the floor. Drinks and snacks took up one end of the table where the children had been drawing artwork with crayons. Their drawings were taped to the walls. Compared to the cell-hut at the Boko Haram village, this prison was a cozy little domestic scene. It immediately aroused Rip's suspicions. Nasry and Barayev hadn't struck him as the sort to provide amenities, even to children, without an ulterior motive.

"Books, too," Na'omi said, rising to where Rip knelt on the floor with the girls. She went to her knees and added her arms to Rip's in encompassing the children and each other.

"They asked me to keep teaching the girls," she explained.

"They haven't hurt you . . . ?"

All too clear in his mind was her being raped by Aabid and his soldiers at the abandoned village.

"No," Na'omi assured him. "They've been . . . nice."

Her brown eyes seemed to melt with his into a pool of intimacy and connection born out of shared hardships and forced togetherness as captives of Aabid and Boko Haram in Nigeria—and now again in Chad as prisoners of a new batch of terrorists.

"Who are they?" Na'omi asked. "What do they want from us? They won't tell me anything. Do you know?"

Taggart had no answers he was willing to share at the moment. Best he could figure, so far, was that the girls were collateral to his being taken for Nasry's personal revenge. But the Chechen ops against Boko Haram went too far for mere revenge, so there had to be something else.

"Richard . . . ?" Na'omi took his hand.

Esther clutched his other hand and showed him a crayon drawing. "It's all of us," she explained happily. "See?"

Indeed, it was a depiction of all of them together in this simple, unpolished sketch of a child: three girls, Esther, Abiye, and Kamba; their pretty teacher; and a broad-shouldered, heroic-looking man. The schoolteacher and the American were holding hands. Esther insisted Rip keep the sketch so he wouldn't forget them.

Taggart was right in assuming the little reunion had been arranged. Elsewhere in the cement plant, Nasry lay sprawled on the cot in his room, head propped up on a pillow while he studied the screen of the laptop resting on his chest. A soundless live feed from a remote hidden camera played in black-and-white the display of affection between Taggart, Na'omi, and the girls.

A thin, humorless smile of satisfaction crossed his thin face.

Chapter Seventeen

Chad, Africa

Michel Nasry's plan began to unfold with increasing clarity when two Chechen soldiers led Taggart, again zip-tied, to the offices Nasry referred to as his "Nerve Center" in the cement plant. The first thing Rip noticed was the expensive Nikon camera set on a tripod in the center of the room with a shotgun mic attached. On the wall behind a single empty chair hung a black-and-green Jihad flag like the one Aabid had used as a backdrop when he videoed Taggart for his ransom demand. The flag and the camera were familiar accoutrements used in previous beheading videos. Michael's entering with the long shimmer of a battle knife in his hand confirmed that this was in all likelihood a kill house. His allowing Taggart a few minutes with Na'omi and the girls must have been a sadistic part of his personal revenge.

"After you do this," Taggart requested, "you let those girls go. That's all I'm asking."

"Do what?" Michael responded slyly. "Oh, this!" He brandished the knife and tested the sharpness of its edge with his thumb while he peered up through his black eyebrows. "You think I'm going to cut your head off and post it online?"

Rip stared at him, ready to accept his fate with the courage of the SEAL he had once been.

"Come on, dude," Michael taunted. "That's so cliché. No, look. It's a Soviet combat knife. Found it in one of the offices. Crazy, right?"

He balanced the knife in his open palm, the point toward Rip, then abruptly stepped forward and sliced the zip-ties from Taggart's wrists. He handed the knife to one of the Chechens and pushed Rip onto the chair in the middle of the room facing the camera.

"I just need you to read this for the camera," he said, as an apparent alternative to beheading him. He handed Rip the printed document. "Look it over and let me know when you're ready."

Rip glanced at it, saw what it was, and then crumpled it into a wad and let it fall to the floor.

Michael pretended to be hurt by the affront. "I took a lot of time with that. Most of them, you can tell they're coerced. Bad grammar, no sense of style or flow. They're just checking off boxes on the terrorist checklist. You know what's missing from them?"

He thrust his phony smile at Taggart and arched his brows. "Sincerity. That's what's missing."

Taggart struck back, the best defense being an offense. "Why'd you let your brother take that bullet? How does that feel, knowing you stood by, doing nothing?"

Michael surprised Taggart by looking directly into his eyes, not flinching and replied with complete candor. "I'll never forgive myself. Ever."

It wasn't the response Rip expected. "Good," he said, rubbing it in.

"But I might forgive you," Michel added judiciously. "Just pick up the paper."

"You want it, you pick it up."

Michael nodded thoughtfully. "Tell me, what do you call the innocents who get caught up in our conflict? You know, women, children, civilians? Collateral damage, right?"

"Above my pay grade."

"Right, collateral. I looked it up in the OED. Parallel, side by side, related, but different. The families eating in a Paris café, the guests at a wedding in Afghanistan. Whether a bomb strapped to a chest, a drone controlled from Nevada—Poof! Both dead and gone, thanks to us."

"Is that a fancy way of saying I'm like you? I'm not. You can take your Oxford English Dictionary and stick it up your terrorist ass."

Michael remained implacable, like he was holding an ace and waiting for the showdown to play it. He opened his laptop. "Hey, Akmal—?"

Akmal's broad-faced image appeared on the screen, a smartphone selfie relayed elsewhere in the plant. Michael tilted the screen toward Rip so he could see it.

"Show him," Michel instructed.

Akmal panned from his own face to reveal the frightened faces of Na'omi and Esther. The camera went to wide angle to show the teacher and her student zip-tied in straight-backed metal chairs facing each other, their knees touching. Esther was so small that her toes barely touched the floor. A rag had been stuffed into Na'omi's mouth and duct taped in place. Rip's eyes narrowed, but otherwise he successfully denied Michael the satisfaction of a reaction.

"Hi, Esther," Michael sang out like a friendly uncle. "Say 'hello' to Mister Rip, Esther."

Esther's lips trembled. "Hi, Mister Rip," she managed.

"Na'omi can't say hello," Michael apologized. "We had to gag her. Na'omi, you can nod."

Na'omi looked directly into the camera lens, as though trying to send Rip a message. She emphasized her resistance by shaking her head from side to side. *No, Richard. Don't do it.*

"Very well," Michael said reluctantly, as though being forced to show his ace when there was no need for it if people would just cooperate. "Akmal, show us what Esther and Na'omi are wearing."

The camera closed in tight. Esther wore a suicide bomb vest. So did Na'omi. Michael watched Rip's face for a reaction. "Akmal has the detonator to these," he said. "You ready, Akmal?"

"Just give me the word."

Fierce emotion welled through Rip's entire being, exactly the response Nasry hoped to elicit.

"You piece of shit—" he raged, springing from his chair intent on tearing Nasry to pieces.

The sharp slap of palms on rifles stopped him. The Chechen guards crouched at the ready, AK-47s trained on him. One more step, any further hostile move, and Rip knew he was a dead man and of no further use to either himself or to Na'omi and Esther. He was the only thing that stood between them and savage abuse and eventual death or slavery. He must stay alive as long as he could—for them. Rip backed down, collapsing in the chair, but his body remained tense and ready.

Nasry nodded his approval. "Hey, you want to paint me as the faceless bad guy without a conscience? ISIS? Bin Laden's bogeyman? Go ahead. But I'm just a Muslim from Michigan who found out the American dream is a lie for someone like me. A few different turns and I could have been you. America made us both. Actually, you could say we made each other."

He rose and picked up the document Rip had crumpled and thrown on the floor. He smoothed it out.

"I never thought you and I would have this opportunity," he said. "But here we are face to face. And you were right. It is about us. You and me. I don't want them—the girls—to be a part of it. I really don't."

He extended the paper to Rip. Rip remained in turmoil. What was it with these people that prompted them, actually encouraged them, to go out and kill innocent people? What was it in them that inspired such profound evil? He knew Nasry wasn't bluffing, Akmal would kill Na'omi and Esther unless he caved to the terrorists' will. First one—Na'omi or Esther. Probably Esther. If that didn't work, then Na'omi. Taggart couldn't let that happen in order to save himself, or to preserve battlefield secrets.

After another moment, he relented and accepted the paper.

"But sometimes there is collateral damage. Right, Rip?" Nasry smiled and gestured at the paper. "Read it. Make me believe it, okay?"

He pressed *Record* on the tripod-mounted Nikon and focused the lens directly on Taggart's face. The camera's red light began to blink, indicating it was starting to film.

Chapter Eighteen

Virginia Beach

Buck's death and all that accompanied it—the funeral, the wake, the firing of his ashes through the cannon—it all ended. Life for those who remained behind began to mend itself by confronting challenges and exigencies still at loose under one exacerbated by intrusive tragedy.

Sunrise over Malvern Hill Civil War Park split up team members into the new day and their private lives. They shook hands solemnly with each other and with Buckley's daddy before they went off to nurse hangovers and the aftermath of violent death, to suppress its implications and prepare for the next round in a war that, for SpecOps, never seemed to end.

Graves drove his GMC truck to Drake Elementary School where his wife Lena taught. Carrying a Mylar balloon as a peace offering and still dressed in the slacks and open shirt he wore to the funeral, now mussed and soiled from a long, sleepless night, he strode down the hallway where classes in session hummed behind closed doors. He paused outside Lena's classroom to peer through the window.

He saw that Lena and her students were engrossed in a mock trial to study the procedures of the US justice system. Pretty heavy stuff for second graders.

"When you call up your witness," Lena was explaining, "you'll want to swear them in first. Like this."

Acting as judge, she raised her right hand in demonstration and nodded for the "witness," a rowdy-looking redhead named Derek, to do the same. She swore him in.

"Do you swear to tell the truth, the whole truth, and nothing but the truth?"

The redhead nodded. "I do."

Watching, Graves noticed that Lena left off the last sentence of the oath that had been used since the founding of the nation—*So help me God.* Bear had sworn into the military on that vow. He wondered if the reason Lena left it off now was to comply with new standards of separation of church and state.

Lena turned to a shy little student named Jennifer, also a "witness" in the mock trial, who hung her head and clasped her hands behind her back. Lena smiled encouragement and opened her arms to the "witness." Jennifer responded immediately and rushed into the embrace, after which she bravely lifted her hand to be sworn in.

"Please be seated," Lena invited, and Derek and Jennifer did.

Lena smiled her pleasure at them and turned to another little boy and girl waiting in their places. "Would the attorneys like to give their opening statements?" she asked.

Instead of hands flying up and voices chirping, little heads turned toward the door to regard Bear Graves as he strode into the classroom. He stopped inside the door holding the string of his balloon, smiling foolishly and looking as awkward as a second grader on his way to the principal's office.

"Uh . . . Hi. Who's on trial?"

Lena looked at him and smiled. "Counselors, we'll take a five-minute recess."

Her students cheered. Lena laughed and expanded her remarks: "*In* the courtroom."

The students pretended to grumble, but Bear saw by the interaction between teacher and students that the kids clearly adored Lena, and she them. Lena would have made a wonderful mother—if only . . .

Bear wondered if Lena delivered flowers as usual to Sarah's tiny grave on her way to school this morning.

As soon as she stepped into the empty hallway with him, Bear enveloped her in his arms and kissed her passionately, with a deep and needful hunger. Astonished, she pulled back to glance self-consciously at her classroom window. Sure enough, little faces with pressed noses against the window ducked back with choruses of titters and giggles. Flushed and trying not to laugh, Lena splayed a hand on Bear's chest to ward off further advances.

"I'm sorry about the other night," Bear attempted.

Lena looked puzzled, not quite sure what "the other night" he referred to. Sarah's death had created a strain in their marriage, the rift of which continued to widen in their efforts to have another baby. The truth was, Joe's sperm could not swim. A macho man like that and his sperm were deficient.

She gave him a sly look and shook her head. "Joseph Graves, we'll talk about this at home."

She patted him on his unshaved cheek and returned to her classroom and the trial.

Ricky Ortiz arrived home after the cannon shooting night in the park to find Jackie and R.J. finishing breakfast at the kitchen table. Jackie was fussing at R.J. for paying more attention to a handheld video game than to what was left of his waffles and syrup.

Jackie looked up and spotted her husband coming down the hallway from the front door. She ladled a couple of waffles off the electric griddle onto a clean plate. "The kids are late for school," she informed him.

"Way late," R.J. confirmed. "Hey, Dad!"

"Hey, buddy." Ortiz ruffled the ten-year-old's unruly hair.

He pecked Jackie on the cheek and sat down at the table. Jackie slid the fresh plate of waffles in front of him and went for coffee.

"I can take them to school," Ricky offered.

"Mom's taking us," Anabel's voice countered from the hallway. Dressed for school in her usual jeans and sneakers, she entered the kitchen yawning and rubbing her eyes. Ignoring the rest of the family, she plopped down in her chair and began texting.

Jackie forked one of Ricky's waffles off his plate and onto Anabel's. "Anabel, you've got two minutes. Say hello to your father."

"Hello to my father," Anabel murmured without looking up from her cell phone screen.

It was like events of the past few days had never occurred. Not the deployment, Buck's death, the funeral . . . Everything was right back to normal, as though Ricky had never been gone. Ortiz leaned back and took in his little Latino family: *Mamacita, hija, y hijo.* Pride swelled his breast, replaced by a creeping ill-defined unease as Jackie, dressed for work, sorted through her briefcase for a particular document. She located it, closed the briefcase, and was ready to go out and meet the business day.

"Time's up," she informed the kids.

R.J. jumped up obediently, shrugged into his backpack and rushed off down the hallway to the front door. Jackie gave Ricky a perfunctory good-bye kiss and hurried after R.J. Anabel yawned widely and stood up from the table to follow them.

"Dad?"

"Yeah, sweetie?"

"You smell really bad."

Alex Caulder's red-and-purple Bronco with the chopped top pulled up to his beachfront shack where the surfboard and old car seat with the rusty springs on the porch framed the doorway. Caulder got out of the Bronco toting a bag of two coffees and muffins. He threw open the front door and called out, "Swell's coming in. I got an extra board . . ."

Silence swallowed the rest. The house echoed with emptiness. The stuffed bear in the corner stared at him. Dharma should still be asleep on the sofa this early in the morning after their late night at the wake.

"Dharma?"

He quickly went through the rest of the house. He first noticed her backpack and clothing were gone. On the kitchen table among stacks of dishes that had not made it to the cupboard he found an iPad with a note attached to it. The note read: *Play me. Don't worry. I won't tell anyone.*

He sank down at the table with sudden misgivings and pressed *Play* on the iPad. Tammi Buckley appeared on the screen wearing the sheer slip from last night before the wake. *Damn! Where the hell had this come from?*

Then he recalled surprising his daughter in Bear's garage workshop sorting through Buckley's stuff looking for photos to use in her commemorative video of Buck's life. *Damned Buckley.* He must have been spying on his own wife with a hidden security camera that fed into his iPad. There had been talk in the team that she may have been screwing around on Buck. When Caulder came into Bear's workshop, Dharma had quickly stuffed the iPad back into the box. *This* iPad?

Curiosity kept Caulder glued to the screen, although he knew where the scene was going.

"I can't decide," the Tammi on the video was saying. "Can you? I need your help."

Footsteps could be heard entering the bedroom. The lamp on the dresser cast a man's shadow on the floor. Caulder paused the tape, unsure of how much more of this he could stand to watch. After all, Buck was dead, and this was his mourning widow.

Sickened by it but still intrigued, Caulder hit *Play*. Tammie dropped a dress on the bed and turned toward the unseen visitor. "I just . . . can't be alone right now," she wailed in a voice hoarse from crying.

Caulder walked slowly into sight of the camera. He stopped again, maintaining his distance.

"I need you to hold me," Tammi pleaded. She eased toward the screen Caulder, reaching out for him with a trembling hand, sniffling back tears. "Will you hold me? Please? *Please?*"

Caulder looked uncertain. "Tammi . . ."

She seized his hands impulsively and placed them on her breasts.

"I can't do this," he agonized, attempting to pull away.

She held onto him to keep him with her. With savage need, she threw herself at him, pulling his face down to hers and kissing him with lust born of grief and aloneness. "*Please . . . ?*"

He went along with the flow, responding with a hunger to match hers. After all, he was only human and male. She was tiny and stacked and willing and . . . Everybody knew what he was, that he was a player. *But, damn!* This was taking things to a new low. *What was he doing?* If the others found out about this . . .

Watching the replay now, shame, humiliation, regret, emotions with which he had little in common, filled him with disgust. He had seen enough when, clinging to each other and slinging off clothing, they headed for the bed. Now alone in his cabin, he slapped the iPad off and stared at his reflection in the black screen.

Chapter Nineteen

SEAL Command, Virginia Beach

Bear Graves stopped in the hallway down from the office of White Squadron's Commander Lee Atkins and waited for Atkins and another officer outside his door to complete their conversation. So far, there had been no official determination about Buck's death. The waiting wore on Bear, although the team had only returned from Africa a short time ago.

Atkins finished his conversation and motioned at Graves. Instead of entering the formality of the commander's office, the two men strolled down to the end of the hallway to talk. It was a brief conversation.

"Captain Pearson had a few questions about how things were handled," the commander informed Bear. "He recommended you take a few weeks off."

Graves pulled up short. He couldn't do that. Rip was still *out there.*

"But I said no," Atkins added, taking in the horrified expression on Bear's face.

"Thank you, sir."

They returned to the door of Atkins's office. The commander turned to face the senior chief. "Bear, can I trust you to keep it together? Look me in the eye and tell me I can trust you."

Graves's strong jaw thrust forward with determination. "You can trust me, sir."

Atkins stuck out his hand and shook Graves's. "Your team supports you," he said, "and so do I."

With that and a nod of affirmation, he entered his office and the door closed. Bear stood in the hallway a moment before he heaved a long sigh of relief. He and the team still had a job to do.

Bear was walking down the hallway with a new brisk step when he heard angry shouting erupt from the Team Room. He rolled his eyes. *What now?* He hustled toward the uproar, entering to find Fishbait Khan, Ghetto Chase, and two other off-duty White Squadron SEALs on their feet and shouting at breaking news from the wide screen TV.

"I can't believe this shit," one of the SEALs protested, shaking his fist at the TV.

The talking head on the screen wore a wig and a smirk. "*. . . has been portrayed as an American hero. TON News has one exclusive first look . . .*"

A crawler on the screen read: Former SEAL Team 6 operative admits to war crimes.

Rip Taggart's image flashed onto the screen. He looked all cleaned up compared to the last time he appeared on video when the Boko Haram leader threatened to behead him unless the US forked over a ten-million-dollar ransom payment. Rip's voice sounded flat and without emotion. He was obviously reading from a prepared script.

"My name is Richard Taggart and I am the face of America. What I am about to share comes from the heart . . ."

"The hell—!" Fishbait exclaimed.

Rip continued reading. "For seventeen years I was a soldier on SEAL Team Six, the most elite special operation team in the world. On September 3rd, 2014, in Kunar, Afghanistan, I murdered an unarmed American who had surrendered peacefully."

Fishbait glanced at Graves, whose slitted eyes remained glued on the TV screen.

"I realize now, and this is hard to admit, that I was a hired assassin who committed war crimes. To the world, rise up and fight America's endless war against innocent Muslims. To America, take back your own soul, your dream of justice and freedom. To my brothers on SEAL Team Six, please look inside your hearts. Let your better nature, let the truth, shine through. It's not too late. I'm proof of that."

"Shit's coerced, man," one of the White Squadron SEALs decided. "You can tell."

"Total bullshit," the other agreed.

Graves continued to stare at the screen even as the camera switched back to the talking head. He knew, as did Caulder and Ortiz, that Rip was telling the truth.

The TV played in the living room of the Ortiz household. Ready for work and on her way through with her briefcase to see if Anabel and R.J. were dressed for school, Jackie paused when she heard Rip Taggart's voice coming from the TV set. The disturbing news about him had been on TV and radio news flashes all morning. She waited to see if anything new had developed. She was so preoccupied with the TV that she startled when the children burst into the living room with their books and book bags.

"*. . . who committed war crimes . . .*"

The kids froze when they heard the familiar voice. This was the first they had heard about Rip's being taken hostage.

"*. . . to America, take back your own soul . . .*"

Enough. The kids didn't need to hear this. Jackie switched off the TV and herded them out the door, ignoring their barrage of questions.

Rip had been like a brother to Lena Graves as well as to Joseph. Before their divorce, Rip and Gloria had socialized with Joe and Lena, as well as the Ortiz family. The three families often shared meals and holidays at one another's homes. And through all that madness that began from Afghanistan and led to Rip's resigning from the Navy and the SEALs and being kidnapped in Africa, the other SEALs had never told the wives the details of what happened in Kunar Province. SEALs kept all such information even from their own families—or perhaps especially from their families. Whatever happened, Joe, Caulder, and Ortiz kept the story carefully guarded.

Lena sat at the kitchen table grading papers before school. She had the small TV playing the news in a corner of the kitchen when a news flash caught her attention. She looked up when she heard Rip's voice. He appeared on camera reciting what appeared to be a structured script. She froze in astonishment, pen poised in her hand, staring at the screen.

. . . your dreams of justice and freedom . . ."

The sun was well up and the Atlantic tide slapping in against the beach when Bear Graves and Buddha Ortiz drove up to Alex Caulder's ramshackle beach house to discuss the news with him and how it might affect the team and the SEALs in general. A gull perched preening on the exposed springs of the old car seat on the porch shrieked its displeasure at being disturbed. It flapped its wing and sailed over Ortiz's head and downwind low to the sand while it continued to scold. Bear pounded the side of his fist against the door, rattling it. Sand sifted down on his head. Caulder opened up immediately wearing Beach Boy cutoffs and flip-flops, no shirt, his angular features sharper than usual with traces of his mischievous Dennis the Menace erased. Obviously, he had already heard the news.

"I'm watching it right now," he said, and led them to his computer where a video played Rip's "confession" in its entirety. The three viewed it grim-faced.

". . . to my brothers on SEAL Team Six, please, look into your hearts. Let your better nature, let the truth, shine through. It's not too late. I'm proof of that . . ."

None of them spoke until the screen went blank. Caulder sighed and turned the machine off. "I don't even want to think about what they did to him," he said.

"Whatever we're thinking," Buddha said, "it had to be worse."

Caulder appeared to have already made up his mind as to a course of action they should take. "Truth's going to come out what happened," he said. "We got to come clean. Get ahead of this thing."

Graves scowled at him. "We do that, we might as well turn in our Tridents."

He had also made up his mind. He locked his gaze into Caulder's, then into Ortiz's. "No," he said fiercely. "We keep our mouths shut. Like we agreed."

"Cover up's worse than the crime," Caulder pointed out. "What's done is done, but we can still—"

"There was no fucking crime!" Bear exploded, jaw set. He grabbed Caulder by the arm and shook him with barely restrained fury.

Ortiz the peacemaker moved in between them. "This isn't getting us anywhere," he said. "They want us at Command, so we got to decide. Right now."

The three SEALs stepped apart and regarded each other warily, the long trust between them on the verge of being tested.

Chapter Twenty

Panama

Much of Central America was steeped in poverty and riddled with government corruption. In Panama City, hapless people at the edge of the canal lived all crowded in on each other in rat warrens constructed of old crates, rusted tin, scraps of canvas, and even abandoned oil drums. Scrawny, hungry kids without shoes and often no shirts scraped around in waste scrounging for scraps to eat. Old people with neither a future nor much of a past stared into emptiness.

Poverty and deprivation seemed not to have touched the residents of a stately Mediterranean-style villa on an aquamarine-blue lagoon that opened into the ocean. The villa's red tile roof and bright white-washed walls reflected back the morning sun like a jewel cast onto the green of a perfectly manicured lawn. The TV inside the house blasted loudly enough to be heard in the kitchen where Nilofar, a Chechen Muslim mother in her thirties wearing the traditional head-to-toe *abaya*, was preparing a peanut butter and banana sandwich for her ten-year-old daughter Fatima. Her husband was a Chechen commander fighting with Allah's armies against the infidels. Last she heard of him he was bound for Africa to meet her brother, also a warrior of Allah.

The news program on TV was broadcasted in English with Arabic subtitles. A commentator was providing a rundown and update involving an American SEAL who had confessed to war crimes. "*The*

SEAL confession has gone viral," he droned on in his most professional Doomsday voice. "*Yesterday, demonstrators rocked capitals throughout the Middle East when a video of ex-SEAL Team Six member Richard Taggart surfaced in which Taggart claimed to have killed an unarmed American in Afghanistan. Though Taggart appears to be speaking honestly, many argue that the statement is coerced . . .*"

Nilofar walked through from the kitchen and turned down the volume. She switched channels to Al-Jazeera TV, which was airing scenes of worldwide demonstrations in Muslim nations, similar to those that followed the Charlie Hebdo-Muhammad cartoons in France. Cameras switched from place to place around the globe—American flags being burned and Uncle Sam hanged in effigy, little kids armed with make-believe rifles "shooting" infidels, crowds storming the streets in Saudi Arabia, Turkey, Iran, Lebanon, and elsewhere with much wailing and gnashing of teeth and waving of Jihad flags and protest signs in Arabic, blazing piles of old tires pumping black smoke into the air . . .

Nilofar, a rather bony woman with a sharp face, returned to the kitchen to finish building Fatima's sandwich while a young Panamanian nanny from Colon rearranged a stack of children books behind the TV and wiped clean the lenses of a four-feed security monitor hidden within a nearby wall shelf. She then followed Nilofar into the kitchen to pick up her purse. Every Wednesday evening the nanny took Fatima out to a movie.

Although Wednesday evenings were Fatima's favorite part of the week, the pert little girl wearing an *abaya* that matched her mother's remained in the living room to get in another minute on a computer game. Oddly enough, the game featured a big-headed avatar carrying an axe, a game generally more seductive of boys. She happened to glance up from the computer in time to see a clip of Richard Taggart's "confession."

"*. . . I was a hired assassin . . .*"

Curious, Fatima called out to her mother in Arabic, "Who's that, Mother?"

Arabic was not a common language in Latin America, where Spanish followed by English were more acceptable.

"*Fil hothy dinye . . .*" Nilofar replied, also in Arabic. "The world has many good people. But some are not. Which is why we are here in Panama. Eat your sandwich. You'll be late for the movie."

"When will we see Father?" Fatima wanted to know.

"*Insh'allah.* Soon I hope."

Chapter Twenty-One

SEAL Command, Virginia Beach

White Squadron Commander Lee Atkins stood tall and rugged-looking in dress blues at a table up front in the Command Briefing Room. All White Squadron troops not on mission profile were assembled. The bomb that was Taggart's "confession" reverberated throughout the SEALs and the Special Forces community in general. The first reaction of any strak outfit like SpecOps to an attack from outside was to harden the walls.

"The President of the United States wants to go on TV and tell the world that Richard Taggart is an American hero and that this confession is pure bullshit," Commander Atkins began.

He paused to let that sink in. His severe gaze raked the table where Senior Chief Bear Graves's team was assemble—Graves, Caulder, Ortiz, Fishbait, and Chase, all in pressed cammies work uniform. The teammates remained still and silent, looking back at their commander. Behind Atkins, a still shot of Taggart during his "confession" overlooked the room from the big briefing screen.

"It is pure bullshit, right?" the commander pressed, looking directly at Graves.

Bear spoke for the team. "No way Rip would say that—"

Caulder finished the thought. "—not unless they coerced him or worse."

The team had coalesced around the team leader. That was the story—and they were sticking to it.

"We checked the ISR footage," Commander Atkins proceeded. A Predator drone from Intelligence, Surveillance, and Reconnaissance had overflown the 2014 op into Kunar Province, as it did most SEAL Six missions. "There's a gap in the coverage when this was supposed to have happened, the other Muj was turned over to the Afghan police, SOP. Anything you want to add? Now is the time."

"Sir, we got to get Rip before they torture him anymore," Graves spoke up. "Any lead from the dead Chechen we bagged and brought out from the village?

"Working on it," Commander Atkins replied. "Got a lead on a Chechen named Barayev. We thought he was dead. Turns out he might not be."

Fishbait drew attention to the black-and-green Jihad flag that backgrounded Taggart in the video still shot on the big screen. "That flag behind Rip? It's the same one from the group that did the Tanzania embassy bombing."

Atkins nodded. "Working on that too."

The meeting broke up with Graves, Caulder, and Ortiz banded together tighter than ever over what occurred that night during the hunt and chase for Hatim al-Muttaqi. The team made its way in a group to the Cage Room where Buddha attempted to shut the door to bar Fishbait and Chase.

"Fishbait, Chase, give us a minute," Ortiz said.

Chase bulled his way on in. "You trust me with your life, Ortiz?" he asked stubbornly.

"Yes I do."

"Then trust me, dammit."

"That's right," Fishbait put in. "We're either part of the team or we're not."

Fishbait and Buck had arrived at the shooting in Kunar after it had already gone down. Chase had not even been a member of the team at the time.

After a moment's hesitation and an exchange of looks among Graves, Ortiz, and Caulder, the three SEALs stepped out of the way to allow Fish and Chase to accompany them into the Cage Room. Graves closed and secured the door to prevent anyone walking in on them. He finally broke the uncomfortable silence of everyone waiting for someone else to open the discussion.

"What's on your mind?" he innocuously asked Fish and Chase.

Ghetto Chase glanced at Fishbait, then back at Bear. "Everything Rip said, it's true, right? Otherwise you wouldn't be shutting us out."

Finally, Ortiz nodded when it appeared none of the others was coming forth.

"Of course, it's true," Fishbait said. "Caulder, what did you do with the photo of the dead guy? The one I took for the After Action shooter statement?"

"Erased it."

"Who else knows about this?" Chase asked.

"Just that other Muj with him," Buddha volunteered. "The driver."

Fishbait shook his head. This shit should never have happened. "What Rip did, scalping the guy, shooting the kid, it's not what I signed up for. But I love this country. I love my religion, too. And I hate these assholes who give Islam a bad name."

He wheeled about in frustration and walked off a few paces before he came back. "Look, we screw up sometimes, but, bottom line, we're on the right side."

Caulder was ready to lighten up things, ease the tension. "Wow, Fish. I thought you were just in it for the money."

Fishbait shot him a look: *smartass.*

Ghetto Chase could always fall back on his Harvard degree. "Me," he said, "I signed up to help people who can't help themselves. Like those girls that got kidnapped."

"We all did," Graves said. He clapped a hand on the kid's shoulder and offered him a way out. "Chase, this is on us. Not you."

Caulder nodded assent, serious again, "You've got a big future, kid. Don't screw it up."

"Walk out," Ortiz suggested. "You weren't over there. For all anybody knows, you were never here either. You know nothing about it."

Chapter Twenty-Two

Virginia Beach

Jackie Ortiz distributed takeout to her family for an early dinner. Lately, she had been too busy to cook, what with her new sales rep position at the pharmaceutical company keeping her on the run with meetings and clients. Husband Ricky and kids Anabel and R.J. popped the still-warm containers onto their plates and opened the tops. Ricky picked up the black plastic fork and made a face. This wasn't the way Latino family life was supposed to be. And, he conceded, it was all his fault. Jackie wouldn't have gone to work outside the home in order to pay for Anabel's dance lessons if Ricky had quit the SEALs as he promised and taken the security position.

But he couldn't quit, couldn't desert Rip when Rip needed the team. After Rip was home again and safe, Ricky promised himself for the sake of the family that he *would* promptly take that normal job for a normal life. Until then—

He gave the fork another unpleasant look and sighed.

"That big sale with the hospital," Jackie was saying enthusiastically as she sat down at the table and waited for Ricky to say grace. "I've got a shot at it."

"That's great news, *Bonita.*"

He only half-listened to family life going on around him, distracted as he was considering his team's early conversation and renewed pact in the Cage Room at Command. It was bad enough, he thought, that he, Caulder, and Bear had covered for Rip when it went down. Essentially, they lied in After Action reports and in post-op briefings. That was easy enough to rationalize. War was an ugly thing that involved killing people and blowing up things. A terrorist war was much uglier. Terrorists were fanatics; each one left alive would be back out sooner or later blowing up busloads of innocent people or hijacking airliners and crashing them with all aboard. You could count on it. This was what made soldiers cynical. Army General Killian had his phrase: "Treat everyone you meet kindly and with respect, but be ready to kill them." Rip also had his: "Kill 'em all, let God sort 'em out."

But to bring Fishbait and Chase into the cover up after the fact? Buddha harbored an uneasy feeling that this thing was not ending well for any of them.

Jackie's thoughts were stuck on the prospect of her big hospital sale today. "It'll pay for your dance school tuition," she assured Anabel.

"Yeah. Great." Anabel said as she sorted through her paper container with her fingers.

"Anabel! No, no, no," her mother scolded. "Don't eat out of Styrofoam. Spoon it out onto your plates."

The wall phone rang. "Anabel, you get that?" Jackie sang out. She was busy making sure R.J. followed proper protocol for eating takeout.

Anabel jumped up and answered the ring. "Ortiz residence . . .Who's calling? You're from New York . . . ?" She lifted a questioning brow at the rest of the family. "Oh? *The New Yorker* magazine?"

That caught Jackie's attention. Ricky bent over his plate, pretending he had no idea what it could be about and that he had no interest in finding out.

"About who?" Anabel asked into the telephone receiver.

Ricky accepted that he was going to have to handle this. He stood up. "Give it to me, Anabel . . . Who are you asking about?" he barked irritably into the receiver. "Never heard of him. You must have the wrong number."

He hung up.

"He asked about Rip," Anabel informed her mother.

Ortiz disliked his family hearing him lie. "Let's just have dinner, okay?

Anabel looked at him, curious. "I'm not hungry," she decided.

"What's wrong?" Jackie asked her, concerned. "You not feeling well?"

"Everyone was talking about Rip at school today," she probed.

R.J. became all ears, like the family might be trying to leave him out of something important or interesting. "What about Rip? Tell me?"

Ortiz put down his plastic fork and pushed away from the table. "Listen, all of you. Don't worry about this. It's a tough situation. They're forcing Rip to say some bad things. But we'll get him back, safe and sound. Then I'll take that contractor's job. Be home more. Mom won't have to work so hard. No more Styrofoam."

He forced himself to smile and change the subject. "R.J., how's the video game? You got to the next level? Anabel, how's dance? I want to come pick you up again."

R.J. scooted away from the table. "Can I be excused?"

"Me, too," Anabel chimed in. "I've got homework."

They hurried from the table. Ricky picked at his food and helped Jackie clean up.

"It was an American, wasn't it?" Jackie said as she wiped down the table. "Who might have come over here to kill Ricky Jr. and Anabel? I don't care if Rip killed him. I care about you. About us. But the kids, they're upset. They don't like thinking of you this way."

"Which way?"

Jackie carried plates to the sink and tuned on the water. With her back to him, she said, "I made peace with what you do a long time ago. Anabel and R.J. are still figuring it out."

Ortiz had nothing to say, nothing he could tell her. But Jackie knew from the way Ricky and the rest of the team behaved when they were together, the low voices and tension, that Rip's video confession was the truth. She turned from the sink. Water continued to run from the faucet.

"Ricky, look at me."

After a beat, he did.

"Ricky, I know what I'm supposed to do, okay?"

What she was telling him was that she was part of the conspiracy of silence and could be trusted.

Chapter Twenty-Three

Chad, Africa

Chad's Sahelian belt, a great plains almost denuded of forest in some areas, had once been habitat to a variety of Africa's large mammals—elephants, rhino, lions. Poaching and deforestation had reduced the fauna population to near-extinction in the region—and into that vacuum of forlorn landscapes and deserted structures migrated terrorists and revolutionaries to plot and plan and train.

From the outside, the abandoned cement plant and its overgrown and falling fences, kilns, tanks, and buildings appeared bleached and torn and lifeless like the bones of some alien giant slain and left to the harsh African sun and wind. Life, however, at least to some minimal extent, had returned to the inside of the bones.

Inside the main building, which Michael Nasry referred to as his "training facility," Chechen soldiers in combat gear drilled in close-quarter urban tactics. They stormed about in squads and stacks, busting through doors, clearing rooms, stalking snipers . . . Swarthy Akmal Barayev, instructor and referee, raced about the great barn-like building in the soldiers' wake shouting commands, cajoling, lecturing, and correcting. As a former Russian Spetsnaz operative, it was his responsibility to ensure Emir Hatim al-Muttaqi's "army" was properly edged for what lay ahead. War and general bedlam made the planet a much more dangerous place and formed a kind of backdrop for terrorism's upward trend.

Inside Michael Nasry's office, his "nerve center" where his recruiters had set up shop with their laptops and files, the Taggart video confession played on the TV screen before a captive audience that consisted of Taggart zip-tied to a rusted metal chair, Na'omi, and her three students who huddled together across from him against a wall scabbed with peeling paint.

Nasry took pride in knowing that the video produced and distributed by him from an old vacant cement plant in a remote corner of remotest Africa was an international phenomena. Recruiting by ISIS, al-Qaeda and their affiliates had nearly doubled since the video made its premier. That was success Emir al-Muttaqi could appreciate.

The office remained eerily quiet except for Taggart's voice spilling from the on-screen video. "*. . . to my brothers on SEAL Team Six, please, look inside your hearts. Let your better nature, let the truth, shine through. It's not too late. I'm proof of that . . .*"

Michael paused the video while Esther and her two classmates eyed the big American tied to the chair. They looked uneasy and wary. Na'omi strived to make eye contact with Rip, to let him know that she still believed in him and that she realized the only reason Esther and she were alive was because Rip submitted to making the video for Nasry. Rip declined to look at her. Stone-faced, he stared off into a gray distance.

Michael paced back and forth in front of his prisoners, hands clasped behind his back in the manner of a professor delivering a lecture on quantum physics or the history of the Peloponnesian War. He stopped in front of Taggart.

"Congratulations," he announced expansively. "You're a real hero now. It's already the most popular video in the world. Recruiting is through the roof. The SEALs, your families—they'll—"

Rip's eyes flashed. "They won't believe it. I only said it because you put suicide vests on her—"

Na'omi.

"—and her—"

Esther, who shuddered at the recollection.

Michael turned to Na'omi. "I apologize for that. I know you love those girls," he said with contrived regret, then continued in a macabre justification of why he had to do what he did. "My brother's name was Omar. It means 'long-lived.'"

"Omar was born premature," Michael explained to Na'omi, ignoring her lack of interest. "Spent the first four months of his life in a plastic bubble. My first memory is going to the hospital and watching my mother cry outside the ICU. She could only hold him for twenty minutes a day."

His chin dropped to his chest. His voice lowered to barely above a whisper. "It almost bankrupted my father. But Omar made it. He was the smallest kid on the block, but he never backed down. He hated injustice. He hated the strong preying on the weak."

He wheeled unexpectedly away from Na'omi and toward Rip, his features twisted with fierce hatred. "*And you murdered him*!" he bellowed.

Rip looked at him with a mixture of pity and disgust. "If you're looking for blood, pal, look on your own hands."

Michael relaxed after a moment and smiled disdainfully. He returned to Na'omi. "You're a good woman, a teacher. But you have no idea what kind of man he really is."

"He's twice the man you'll ever be," she snapped back. But her eyes shifted away from Rip to settle their painful gaze on her hands.

Michael clicked off the TV video. He assumed a wide-legged stance in front of Taggart's chair and glared down at the SEAL. "This video is your confession before man and God. For murdering a beautiful human being. You will help me train our men. And you will be confessing more, a lot more."

He nodded toward guards stationed at the door, who ushered Na'omi and her students from the room. Esther kept looking back at Rip bound in his chair. Tears streamed down her cheeks.

While Michael waited for the guards to come back, he ignored Taggart and began playing a video game on one of the computers.

Taggart glimpsed a big-headed weirdo on the screen armed with an enormous battle axe.

Upon their return, the guards escorted Taggart to the girls' makeshift dormitory. They re-tied his hands from his front to behind his back and threw him to the floor where they bound his bare feet together. Na'omi and the girls watched in dead silence, afraid to move or speak or do anything to attract the guards to them. Rip joined their silence even after the guards left, bolting the door behind them. He took note that a guard kept vigil outside the door.

Rip sat trussed on the floor staring into space past the long table where the students received their lessons and colored more pictures for the walls. He realized what Nasry was doing, putting him in with the girls—conditioning him to do literally anything in order to save Na'omi and her students.

Esther, with the encouragement of her teacher, shyly approached Rip with her hands clasped in front of her gray tunic. Na'omi nodded for her to continue.

"Thank you, Mister Rip, for saving us," she blurted out.

Rip brought himself back from space. "You're a brave girl, Esther."

Na'omi walked up and placed a gentle hand on the little girl's shoulder. "Esther, there are books on the shelf. Get the others to do some reading."

Esther rushed to her friends to do as teacher asked. Na'omi settled on her knees by Rip's side. She smelled clean and fresh from the shower and looked pretty even in the loose gray linen trousers and tunic supplied by the Chechens. Nasry, Rip suspected, was manipulating both of them.

"That must have been hard for you," she said softly, referring to the video. "But it's only words. The first time Boko Haram raped me . . . I wanted to die. Then you told me I had to be strong for the girls, and so I was. Now you have to be strong for them."

"Na'omi . . ."

She touched his cheek. "I don't care what that man says. I know one thing sure about you. You will do anything to save us. Richard, I believe in you."

The human heart was not symmetrical or neat. It turned back on itself in folds and knots that Rip felt deep in his core. She must have felt the same way. Tears glistened in her dark eyes.

Chapter Twenty-Four

Virginia Beach

Imagine! A SEAL whose sperm weren't strong enough to *swim!*

Bear Graves left his local hardware store with a bag of do-it-yourself items for his garage workshop. He had thought to complete the baby crib he was building for the as-of-yet unborn child to take Sarah's place. A child that might never be born. Still, it gave Bear something to do with his hands other than train with the team while time dragged. It also proved to Lena that he was at least thinking of Doctor Banershee's recommendation that he do something about his infertility.

Besides, there was nothing Graves and his team could do about Rip except wait for the geeks and spooks to come up with a lead. Every morning Bear checked with Commander Atkins for any new developments. The commander simply shook his head.

Bear climbed into his pickup and tossed the bag to the passenger's seat. He started the truck, plugged in his cell phone and tuned it to CarPlay radio. A talk show was on, the host a know-it-all with an attitude discussing Taggart and his "confession."

"If we don't get a handle on these professional assassins," he was saying, "we're going to be hearing about a lot more war crimes."

Bear dropped the GMC into reverse and backed out of the parking space. A guest on the program provided his take on the terrorism problem. "I'm sick of our heroes being vilified for doing what it takes to protect America—"

"This isn't what we stand for, Andy—"

Fuck off, buddy! The guy was probably some fat asshole with a big mouth and the guts of a sparrow. Throughout US history, one go-to formula for victory was to kill enough of the enemy to make him stop fighting.

When Bear arrived home, he discovered Lena having coffee at the kitchen table with their pastor. He shot Lena a questioning look. *What have you told him?*

"I asked Pastor Adams over for a chat, Joseph," she said innocently.

Trapped, Bear shook hands and sat down. "Hello, Pastor."

"Hello, Joe." The minister was a small, balding, kindly man in his fifties.

Lena rose from the table to fetch her husband a cup of coffee. He cradled the cup in his big hands and gave her an accusing look. So now he needed an intervention by their minister?

"My cousin is a Ranger," Pastor Adams began off-handedly. "Did I tell you that?"

Bear shook his head.

"Four tours. Iraq. Afghanistan. He lost a lot of buddies."

"That's tough. I feel for the guy."

Bear had a feeling he knew where this was going. Lena had been concerned about him since the team's deployment to Afghanistan. Taggart left mysteriously shortly after that. Then came Sarah's death, followed by Bear's inability to provide Lena with another child, Rip's abduction, Buck's dying in Nigeria, Rip's "confession" video . . . that was a lot to cope with, even for a guy like Graves.

Reverend Adams appeared to be studying Bear, as though attempting to read his soul. Then, just as Bear suspected, here it came. "It can be a heavy burden, even when the cause is just," the pastor said in his gentle pulpit manner. "And it *is* just. What helped, what really grounded him was coming into the church. Not just the prayer, but being with people, Joe. Picnics, socials. You can't isolate yourself."

"Pastor, I'm not sure what Lena told you. But, really, I'm fine."

"I'm glad to hear that, Joe. But, we're the ones who have asked you to go into the world and do what must be done in the Lord's name. Let us help you. Pray with me, Joe."

The preacher bowed his head at the table and offered an outstretched hand each to Bear and to Lena. Lena took it and bowed her head. Graves hesitated. Then he gripped the pastor's proffered hand and clasped Lena's other hand across the table to form a prayer circle. Reverend Adams led the prayer.

"Jesus, we ask you in the name of the Lord to bring peace to this member of your flock . . ."

Graves opened his eyes to look at Lena, his face inscrutable, hers at peace with her eyes closed.

Chapter Twenty-Five

Virginia Beach

Alex Caulder went surfboarding in the morning with the incoming tide, but his mind wasn't on it. He kept thinking about Dharma and the iPad video showing Tammi Buckley and him together on the day of Buck's funeral. He returned to his beach shack and propped his surfboard to the side of the front door opposite the rusted car seat. Usually, retreating to the ocean and its waves helped him to lose himself. It hadn't worked this time.

His nearest neighbor lived a half-mile down the beach, which afforded him the isolation and luxury of an outdoor, open-air shower. He stepped underneath the sting of the pressured water, got out, toweled off, and stood for a long time looking out to sea, thinking.

That afternoon he banged the blonde waitress from the Gulfstream Diner or, rather, he *attempted* to. That left him on a flat sea. He rolled off and lay naked on the bed next to her.

"Don't worry, hon," she sympathized. "It happens."

"Not to me. Look, I've got to go."

He lay watching her while she dressed. "A reporter came by the diner," she said. "Asking about your friend."

"What friend?"

"You know. Short stack, three eggs over medium, crisp bacon. He always ordered that whenever you get back from . . . Well, you know."

"You know—what?"

She sat down on the side of the bed to put on her work tennies. "Missions and everything," she said. "What you guys do."

Annoyed, Caulder reached for his underwear and jeans. "I work in *weapons development.* So keep your . . . mistaken assumptions to yourself. I mean it. Okay? Got it?"

"Sure, hon. I'm a waitress. I know how to take orders."

Caulder's day didn't get any better. He couldn't have explained why he did it, but he drove to Buckley's little house that Buck and Tammi purchased just before what turned out to be Buck's fatal deployment. Her car sat on the front lawn with a U-Haul trailer attached to it and backed up to the front door. Tammi was loading the last of her household belongings into it. She looked more depressed and alone than ever.

"I didn't know you were leaving," Caulder said. He took a taped box from her and carried it aboard the trailer. "I could've helped," he offered.

"Oh? The Viking warrior looking after the widow of the fallen comrade," Tammi scoffed, every word dripping with sarcasm. "It's an ancient tradition, yes?"

"I thought it was what you wanted."

"That's so . . . so Caulder. Always someone else's fault."

She seemed to have gotten bitter almost overnight. She slammed the door to the U-Haul and rested her forehead wearily against it. In a low, faraway voice, she said, "It's funny. I never cheated on him. I know he thought I did. All of you. But I never did." Her voice carried her, drifting even farther away. "Never—until he was dead."

"Buck was my friend." Caulder felt like a hypocrite saying it. "I feel bad too. If you want me to take the blame, I will."

Tammi kept her back to him with her head lowered. "This Rip thing?" she pondered. "It all came clear to me. You're *all* him. You're all just one step away from a confession video."

She finally turned to face him. The tone of her voice changed to include sorrow and regret. "Alex, I'm sorry. It's not your fault. I wish I was you, helping someone else pack up their life."

She stepped forward and touched his face with her fingertips, a gentle gesture that also expressed pity. "You're the lucky one," she said.

He frowned. "Why's that?"

"You don't have anything to lose."

Chapter Twenty-Six

Virginia Beach

Caulder and Buckley may have tagged Robert Chase Jr. with his team handle, *Ghetto*, but his life had been anything but what that signified. He grew up in a posh Virginia Beach community, the only son of a prominent and well-connected government lawyer whom the *Washington Post* speculated may become the next attorney general of the United States. Living so near the home of the East Coast Navy SEALs and of SEAL Team Six, the most elite counterterrorist unit on the globe, Robert Jr. as a kid often went about with his nose stuck in a book about the SEALs. They were his heroes. His classmates read *Harry Potter.* The future Ghetto Chase absorbed *Brave Men, Dark Waters*, or *First SEAL*.

Robert Sr. held expectations that his son would follow his path into the practice of law. Ghetto even seemed headed in that direction. He completed his prelaw degree with honors at Harvard, his father's alma mater, and was excelling in his *juris doctorate* when he disappointed his dad by enlisting in the US Navy, refusing an officer's commission in order to become a SEAL operative. Although Robert Sr. may have been dissatisfied by his son's choice, he could never say he was surprised by it.

Ghetto may have given up his parents' lifestyle, but he still enjoyed some of its trappings. Such as the new baby blue Prius he parked in front of his parents' suburban colonial home during his free time from training at SEAL Command. Caulder jokingly referred to Ghetto's juxtaposition of his two different lives as a "continuing cultural shock."

On a morning after the "Taggart Confessions" went viral around the world, creating chaos and rioting, Ghetto drove home for a serious conversation with his father and to request a favor. He delayed getting down to the purpose of his visit until after the ritual of coffee at the formal dining room table. His mother hovered over the two men in her life with a hot pot. She was a slim, attractive woman in her fifties with an aquiline nose and hair that still showed no gray. She traced her family lineage back to colonial Virginia and the slaves of wealthy plantation owners. Thus the source of her name, Virginia.

"Judge Martinez and her husband were here for dinner," Virginia said, affectionately stroking her son's short-cropped military haircut. "They asked after you."

Robert Sr. was a self-professed workaholic. Even at coffee with his son, he sorted through deposition files spread about on the table. A distinguished-looking gentleman with gray at the temples and a well-trimmed mustache and goatee, he and his son shared the same athletic build.

Robert Sr. looked up from his work. "She said she'd love to have you clerk for her. You were only a semester away from your JD. You could finish up," he added hopefully.

"Dad, we've been through this. I'm not going back to law school."

Virginia had been the parent who championed her son's choosing his own path. She knew even when her husband persuaded him that law should be his profession that his heart wasn't in it. Now, she moved in smartly to divert the conversation to more neutral grounds.

"Did you know this . . . SEAL?" she asked out of genuine curiosity. "The one who confessed?"

"No."

"I just hate to think of you . . . caught up in things like this."

"What your mother means to say," Robert Sr. interjected, "is we're worried about you."

"'What she means to say,'" Ghetto repeated hopelessly. It was his father's way of directing the conversation back to the same topic. "Look, Dad. What I'm doing, it's just as righteous as when you marched to Selma."

"Son, that was the Civil Rights movement. There's no comparison."

Chase fortified himself with a deep breath before plunging ahead toward the purpose of his visit. He and his dad had always been comfortable in discussing most subjects, the one exception being law school. Chase always tried to avoid that area.

"A buddy of mine," he broached. "He died in my arms a week ago."

A concerned look swept his father's face.

"Then," Chase continued, "I took out a guy while trying to save some kidnapped girls."

Virginia looked horrified. She was a gentle person who always attempted to look at the more pleasant side of life. She braced herself against the edge of the table, her lips trembling with emotion. Her son, a killer?

"I killed someone," Chase reaffirmed. "And I'll do it again."

Virginia fled the room with hands over her face. Chase hadn't brought up the subject to shock his mother or his father, but instead to prepare the way for what concerned him. He regretted not having taken his father aside before bringing up the discussion.

"She'll be okay," Robert Sr. assured his son. "I'll talk to her."

Chase gave the moment some space before he resumed. "Listen, Dad. Did you ever have any doubts? In the Movement, that you were doing the right thing?"

"I never had to kill anyone. I don't know how that feels."

"That's not what I'm asking. I signed up for that."

Father and son waited. Robert Sr. chose his words carefully, as a lawyer would. "Doubts? Sure, there were some dark moments. But regrets? No. If I allowed injustice to happen, then it was on me. I couldn't stand by and do nothing. We were warriors, too, in our way. I would have died for them, and they for me."

Chase thought about it a moment. Now for the other reason for this morning's visit.

"Dad, I need a favor. Your old Harvard roommate—Charles Billington. He's still at the embassy in Kabul, right?"

"Yes."

"I was wondering, could you ask him to check something with the Afghan police? An interview with a Mujtahid captured in Kunar. I have the date."

Robert Sr. wasn't a brilliant lawyer for nothing. "That date wouldn't happen to be September 3, 2014, would it? The same date mentioned in the SEAL video?"

Chapter Twenty-Seven

SEAL Command, Virginia Beach

The geeks and spooks were working after all. White Squadron Commander Lee Atkins summoned Bear Graves's team to the Command Briefing Room, where Lieutenant Camille Fung, a Command intel officer, was prepared to commence. Fung was a no-bullshit woman and got right to the point.

"The target is Nilofar Kazbekov."

A photo snapshot flashed onto the big screen showing a rather bony Muslim woman in her thirties wearing a full head-to-toe *abaya.*

"Her husband was that dead Chechen you brought back from Nigeria. He was last seen with Akmal Barayev, Nilofar's brother, who is high on our target deck. Agency sources tell us Akmal . . . here—" A photo came onto the screen of a man in his late twenties, early thirties, with a long, full face, a swarthy complexion, and a tight crop of curly black hair. ". . . is very close to his sister and may have information leading to Rip in West Africa."

Commander Atkins cut in from the sidelines. "She lives in a villa in Panama paid for by charities tied to terrorist groups."

He nodded for Lieutenant Fung to go ahead. She brought up Google Earth images of a startlingly white, two-story villa with a red tile roof situated on well-manicured grounds near an ocean lagoon. Additional agency surveillance photos provided more details of the layout, including footages of Nilofar and her preteen daughter Fatima laughing and doing dance moves on the lawn while the nanny and two armed guards lounged nearby.

Not bad digs, Bear Graves noted to himself. Terrorist "charities" must be doing remarkably well.

"On Wednesday night the nanny usually takes the daughter to a movie," Commander Atkins informed Senior Chief Graves and his men, "so they should be out of the way. We estimate a three- to five-man security detail to accompany you. We're going in low vis with non-attributable gear."

That meant if they were caught, the US publically disavowed all knowledge of their existence.

Chapter Twenty-Eight

Panama

In 1989, the US Seventy-Fifth Rangers parachuted onto the Rio Hato military airfield in support of Operation Just Cause to depose the iron-fisted dictatorship of General Manuel Noriega. More than two-and-a-half decades later, a clandestine force of ten US Navy SEALs from Team Six slipped onto the small airfield in a C-17 arranged by CIA spooks and assets on the ground. A smaller plane, unmarked and operated by local CIA assets, waited inside a hangar ready to supply the SEALs a platform for their water-night parachute jump with the Kazbekov villa as their target.

As the sun set in the Pacific, Senior Chief Bear Graves's team and five operators from White Squadron to man the security detail received warning orders to 'chute up and prepare to board. They would be jumping light, which meant one-piece black jumpsuits, weapons, helmets with NVGs, water wings, radios, swim fins strapped to their thighs, and little else. If all went according to plan, the team would seize Nilofar while her daughter and nanny were away at the movies, whisk her back to the airfield, and be well on their way to the US by dawn. She was the best lead Intel sources had come up with so far as to where Taggart and the African females were being held after Chechens stole them from Boko Haram.

Graves conducted jumpmaster checks before the SEALs filed up the open back ramp of the aircraft and took seats in the passenger webbing for the short one-hour flight out over the Pacific and then back in to jump in waters off the beachfront villa purchased and maintained by terrorist "charities."

Shortly after full darkness, the aircraft took to the sky. Ghetto Chase fell immediately asleep with his head bobbing on Ortiz's shoulder. Ortiz nodded off. Fishbait and Caulder in the webbing across from them slouched down in the darkened cabin, waiting, as did the five SEALs of the security detail. Bear waited quietly on the JM jump seat near the back ramp for the green light to signal the plane's approach to the drop zone at the mouth of the targeted lagoon.

Red and green lights above the jump door signaled the action. When the red light blinked on, Graves stood, faced the interior, and lifted two fingers. "Two minutes!" he called out.

Eyes snapped open and locked on him as the back ramp open. Paratroopers laden with battle equipment plus main and reserve 'chutes and weapons followed the JM's jump commands.

"Stand up!"

Paratroopers checked straps and buckles and handles of their own reserve and the mains of the jumpers ahead. The two sticks then turned around and went over the same routine with the paratroopers behind.

"Sound off for equipment check!"

Troopers sent the count up by slapping the 'chute or butt of the man ahead until the first man in the stick thrust thumbs up to Bear. NVGs covered eyes to provide vision in the dark. The open back ramp with wind howling past like a cataract increased the noise level inside by several factors. Calm and ready, facing the open ramp in twin sticks, the SEALs waited for Graves to shout the final commands.

He leaned out against his safety strap to peer around the edge of the open ramp into the prop wash underneath the left wing, his eyes scanning. *There!* A strobe light attached to the prow of a fishing boat operated by a CIA agent blipped six thousand feet below and ahead.

Graves pulled himself back inside to face the plane's interior and men prepared to leap into the unknown night. The green light above the ramp popped on with terrible presence. Bear thrust out both palms, craned one arm in an exaggerated movement across his chest and swept it toward the open door.

"Stand in the door!"

The sticks pounded forward.

"Go!"

Caulder went out the door first in his stick. Fishbait was his opposite first man. Seven others followed them out in a shuffling rush into the black wind. Graves came as the last jumper out. He cleared the door before walking quickly off the ramp into space. It always stunned him how rapidly and furiously paratroopers exited an aircraft.

Free falling, Caulder counted off the seconds—one . . . two . . . three seconds . . . He pulled his rip cord handle. His square 'chute tore from its pack, jerking him up hard in the wind and snapping his legs up as it blossomed. Hanging in his harness, he heard the rustling pops of other opening parachutes.

He toggled S-turns to allow the other jumpers to fall into his stack. A staircase of parachutists floated toward the blinking strobe in the water, each separated from the next by only about one hundred feet of air.

As point man in the stack, Caulder guided on the strobe. Other jumpers guided on him. In rapid sequence, the outline of a speed boat appeared on the water. It loomed larger and larger in the dark. Caulder's feet knifed into the waves twenty feet from the boat's stern. His heard other splashes as the rest of the team joined him in the drink. Quick-release parachutes floated free and collapsed. SEALs swam for the boat and were helped aboard by its crew.

Graves was last man out of the plane and last man of the stack into the ocean. Caulder and Ortiz hauled him out of the drink and into the boat. The team chief conducted a quick head count and threw a thumbs up to the CIA guy at the boat's helm. The boat's engine kicked in and propelled it and its cargo toward the opening of the lagoon that led to the targeted villa.

Chapter Twenty-Nine

Panama

The entrance to the lagoon was narrow and sheltered by foliage. The boat eased back throttle and slipped along the shoreline in the shadows of overhanging trees and dripping moss. When the CIA helmsman cut power, SEALs slipped over the gunnel into the black water with barely a ripple or sound to give away their presence and finned their way up the length of the lagoon toward the villa. Bear called a listening halt when it came into view, the team and attached security treading water with only their masks above the surface.

Windows squared with light burning brightly inside on both the lower and upper floor cut long rectangles on the lawn. Blue illumination glowed in the Olympic-size swimming pool. So far, nothing seemed to be moving. It was Wednesday, so the nanny ought to be at the movies with Rafina, which left the target, Nilofar, at home alone with her guards.

SEALs bellied out of the water onto the edge of the lawn like a pod of finned, masked amphibians, creatures from the Black Lagoon. Graves and Caulder pinpointed two guards and pointed them out. One patrolled the upper outside deck. He opened a door and disappeared inside.

The other guard at the pool paused with rifle slung on one shoulder to light a cigarette. His lighter sparked but refused to ignite into a flame. The repeated sparking flared over a broad bearded face that appeared Arabic, but might have been Chechen.

Fishbait continued to observe him from a starting position at the edge of the water while the rest of the team slipped off into the darkness to get into position for a building entry. Minutes later, Bear sent him a *Ready* signal through his helmet comm—a double click.

The guard made repeated attempts to make his lighter work. A red IR dot appeared on his forehead, unobserved by anyone not equipped with IR NVGs. Fishbait squeezed the trigger of his rifle. The noise-suppressed weapon issued a barely-audible *Thump!* The guy flicking his Bic looked momentarily stunned before the cigarette dropped from his lips and he crumpled without a sound, dead from a brain shot, and sloshed into the blue glow of the pool where he floated face down with a stream of blood crating an aura around his head.

Fish moved on up toward the house to post himself behind a tree to cover his teammates as they moved tactically toward the villa. Oozing like sinister shadows, a part of the night, Bear and his men swung toward the backyard, clearing windows as they went and avoiding the single outside security camera that pre-surveillance had located. A couple of SEALs from the security detachment spread out around the grounds to maintain surveillance and provide a blocking force.

Double sliding glass doors off a wooden deck provided a view of the lighted kitchen interior. A young Latina woman was busy building a plate of cookies and milk at the kitchen island with her back to both the door and an interior security monitor. A husky bearded guard wearing jeans and an official-looking ball cap, pistol on his hip, swiped a cookie off the plate on his way outside through the sliding doors.

"Carlos!" the young woman scolded, laughing. "You'll get fat!"

Carlos grinned, unaware that SEALs were closing in on the back deck, slipping along the side of the house. Ortiz was now on point with Graves close behind and Caulder and Ghetto trailing as rear security. Carlos slid open the glass door and stepped out onto the deck in the night air, munching on his pilfered cookie. A deadly red dot appeared on his forehead, followed by the quiet *Thump!* of Ortiz's short carbine. The guard tumbled off the deck and lay still on the lawn. Inside the kitchen, the little cookie maker's head went up in alarm.

"Carlos?"

SEALs flowed onto the wooden deck and into the kitchen. Caulder split off in a trot to one side to cover a set of stairs leading up to the second floor. Graves, Chase, and Ortiz rushed the surprised woman.

"Hands!" Ortiz commanded.

She stood frozen in alarm behind the island and the plate of cookies and milk that concealed her from the waist down.

"*Manos!*" Ortiz tried again, this time in Spanish.

Stupid mujer! There she was, overrun by a coterie of space age-looking soldiers straight from a *Star Wars* movie—and she went for a gun. Her hands flashed into sight with a semiauto pistol in one of them.

"No, no, no . . . *No!*" Ortiz yelled at her.

It was over very quickly, as such things almost always were. She fell to the floor with Graves's bullet through her heart. Spewing blood soaked her blouse and flowed across the tile kitchen floor. *Damn!* Bear noticed she had a pretty face with full lips and big brown eyes that remained wide open. This could be a dirty job at times.

Bear regained control of himself. His eyes swept the kitchen—newspapers on the table, computers on the breakfast island and countertops. He motioned to Chase and Ortiz.

"You've got all this," he told them.

Ortiz and Chase began collecting computers, papers, cell phones, and anything else of potential intel value while Graves linked up with Caulder at the open stairs that led to the second floor. Three security SEALs had by now made their entry through the front of the house and joined Bear and Caulder on the stairs, ascending slowly and cautiously, covering one another in the event of other hostile action. At least one guard remained alive and dangerous inside the house—the one on the upper outside deck who disappeared inside through a door. He was not the hefty one now cooling out on the back deck to the kitchen; he had been younger, leaner. A house under such heavy guard either had a lot to protect, or a lot to hide.

Stuffed animals were perched on stair steps all the way to the second floor, an eerie menagerie of lions and tigers, elephants and bears, zebras and pandas . . . All seemed to glare hate at the SEALs as they advanced upward.

Suddenly, the surviving guard appeared at the top of the stairs, his head lowered and his eyes on his cell phone. When something caused him to glance up, he cried out in surprise and reached for his holstered weapon. Caulder proved quicker on the trigger. The guy did a weird little dance as bullets tore into him. The body tumbled down the stairs, stampeding the menagerie of stuffed animals. Caulder stuck out a boot to stop it before it reached the bottom. A dislodged jaguar continued rolling all the way to the floor below.

Bedrooms lined the long hallway on the second floor. The three security detail SEALs dropped off to clear the first rooms while Bear and Caulder rushed toward two open doors at the end of the hall, which Intel indicated belonged to Nilofar and her daughter Fatima. Both rooms appeared to be draped in darkness except for an odd faint light flickering dimly from somewhere inside. Graves indicated he would take this room while Caulder searched the other one.

Bear eased through the open doorway, his senses alert for danger. The odd flickering light emanated from underneath the bathroom door. Through NVGs, Bear saw a tiny girl in pajamas sitting up in bed with a toy dog under one arm and a rhino under the other. The SEAL in all black with helmet and wide-eyed goggles must have seemed to her a monster from another planet. The man and the little girl stared at each other through the darkness, each too astonished to move or speak, the child wide-eyed and obviously terrified. Bear could only imagine how his daughter Sarah might have reacted to such an intrusion had she lived.

Caulder cleared the other bedroom. It was well-stocked with stuffed animals and was apparently the child's bedroom. No one was there. The little girl and her nanny were expected to have gone out to a Wednesday night movie.

Caulder moved on and into the other bedroom where he discovered an odd standoff of sorts between Graves and a little girl sitting up in bed. The child seemed to have gone into suspended animation. Caulder touched Bear from behind. Bear slowly turned his head.

Caulder gestured, his expression, hands, and shrugged shoulders all asking the same question: *What the fuck is she doing here? Wasn't she supposed to have gone to the movies?*

But if daughter was home, that likely meant the little dead cookie maker in the kitchen was the nanny.

The toilet in the bathroom flushed. Both men wheeled to face an intruder, weapons ready. The door opened and out stepped a bony woman wearing a nightgown. Both SEALs recognized her from her photo at the mission briefing. Caulder grabbed her before she could scream and flung her onto the bed while Graves attempted to calm the daughter, Fatima.

"It's okay, it's okay," he soothed.

"Little help here?" Caulder called out.

The woman had gone totally ape shit. It was all Caulder could do to hold his own without being forced to harm her. Fatima added to the turmoil when, terror-stricken, she lunged toward her mother, desperately crying and screaming and reaching for mommy.

Caulder changed his mind about needing help. "Get the kid, Bear."

Graves snatched the little girl off her feet and tucked her underneath one arm while she continued to kick and flail about with her tiny fists. Once they subdued mother and daughter, the two SEALs hustled them down the hallway.

"Touchdown!" Graves reported via radio. "Prep for exfil."

Things went on fast forward. A pair of dark vans waiting down the road rumbled up the drive to the now-unguarded house, driven by more Agency assets. Graves and Caulder dragged or carried Nilofar and Fatima down the stairs, stepping across the dead guard. Fatima stiffened in shock underneath Bear's arm. Her mother wailed with fright and fury.

"*Delta Four, Delta One, collapse into the house*," Graves radioed to all operators.

Fishbait, who maintained vigil by the swimming pool, responded, *"Delta One, Delta Four, stand by . . . We have a dog."*

Caulder cast a *What the fuck?* look at Graves.

A mangy-looking, long-legged black cur raced across the lawn in front of Fish and headed for the pool. It spotted Fishbait and skidded to a halt, its hackles bristling.

In the villa's kitchen, Chase and Ortiz had just finished bagging possible intel materials, including a child's pink computer, when Caulder and Bear burst through with Nilofar and Fatima, both of whom had ceased resisting and were instead shaking with fear.

"What the hell?" Ortiz exclaimed, seeing the child.

"The girl—" Chase chimed in. "She's not supposed to be here."

"She is," was all Caulder said.

This thing was getting out of hand. They heard Fishbait's dog baying outside. Fish was taking aim at the mutt to shut it up when a young boy appeared after having pushed through privacy hedges from next door and began calling his pet.

"Chico! Chico!"

Fishbait let off the trigger. He ducked behind a tree and slipped inside the house through an unlocked side door.

"*Delta One, Delta Four, coming in*," he radioed. "*We gotta go. We got lights at the neighbors.*"

He did a double take when the rest of the team emerged from the kitchen area with the target *and* her daughter in tow.

"We take her," Ortiz explained. "Can't leave her in a house full of dead people."

"You get the security hard drive?" Bear asked Chase.

"Yeah."

The dog now in the backyard was howling and barking up the entire neighborhood. The SEALs broke in a dead run for the two vans, dragging Nilofar and Fatima along with them. Bear and Caulder loaded their captives into one van and climbed in with them. The other operators loaded into the second van. The two vehicles pulled down the drive and out onto the road to merge into the night on their way along a back route toward the airfield where they would be exfiltrated.

Chico the dog raced around the house, the boy chasing him, and discovered the guard's body floating in the blue glow of the swimming pool, which incited another round of baying. The boy ran up to poolside and stopped to stare at the corpse floating in a spreading patina of blood.

Chapter Thirty

Chad, Africa

Six helmeted and goggled fighters maneuvered in the darkness of a massive open building, the lasers of their weapons tracing red lines against the walls. With the aid of greenish liquid night vision provided by early-generation NVGs, the Chechen advanced in a protective stack with weapons bristling out in all direction, like a herd of Cape buffalo defending a threatened calf.

When the stack reached an industrial-steel stairway, it advanced toward the roof in a cautious, leapfrogging overwatch. One element advanced while the other covered and prepared for combat. Then the lead went to ground and covered for the trail unit to press on through. In this manner an advance was always prepared for defensive or offensive action. Such maneuvers had been perfected by US SpecOps troops and US Marines during the wars in Iraq and Afghanistan.

A padlocked steel-screen gate blocked the stairs' top landing. One of the Chechens fumbled with a bolt cutter to snip the lock. Helmet radios crackled a command in Russian.

"*Stop! Freeze!*"

Dim lights suddenly illuminated the abandoned cement plant in Chad that the American radical terrorist Michael Nasry and his Chechen cohort Akmal Barayev had transformed into a terrorist training facility. So far, with the exception of 9/11 and a few other attempts, suicide bombers had not directly attacked the United States to any large extent. But if Nasry, Barayev, and their superior, head of operations Emir Hatim al-Muttaqi, played out their grand design, it was only a matter of time before many American soft targets—sports arenas, training facilities, movie theaters, schools—would be attacked, as they had been in Europe.

When the lights came on, Michael and Akmal watching in critique from the sidelines shoved their NVGs up onto their foreheads. Rip Taggart garbed in baggy shepherd trousers and a black tunic stood with them, but he wore no NVGs and seemed uninterested.

Seeing no reason why someone might have turned on the lights to halt training, Akmal ignored it and radioed his assessment of the training so far. "That was good," he said, still in Russian. "But you're still moving too fast. Walk to victory. Your enemy knows that."

The dim light in the great empty building created harsh shadows in the hollows of Michael's hatchet-like face when he turned to Taggart. "You get the idea," he said. "All these new recruits you are bringing us, we will make many more of these teams. American ones. To bring on you what you bring on us."

Taggart glared silently back at the terrorist. He turned his back.

Akmal was prepared to celebrate. "Michael!" he enthused. "The way you have made use of this SEAL, all the new recruits. I was wrong to doubt you."

Michael smiled his satisfaction. He looked at Taggart's back. "It's only the beginning," he said. "Right, Richard?"

Taggart remained stubbornly silent.

"Did they move correctly?" Akmal asked him. "How do you clear rooms? What about the spacing?"

A door opened and a loud voice announced in a manner that proclaimed its owner was accustomed to giving orders and having them obeyed. It was he who turned on the lights.

"Turn up the lights," he further declared.

More light flooded the huge barn-like arena. Into this brightness strode a stocky, medium-sized Arab in his early forties wearing a checkered *kaffiyeh* and a long, flowing white robe in the manner of Osama bin Laden. He was a dark-skinned man with a bearded, cadaverous face. Taggart recognized him instantly. SEALs had chased Hatim al-Muttaqi, the Butcher of Khost, all over Afghanistan.

"*Assalamu alaikum*," Michael greeted him, turning deferential.

Al-Muttaqi stalked directly at Nasry, his combat boots clacking angrily on the concrete floor. A detail of bruisers in khaki-like uniform and armed with AK-47s trailed along with him, alert and watchful for any threat to the Emir.

"This is . . . unexpected," Michael stammered in Arabic. "You should have let me know. I could have—"

Al-Muttaqi chopped him off with a scowl. "The Prince wants to cut off my hand," he snapped, also in Arabic. "For stealing. He says I stole his trust. I didn't tell him it was because you stole mine."

"Emir," Michael protested, "your trust is sacred to me."

Taggart understood little Arabic, but he took note of the tone of the exchange and the body language. He sensed betrayal of some nature.

Al-Muttaqi looked directly at Taggart and spoke to one of his bodyguards. "Take him away."

Prodding Taggart with his rifle, the bodyguard escorted him upstairs where a Chechen soldier took over and locked the American in his cell-room. Down below, Michael and Akmal enthusiastically led the Emir on a strolling inspection of the training area.

"The SEAL is even more valuable to the cause than I thought," Michael explained, eager to present his viewpoint to the leader. "Have you seen our recruiting numbers? Would you like to see more of the training?"

Al-Muttaqi lifted a hand. "We will discuss in private," he said, clearly displeased.

Michael chased his recruiters from their computers, laptops, and files in his nerve center. He and al-Muttaqi faced each other across a table.

Al-Muttaqi studied Michael through narrowed eyes. Michael felt himself begin to sweat. He wiped his brow nervously on his tunic sleeve. The Emir held power of life and death over his subordinates.

Al-Muttaqi finally began to speak in a flat voice. "You are aware, are you not, that our alliance with Boko Haram is the key to our expansion into Africa?"

"Of course, but—"

Al-Muttaqi cut him off. "So that's why you killed one of their key commanders and his men?"

On the defensive, Michael smelled his own sour sweat. "I made a tactical decision. It wasn't safe to contact you. If you'd let me explain—"

"I raised you up. Like Lazarus from the garbage heap." The Emir sounded disappointed and hurt. "They all wanted me to kill you. But I saw something in you. You were like a son to me."

Something like regret joined disappointment and hurt, like al-Muttaqi might now be lamenting his decision to spare the life of the boy Michael had been.

"I will always be grateful," Michael offered, careful not to plead. "I—"

"I may not be able to make this right," al-Muttaqi interrupted. "If we have to leave Chad, the Prince will kill us both."

Michael reverted to silence, his common fallback when, as a twenty-year-old he arrived in Afghanistan to enlist with the Taliban and al-Qaeda to fight for justice. Omar had left Detroit soon afterward to follow him.

Al-Muttaqi's stance softened. He remembered Michael as that idealistic boy willing to fight for social justice. He reached across the table and laid a gentle hand on Michael's shoulder.

"I remember the first day I saw you," he said. "You killed a man for stealing your shoes. I knew then that you had the will that my own son lacked. I knew then that when such fire . . ." He touched a finger to Michael's temple. ". . . is joined with such intelligence, that you could be the lion the cause needed. But I alone saw the black rage inside you. Because of Omar, you've let that rage endanger our cause."

"Everything I've done, I've done for you, Emir," Michael stressed. "Out of respect and gratitude. And we are doing everything we dreamed."

The Emir fell into a long, reflective quiet that Michael dared not interrupt. Finally, al-Muttaqi nodded to himself. "I will try to talk to Boko Haram. Come to some sort of accommodation."

Chapter Thirty-One

Virginia Beach

In a booth at the Gulfstream Diner, neither Alex Caulder nor Bear Graves had much to say as they gazed out the wide picture window at the long stretch of beach and the morning sun coaxing sparkles out of Atlantic white caps. Spooks at NAS Oceana had met the C-17 exfil out of Panama to take custody of Nilofar and Rafina, mother and daughter, for interrogation and disposition. Caulder, Graves, and Ortiz set out in separate vehicles for ritual decompression pancakes. Command debriefing came later in the morning.

Buddha was running late since Bear asked him to stop by Command to check on the debriefing schedule. Soon, his battered Ford Fusion pulled into the diner's parking lot. Buddha long-legged it across the lot and soon slipped into the booth across from Bear and next to Caulder. He promptly expressed his opinion of last night's operation.

"Well, that sucked."

Graves drew in a weary breath. "The girl wasn't supposed to be there."

Caulder scoffed. "Yeah. Intel strikes again."

"Just another day at the office," Ortiz said philosophically.

Caulder looked out the window toward the incoming tide. He smiled to himself. "Remember the dog?"

Ortiz cracked a quizzical brow. *That was just last night, Caulder.*

"Not that one," Caulder averred.

"In Tikrit," Graves supplied.

Buddha rolled his eyes. "You're gonna bring that up?"

Graves managed a dark grin. Like cops who daily witnessed man's inhumanity to man, SEALs had learned to recognize the macabre humor in events that occurred regularly during the War on Terror. To laugh at them kept a man tethered to some semblance of sanity. Otherwise, he went mad in a mad, mad world where nothing made sense.

"You should have seen your face, Buddha," Graves said.

"Yeah, Bear. That dog was licking up brains like they were Alpo."

"Best meal it had had in months."

"Seen worse," Caulder recalled. "How about that Talib Rip splashed with the 50-cal. Just—*Woompf!*"

Bear nodded. "Human confetti."

"Raining men," Caulder said. "Buckley barfed in his helmet."

Silence fell over the table. Blood, guts, and gore. Was that all they could talk about anymore when they got together? The three weary SEALs now changed into jeans and T-shirts stared out the window together, reflective and withdrawn while they waited for their order to be delivered. Caulder's blonde waitress was not working today; her replacement was a brunette. Caulder gave her the eye, but then decided to stick with blondes.

Ortiz had ordered pancakes with strawberry syrup and pecans. The pecans reminded him of brains the dog ate. Strawberry syrup was the same color as fresh blood from a heart wound. He pushed the pancakes aside and sighed.

"What'd Fung say about the girl?" Graves asked him.

"She's about as well as you can expect," Buddha said. But then what could you expect? Her nanny had been killed, dead men were left strewn all over the house, she and her mommy had been kidnapped by rough strangers and railroaded out of the country in the middle of the night. For a ten-year-old, that was *not* another day at the office.

"The spooks are talking to the mother now," Buddha added.

Caulder swigged from his coffee cup. "They get anything out of her?"

"Not yet."

Bear seemed withdrawn, closed in on himself. He had been that way all the way back from Panama, flying through the night with not a word to anyone. Just sitting there collapsed into the canvas seating. Buddha surmised Bear's mood had to do with his shooting the little girl's nanny and being forced to rough up the kid a bit wrestling her and her mom out of the villa. Bear had a soft place for kids, especially little girls. Buddha remembered how overjoyed Bear had been that day in Afghanistan before the op that night when Lena on Skype revealed that she was pregnant with their child and showed him the sonogram of Sarah. And then Sarah died in her crib when she was only a few months old.

"You okay, Bear?" Buddha asked as Graves continued to stare out through the diner window toward the sea.

"Me? Fine. Why?"

Ortiz shrugged. Bear didn't sound fine.

Chapter Thirty-Two

Virginia Beach

Bear Graves had lied. He wasn't *fine.* So much death, dying, *killing* . . . It haunted him so that nights, *some* nights, he awoke drenched in nightmare sweat. The nanny in Panama. *Damn her!* She wasn't even Middle Eastern; she was Panamanian. But the cult of death seemed to infect everyone and everything it touched.

The Jihad enemy had spread so that it now sprawled across continents and nations and the world, lurking in urban alleys, crouching in caves, pouring out across deserts and mountains and forests. Americans and allies alike had been fighting global Jihad for more than two decades, a war that would never end in the enemy's unconditional surrender.

Instead, it would have to be suppressed by men like Rip Taggart, Caulder, Buckley, Chase, Bear, Buddha, Fishbait—men who could and would react to mass murder by hunting down terrorists and killing them. That was the only way to stop them.

That truth made men like Rip Taggart and Bear Graves part of the cult of death whether or not they cared to admit it. For some, it ate out their souls until they became the enemy they were fighting.

That was why Bear Graves was not *fine.*

His garage workshop provided a form of therapy. After his return from Panama, he worked feverishly into the night on the crib he was building for the baby Lena wanted, that she *deserved, needed.* Normally, his hands were steady, his mind focused. Tonight, however, his hands shook as he planed out one of the crib legs. The blade slipped and he stripped out a length of wood from the leg, making it unusable.

He glared at the damaged component, his anger building up against it and the war it suddenly represented. He grabbed the part like a club and, out of control, began smashing the crib slats that he had already set in place. Slivers and chips of wood sprayed across the workshop as he took out his rage on the crib.

Lena rushed into the workshop. "Joseph?"

He kept at the crib, grunting and groaning, shouting underneath his breath, his eyes wild, his face apocalyptic, busting the crib, destroying it until nothing remained of it or himself.

"Joseph . . . *Joseph . . . !*"

She finally got through to him. He turned to face her, panting, hunched over with the broken crib leg clutched in his fist like some caveman confronting a sabretooth tiger. Lena gently took the length of wood from his hand.

"I'm sorry," he said when he caught his breath.

"Please talk to me, Joseph?" Lena pleaded. "What are you thinking right now?"

He looked away. "Trust me, you don't want to know."

"Joseph . . . Joseph, I do."

Gradually, his eyes settled on her lovely face and the brilliant blue eyes, the blonde hair . . . Her children at school loved her. She represented all that was good left in his life. He drew in a breath so deep it might have been his last. He lowered his head. He didn't want her to see his eyes.

"Yesterday," he confided, not much louder than a whisper, "I shot a woman. I took a little girl away from her mother."

Lena went speechless, horrified and not knowing how to react to an admission so starkly presented. Rarely, almost never, did SEALs discuss such things with their families. It was better they not know.

Bear immediately regretted burdening her. After all these years, keeping things to himself to protect her from the horror of his life with SEAL Team Six, to now dump it on her like this. How could she possibly love a man like him, to want his child so desperately?

"I shouldn't have told you," he said, turning away.

"No, you should." She approached from behind, placed her hand gently on the back of his neck. He recoiled from her touch.

"You should," she repeated. "My father never did when he got back from Vietnam. It ate him up inside."

She glanced at the broken crib and gathered her emotions. "Joseph, you do these things for a reason. You're protecting us. Our people, our country."

Graves pulled away from her. "I shouldn't have told you," he said, and walked out to his truck and drove off, leaving Lena with the broken crib.

Chapter Thirty-Three

Virginia Beach

It was late at night and a row of empty bottles and shot glasses lined the length of the wooden picnic table on the back deck of Alex Caulder's ramshackle beach bungalow. It was late enough that Caulder, Buddha Ortiz, and Bear Graves, who together had emptied the bottles and glasses, were about to pass from humor to maudlin. They chortled at a final off-color joke about two priests and a duck at a strip joint before, one by one, they walked slowly to the deck railing and gazed off past the dunes and the beach to where jewels on the tapestry of the heavens curved down to meet the Atlantic. They stood there shoulder to shoulder in the dark, each with his own demons primed by alcohol.

"When Sarah was just a newborn," Graves said in a voice filled with pain, "I would take her out at night and show her the stars. She couldn't understand, but . . . but I wanted her to start seeing that she was part of something bigger. Something beautiful and good. Something I was fighting for."

"I'm sorry, Bro," Ortiz slurred. "She was beautiful."

"She was," Caulder allowed. "Her spirit, it'll live in your next one."

Bear continued reminiscing, the sadness inside his heart a terrible thing to witness. "The night Lena found her, in the crib—that was the same night I shot that kid."

Taggart was gone by then, and Bear was team leader on another failed HVT op against Hatim al-Muttaqi.

"He picked up an RPG," Ortiz noted. "Any one of us would have shot him."

Bear downed another drink and shook his head hard, either to clear it or empty it of bad memories. "Sarah died because of me. To pay for the life I took."

"Whoa, Bear," Ortiz cautioned. "That's bullshit."

Seeking answers, Bear had tried to discuss it with his minister before the team's mission into the abandoned Nigerian village in their effort to rescue Rip, the schoolteacher, and her students.

"Then it's possible," he asked Pastor Adams, not revealing the motivation behind the question, "that God would punish a child . . . for what her father . . . ? If her father . . . committed a big enough sin?"

After services, the congregation had adjourned to the church lawn for treats and socializing. Pastor Adams regarded the big SEAL with compassion and understanding. "Sins have consequences," he acknowledged. "Sometimes even deeper than we can imagine."

Bear had taken the conversation no further. Lena had tried later to get Pastor Adams and Bear together for counseling, but by then the time for that had passed.

Now, on the back deck of his beach shack, Caulder scoffed at the idea that God would punish a child for the sins of the father. "Dude. These things, they're mysterious, man. There is no way. In the midst of life we are in death. Isn't that what the Bible says?"

Graves slapped down another drink. "Rip . . . Rip didn't believe in God."

"At the end," Caulder said, "he didn't believe in anything."

Bear drew in another deep and weary breath. "I always blamed you for what happened, Caulder," he admitted. "I should have fought for Rip. I should have made him stay."

Ortiz nodded. He felt the same way.

"He left *us*," Caulder reminded them. "It was the demons, eating him from the inside. He saw too much and didn't forget enough."

Bear continued as though talking to himself. "Back in that Nigerian shithole of a village? I wanted it to be Rip in that grave. I wanted it to be him so bad."

Buddha and Caulder stared, not knowing how to respond.

Bear leaned on the railing. "I just wanted it to be all over."

"It will be," Buddha assured him. "When we get him back."

His cell phone jangled. He retrieved it from his pocket and checked the screen. "Jackie."

He went inside to take the call, leaving Caulder and Bear at the railing looking out into the darkness, a night for intimacies and confessions. It was vintage Caulder that if he had something to say he came right out with it, skipping preliminaries. Perhaps he was merely drunk, or perhaps he sought absolution over what happened between Tammi and him. Whatever the prompt, he suddenly blurted it out.

"After Buck . . . I went over to Tammi's house."

That caught Bear completely unaware. He squinted, concentrating.

"She didn't want to be alone . . ." Caulder explained as matter-of-factly as if he were explaining how to surf. "'Just hold me,' she said. 'I need to be held.' So I did—"

That sent Bear over the edge. You didn't screw a brother's wife the moment he died.

"You sonofabitch!" he bellowed.

He sprang back from the railing and unleashed a straight right punch to Caulder's face that sent him reeling back. Caulder stumbled over his own feet, crashed on his butt on the deck and rolled off into the sand while trying to regain his feet.

Ortiz overheard the ruckus. He hung up on Jackie and rushed onto the deck to find his two friends rolling drunkenly about in the sand. He pulled Graves free of the entanglement. Caulder struggled to his feet. Graves was breathing hard with pent-up anger. Ortiz looked them over.

"This is way overdue," he decided. "Take it to the beach."

The two inebriated SEALs staggered toward the water, Ortiz following to referee. Caulder stumbled to his knees, jumped right up, and fell again. They staggered on toward the surf, sniping insults at each other.

"You selfish little shit," Graves hissed. "You've had this coming a long time."

"You're always trying to pin your guilt on me," Caulder shot back. "Be a man. Own your own fucking life."

They reached the edge of the surf and squared off as the moon slipped above the ocean horizon. It wasn't much of a fight. Fortunately, these two men trained to kill in so many ways were too drunk to do much more than swing at the air, grapple, splash in the surf, and punch wildly at each other like a couple of sotted fans in a hockey brawl.

Ortiz observed from a nearby dune, his arms crossed, as his teammates stumbled about, half-drowned, full-drunk, and covered in sand and bad intentions.

Graves finally got in a feather pillow punch that caught Caulder just right and sent him reeling into the water. He lost his footing and splashed into the froth. He came up sputtering and shaking his head. Bear waded in after him to finish the job. Unable to get back on his feet, Caulder set out crawling on his hands and knees toward the sand in an attempt to get away.

Buddha jumped between them. "Enough!"

Blind with rage, Graves took a swing at Buddha, who stepped inside the punch and, with a quick right hook, dropped Bear into the surf alongside Caulder. He came up dazed and spluttering saltwater.

"You two done?" Ortiz demanded. "Because if you're not, I'll go with Red Squadron to get Rip. I mean it."

The cold surf had taken the fight out of them. Both were on their hands and knees crawling away from the water with waves splashing against their rear ends. Caulder licked blood from his split lip. Then, always willing to see the humor in a situation, he broke out in Dennis the Menace laughter so infectious that Bear began laughing with him. Buddha joined in.

The three brothers came up off the beach together, arms thrown around one another's shoulders, laughing their foolish asses off as if, Caulder observed later, they had good sense and weren't SEALs.

Chapter Thirty-Four

Chad, Africa

Michael Nasry moved Taggart from his original almost-airless detention in the cement plant to the room adjoining that of Na'omi and the three schoolgirls. An open door connected the two rooms. The only reason he was moved, the best Rip figured, was as a matter of convenience for the guards. Less keepers were required for one set than for two. The change also freed soldiers to participate in Akmal's training program.

Na'omi was holding a class session for Esther and her two friends when guards ushered Rip through the larger classroom and into his cell on the backside of theirs. She chanced a quick look of surprise at Rip before returning to her teaching, trying not to let on to their keepers that any further emotional bond existed between them that could be exploited.

To Rip's astonishment, he was left unfettered and unchained. His cell was even more Spartan than the one Na'omi shared with her students. Its only furnishing consisted of a bedroll spread on the floor in the middle of emptiness. Not even a window let in light, which meant in Rip's calculation that these rooms were interior and, therefore, more difficult to escape from.

As soon as the guards left and locked the outer door, Rip leaned a shoulder against the open door frame that separated the cells and watched Na'omi's class in session. He suspected her efforts were not so much to keep up studies as to establish a little island of normality in a sea of chaos and threat, and to keep the girls' minds occupied. She smiled her pleasure at seeing Rip again as she scrawled a sentence on the wall with a colored marker: *By the grace of God, we will return home to our families.* This connection between Rip and Na'omi, however it could be defined, likewise provided a slice of welcome normality.

Na'omi called on Esther to recite: "Esther, which is the verb?" she asked, indicating the sentence on the wall.

"'Return,' teacher."

"Good. And the subject?"

"God?"

"No. Although we give thanks to Him."

"Grace?"

"We. 'We' is the subject."

The room plunged into immediate silence when Michael and Akmal Barayev entered with the dark-skinned, jackal-faced visitor to the plant. Hatim al-Muttaqi's black eyes seemed to surround Na'omi and the girls like those of a predator owl with a flock of guinea fowl trapped against a wall. Na'omi herded the girls into a corner. Rip turned away from the connecting door and returned to his own side of the cell. The three terrorist commanders followed him.

Akmal carried a large container of water with a towel draped over his arm. A uniformed Chechen guard hurried in with two metal folding chairs. He closed the door against Na'omi and her students so they were unable to see what went on inside Rip's room.

Al-Muttaqi eyed Taggart before nodding to the guard, who unfolded and arranged the two metal chairs facing each other. The Emir swept his white robe smooth around his legs and sat. He gestured for Taggart to take the other one. "Please sit."

Rip slowly sank onto the chair so that their knees were only a few inches apart. He allowed a strange humorless smile to flicker across his face.

"Emir Hatim al-Muttaqi," he acknowledged. "The Butcher of Khost."

Al-Muttaqi's smile mirrored Rip's. "You were famous in Afghanistan as well—the SEAL who hunted me," he said in English. "You'd be surprised how many times you almost caught me."

Rip's eyes took in the three terrorists, the guard, the heavy container of water, and the towel. These guys hadn't come to wash his feet.

"So, what's the agenda here?" he asked.

Al-Muttaqi relaxed and clasped his hands on his lap. "You are going to tell me how we stop your drones, your surveillance, all the technology that helps America beat us," he said in a voice that brooked no resistance or contradiction.

He tilted his head toward Michael, but his eyes remained on Taggart. "Afterwards," he said to Nasry. "I'll give him back to Boko Haram. Plus the ten million dollars. Plus the girls. That may balance the scales between us. We shall see."

Clearly he wasn't pleased with the deal he had made.

"Emir, he is more valuable to us," Michael objected.

"That is for me to decide," al-Muttaqi replied, ending the discussion.

He signaled to Akmal, who brought the water and towel and stood ready. No more Mister Nice Guy. Although this was Taggart's first face-to-face-encounter with al-Muttaqi, he knew from having chased him all over Afghanistan that this was a man who could, and would, slit a child's throat and then sit down next to the corpse for dinner.

"You Americans had the Jordanians waterboard me eighty-six times," al-Muttaqi said. "I vowed to kill a hundred infidels for every towel they put over my face."

"Then kill one more," Rip challenged. "I don't know anything about all this shit."

Al-Muttaqi wasn't giving up that easily. "At what altitude do drones fly?"

Rip sank back into his chair and casually crossed one leg over the other.

"How long can they fly before refueling?" the Emir persisted.

"I don't know."

"The radio frequencies that control them. Are they jammable?"

"I can't tell you things I don't know. I've been out for two years. It's all changed by now."

Al-Muttaqi glanced at the water and the towel, then brought his eyes back to Rip, assessing him before reaching a conclusion.

"Waterboarding didn't work for me," he said. "It won't work with you."

He snapped his fingers, a signal Akmal had been waiting for. He obediently placed his container and towel on the floor and hurried into the adjoining room. A muffled scream announced what was going on. Rip should have known. Waterboarding might not work, but Rip had already demonstrated an attachment to the African females that could be used against him.

Akmal returned dragging the youngest schoolgirl, nine-year-old Abiye, by her arm.

"How can we jam the frequencies?" al-Muttaqi persisted.

Taggart called the bluff. Sooner or later when he and the girls were no longer useful to their plans, these ruthless bastards were going to do what they did regardless of what he told them.

"You don't get it," he said to al-Muttaqi in a level, uncompromising tone. "America is coming for me. For you. Your people killed, what, three thousand of us on 9/11? We've killed millions of you to get even. We will never stop. Not until you and everyone you know is dead."

He let that sink in. Al-Muttaqi's face remained unfathomable.

"Trade me," Rip proposed. "And the girls. For twenty of your imprisoned Jihadi brothers." He gestured at Michael. "Give *him* to Boko Haram."

Michael laughed at such an absurd suggestion. Al-Muttaqi didn't; he even seemed to be considering the advice. Michael fidgeted nervously on his feet.

"Emir, he's stalling," he pointed out. "Trying to save his own skin. Every day we grow stronger."

Al-Muttaqi rose from his chair and looked down upon Taggart, who returned the look. Neither of them flinched. Even tiny Abiye had gone silent with the tension.

"Of course, we will continue this later," the Emir said before he turned and walked out of the room like a Shakespearean actor closing a scene. Akmal followed with Abiye and pushed her into the other room. Michael pierced Taggart with a raw look of hatred, but Rip saw and recognized the fear and uncertainty that had been planted in the American jihadist's mind.

Chapter Thirty-Five

Virginia Beach

A distinguished government lawyer, Robert Chase Sr. had connections. It didn't take him long to produce results after Ghetto asked him to go through his old friend and former college roommate at the American embassy in Kabul to check up on the Mujtahid captured in Kunar Province on the date Rip Taggart was now publically confessing to having shot down an American in cold blood.

Ghetto's dad was working in the den of his colonial house in Virginia Beach. Virginia was preparing dinner when Chase arrived to see what his father had found out. His mother hugged and kissed him and sent him on back to the den with an admonishment for the two of them to wash up for the table. They were having her famous pot roast. It smelled delicious. Robert Sr. looked up when his son entered. He smiled and rummaged through his desk until he came up with a computer flash drive.

"It contains all the Afghan police prisoner interviews in Khost and the Kunar area from the day you asked for, plus a day on either side," he explained. "I don't even want to tell you what it took to get this."

"Thanks, Dad." He reached for the flash drive. His father pulled it back.

"In politics," he said somberly, "sometimes ignorance is power."

"Pop, I'm not in politics."

"Everyone's in politics."

AFRICOM

FBI

Ghetto's brow creased. *What was this?* His old man seemed to be warning him about something.

"Son, think hard about what you're doing. This could be one of those moments where your life goes one way or the other."

He was totally serious. Ghetto held out his hand for the flash drive. He had gone this far . . .

"Son . . . Son, be careful."

Chapter Thirty-Six

Virginia Beach

What with his ex-wife Erica out of pocket, it took Alex Caulder some time to track down his errant fifteen-year-old daughter, Dharma. He hadn't seen her or talked to her since she moved in with him for a few days and then disappeared one day without a word or even a note. Erica probably wouldn't have helped him find her anyhow.

Had he been more introspective, say like Chase or Buddha, he might have asked himself *why* it seemed necessary that he find her. It wasn't like he had been much in the kid's life when she was growing up. Erica was right about that, that she barely knew her father. He had been this mysterious guy popping in and out of her life until one day he wasn't popping in anymore.

Erica, truth be told, had not been much of a mother either. But that was on her. *This* was on him.

Caulder kept visualizing her the way she was that day when he went to retrieve her from the police station. Typically, she had gotten mixed up in a "social justice" school demonstration. When he reached the police station, here was this little gothic teenager with black lipstick, black garb, black eyeshadow, and black about everything else. In spite of the tough talk and false front she put on for the public—like her old man in many aspects—she was actually a scared and lonely little girl underneath all that black. At the police station, that was the first time he saw it in her and recognized it.

He needed to find Dharma, he told himself, just to make sure she was all right.

He learned through her high school principal that she had quit her studies to work at an ice cream shop called Truly Gelato out on the Boardwalk. The Boardwalk was a three-mile stretch of beachfront, glimmer and glamour—hotels, upscale shops, tourists in bikinis, roller bladers, skateboarders, joggers in Spandex. He found her scooping ice cream for a pair of loud-talking barbarians and an almost topless babe. He waited outside watching her through the window until she finished with her customers.

Her appearance had changed. Gone was the black lipstick. Her eye shade had turned pale green. She still wore black, but in a more socially-acceptable combination—black jeans and a black T-shirt underneath a gaily-colored apron.

Caulder shook his head and grinned in recalling his first job. He whacked off his long hippie hair and changed his raggedy, butt crack-exposing jeans for a new pair of Levis. Funny how nose rings, long hair, and crotch-dragging low riders disappeared when a kid had to get a job.

The barbarians and the babe left with their ice cream and Caulder walked up to the counter. Dharma seemed surprised to see him. "Hey," she said.

"Hey."

"If you're here for the gelato," she warned, "this place sucks."

Caulder remembered how at her age he had been just as cynical. Ortiz would have said he hadn't changed.

"Look," Caulder said, mentally kicking the toe of his Birkie in the sand. "I owe you an apology. That video, of me and Buck's . . . uh . . . Buck's widow, I—"

Maybe he deserved the ass kicking Bear proposed to administer that night when they were all drinking on Caulder's back deck.

"Wow, Alex. I thought you came about the video that's been on TV. Of, you know, the SEAL." She made a face and shrugged dismissively. "But I guess you think having sex is worse than killing an unarmed kid."

Her reaction took Caulder aback and rendered him momentarily speechless.

"Anyhow, what's the big deal?" Dharma said. "Tammi probably needed it. People do hook up, right, Alex?"

"Wait . . . Wait! Are you having . . . I mean, are you using protection?"

"Chill out, Alex. Don't try to be a father. I don't need one."

She looked him over for a second. "Is it true about the SEAL?"

"I can't talk about it."

"Fine. You know, I'm pretty busy here."

Another customer came in, a kid with a skateboard parked outside. Caulder waited until the kid got what he came in after and left. He unexpectedly felt the need to explain to his daughter, make her understand who he was, *why* he was. He talked while she wiped down the counter with a cloth.

"Stuff like that SEAL said, it goes on every day. On both sides. Always has. Always will. Nobody wants to know about it. They just want us to do what we do and keep the bad guys out of their suburbs and the truth off the TV."

Dharma continued to wipe, thinking about what he said. "Maybe we're making more bad guys than we're killing," she posited. "It's bad math."

"I don't think about that. I can't. Doubt make you hesitate. That gets you killed."

She kept working, ignoring him. Caulder looked around. He was beginning to think he had been wrong in looking for her. "Look, I made a mistake."

"Which mistake are we talking about here, Alex?"

It became obvious that he wasn't reaching her. He had been a fool to even try. Give it one last shot and then collect his marbles and get the hell out.

"I'm a warrior," he tried to explain. "That's all I am. That's my path. I have to live like I'm already dead."

The way she stopped to look at him made him uncomfortable. "Look, I don't think it's a good idea for you to be around me," he concluded with finality and turned to walk away.

For a moment Dharma was inclined to let him go. But, then, before he reached the door, she straightened behind the counter. "Alex? Okay, Alex, but, uh . . . Alex, you were the one who came to see me."

Chapter Thirty-Seven

Virginia Beach

When they were first married, Rip Taggart and Gloria purchased a modest little two-bedroom in a subdivision off Dam Neck highway near the SEAL base. When they split up, after all that nastiness that was Kunar, Gloria got the house and the car and Rip got the bills and the guilt. By then, he had lost everything else that mattered, so he refused to let this matter either. He didn't know at the time that Gloria was pregnant; he still didn't know it.

Gloria wasn't exactly shocked when Rip's "Confession Video" made world news and generated riots and Muslim protests all over the Middle East, Africa, Europe, and even in the United States. She had known and accepted the nature of her husband's work, if not its specifics. Rip was the tough, closed-mouthed sort who never talked about his work except to his teammates. Worse, even if you were his wife you seldom knew what he was thinking or feeling. She sometimes accused him of not having feelings like ordinary men. That was one of the reasons for the divorce. Afterwards, he seemed to disappear out there somewhere in the world, doing things men like Rip did. Gloria hadn't heard from him, or of him, until he and those other people and girls were kidnapped in Africa and made the news.

The news media weren't supposed to find out where SEALs lived, but they did anyhow. After Rip's "confession," TV trucks and gaggles of reporters homesteaded the residential street in the modest little subdivision of one-story brick homes and blocked traffic in front of Gloria's house. It didn't seem to matter that Gloria explained repeatedly that Rip didn't live here anymore. Reporters and TV trucks still kept showing up trying to get an interview with the wife—*ex-wife*—of the notorious SEAL who admitted to having committed war crimes. Gloria felt besieged with baby Dylan in her own home and left it only when it became absolutely necessary. She hadn't been to her Beachcomber Bar & Grill since this all started. Her manager could handle it until all this passed over. She was thinking of selling out anyhow; bars and clubs were not a good environment for a kid to grow up around.

The doorbell rang. Gloria had had it up to her turtleneck sweater with a bunch of nosy, chicken-necked reporters. She scooped Dylan from his crib and stormed to the door determined on giving the unlucky intruder a piece of her mind. Providing, of course, that she had any mind left to give.

She flung the door open to find Lena Graves. "Can I come in?"

Gloria relaxed with an explosive exhalation. "Of course. I thought you were another vulture at the door."

She laughed and indicated the mob outside in the street and on the sidewalk. A nasty breed, in Gloria's opinion, not only for their overbearing entitlement but also for the candy bar and cigarette wrappers strewn around the neighborhood. Carrying Dylan on her hip, Gloria led Lena into the kitchen to get away from the cackling outside.

"I should have called first . . ." Lena apologized.

"It's been a while, Lena."

It had. Lena had heard through the grapevine that Gloria delivered after Rip left but this was the first time any of the wives had actually seen the baby boy. Gloria also seemed to have vanished after the divorce. Lena understood why she might not want anything to do with the other wives. Too many memories connected with them.

Gloria poured coffee and they sat at the table with Dylan on Gloria's lap.

"With all that's going on . . ." Lena began uncomfortably. "Well, you know. I just wanted to check on you. See if you were okay. I'm sorry about Rip."

"I've got Dylan." Gloria flapped a hand nonchalantly. "That's all I need."

"He's beautiful."

The baby appeared to be about a year old, at that age when kids began to take an interest in the world around them. Gloria had him dressed in a blue jumper suit with, ironically, a seal inscribed on the bib. He studied Lena intently—babies really did look like Winston Churchill—and reached out to her, clasping and unclasping his little hands. Lena felt a knot forming in her throat. Sarah would have been almost this age when . . .

"Want to hold him?" Gloria offered.

Lena accepted immediately. "Sure."

She cradled the baby, remembering, but struggling to keep her emotions under control.

"You trying again? You and Joe?" Gloria asked.

"Hopefully." She let a moment drag by. "Wow! He's big. How many months?"

Gloria read something disturbing in Lena's blue eyes, an unhappiness, almost dread. "So?" she probed tentatively. "Why are you really here?"

Lena's lips trembled, but no sound came forth. Truthfully, she wasn't really sure why she came. Except Gloria must have gone through something similar to what Lena was going through with Joe before she and Rip split up. Tears flooded her eyes and she choked up.

From her years playing the patient and understanding bartender, Gloria had a knack for diagnosing trouble. Especially among SEALs and their wives.

"Let me guess," she said. "Joe's torn up inside. Shutting you out. Like he's got a thousand ghosts in his head. Like when he looks at you he sees you dead. Honey, you think that kind of life you're in, you think it's normal? It's not."

Lena handed Dylan back to Rip's ex-wife, torn by how close Gloria had come to the truth. Suddenly, it just burst out. "I-I don't know what to do. I don't know how to help him."

Gloria understood. She had been there. "Their world," she said. "It's all about death. If you want that . . . ? Or if you want life, get out. Get our now. While you still can."

Chapter Thirty-Eight

Chad, Africa

Like a circus elephant, Rip Taggart had one leg chained to a steel eyebolt set in the floor of his room-cell adjoining that of Na'omi and the three girls, Esther, Abiye, and Kamka, who lay asleep on their bed mats this late at night. Gasoline generators provided electric lights for key areas of the cement plant. The lights flickered constantly and sometimes went off. Na'omi sat on the floor with her arms wrapped around her knees and a blanket over here shoulders as she watched Rip through the connecting doorway knock out Ranger pushups to keep in shape.

Presently, she rose, pulled the blanket tighter around her shoulders, and walked past Esther into Rip's room-cell. Esther stirred in her sleep and opened her eyes. Inside the other room, Rip ceased exercising with his arms stiff in the *Begin* position and looked up. Na'omi wore a thoughtful expression.

"On that . . . video," she began. "You spoke about your brothers. Other SEALs. Tell me about them."

"Not much to tell."

"Start with their names," she suggested.

He rolled over on his side to face her with his head propped up on one hand. "One guy was called Bear."

"He must be really big."

"Yeah. But we called him that because he ran bare-assed naked down the Boardwalk at Virginia Beach during Green Team."

That brought a smile to Na'omi's face.

"Everybody had nicknames," Rip continued. "Me, Buddha, Fish . . ."

Na'omi sat cross-legged with her blanket on the floor next to him. "We do the same in Nigeria. It is a sign of affection."

Rip's mind drifted back. He felt nostalgia sink its roots. "Everybody but Caulder had one. They were good boys."

"They were your family."

"They were my *only* family."

Gloria, he realized, had never really become a part of his family. She even said once that she always felt the outsider, the ugly stepchild that never fit in no matter how hard she tried.

Perhaps now, because of their long confinement together, Rip was beginning to look upon Na'omi as a member of his new team, to trust and accept her in a way he had never experienced with any other woman.

"What I said on the video . . ."

He caught himself. But he couldn't seem to stop the urge to reveal himself to this woman. It became important that she know him, the *real him*. Even the ugly parts.

"It's true," he said. "I shot his brother."

He half-expected her to recoil in horror. Instead, she studied him a moment and then asked, "Why?"

Rip inhaled deeply. "He was . . . just a period at the end of a sixty-word sentence. I don't even remember what he looked like."

A long piece of quiet settled over them. They had come a long way together from that morning at her school when Na'omi angrily and correctly accosted him for being a perpetual drunk with a hangover. A relationship that began on a rocky landscape gradually grew after the kidnapping into something more solid. The catalyst, Na'omi realized now, came during their unsuccessful escape attempt from the Boko Haram village. Rip would most likely have made it if he had gone alone. Instead, he risked everything trying to save her and the girls. She had to search deep, but when she did she discovered that the tough American had a real heart buried beneath his scarred crust.

Rip had absolved her of all guilt after her rape by Aabid and his warriors at the village. She now absolved him of crimes and mistakes he might have made in battle. She moved close and draped her blanket over his bare shoulders. Their eyes met and they looked deeply into one another's soul. There were no easy solutions for the crisis in which they found themselves, no easy way out. But life not always presented easy answers. They knew each other, though, deep down where it counted, and from that connection the bond between them could grow.

In the other room, Esther lay with her eyes open, listening to every soft word spoken between her two heroes. Tears of happiness overflowed her eyes. She knew—she just *knew* it with that undoubting faith of a child—that everything would be all right.

Chapter Thirty-Nine

SEAL Command, Virginia Beach.

Ghetto Chase revealed to the team that he had obtained tapes on a flash drive of all prisoner interrogations of the Afghan police on the night of the Kunar raid when Rip wasted the American Mujahid and the team captured the other. The entire team—Graves, Chase, Fishbait, Ortiz, and Caulder—gathered in the Cage Room around the table in Bear's cage to view it in private.

The first interrogation on the low-res video was of an Afghan in his fifties or so. He cringed in a chair while an off-camera policeman questioned him in Pashtu. Graves squinted at the grainy production, unable to clearly make out the man's facial features.

"Is that him?" he asked, although he knew it couldn't be. The image was bad, but the guys that night in Kunar were young.

Caulder also squinted at the video. "I don't think so," he decided. "Too old."

"What's he saying?" Buddha asked Fishbait, who wore earbuds and acted as interpreter.

"Shut up and let me listen."

After concentrating for a few minutes, Fish shook his head in disgust. "These assholes make me ashamed to be from Afghanistan. He's bragging about torching his own niece for getting raped. Go on to the next one."

Chase fast-forwarded to a close-up of another man being interviewed by off-camera police. At least this one appeared to be in the right age bracket. Fishbait held up a finger as he listened. *Wait.* This might be the one.

Graves studied the face on the screen. Was this the silent one who, according to his wounded buddy, was a mere driver who spoke no English?

"It could be him," he commented.

"Freeze it," Fish requested.

The image stopped on the dead guy's face. Fishbait removed his earbuds. "He's hard to understand," he said. "His Pashtu sucks. He says he's Arab, but his Arabic sucks too."

"What did he say, Fish?" Bear asked eagerly.

"That a SEAL killed a prisoner in cold blood. After he surrendered. And that he was American."

A solemn moment passed as the teammates digested the implications of what they had discovered—a possible eye witness against Rip.

"Where'd you get this?" Bear asked Chase.

"What's it matter?"

"What happened to this guy?" Ortiz wanted to know, indicating the image on the screen.

"From info on the tape, all these guys were interrogated and released," Fishbait revealed.

The men shook their heads in disgust. It happened the way Rip said it would. Catch and release always ended up the same way, with captured terrorists turned loose to continue the Jihad.

Chase tapped a finger at the shot of the guy on the video. "Besides you guys and Rip," he ventured, "he's the only one who knows what happened. Right?"

Graves looked to Caulder for confirmation of what he himself had already accepted. This was the guy all right, the one Rip would have killed next if Caulder and Ortiz hadn't stepped in to save his rotten ass.

"He has Rip," Ortiz decided. "Or he knows who does."

"The raghead driver . . ." Graves mulled.

"What?" Chase couldn't be sure where all this was going.

"Rip was going to kill him too," Caulder explained.

"Why didn't he?"

Caulder turned away from the screen "Because I stopped him."

The fucking irony. All this shit could have been avoided—the abductions, executions, Rip's "confession"—if Rip had eliminated both ragheads at the same time.

Chase's logical legal mind went into gear. "What if he's an American, too? Think about it. He's not from where he says he is. Makes sense, right? Two guys fighting together?"

Ortiz accepted that. "If he is an American, Intel could maybe ID him."

"Could help us get to Rip," Graves added.

"Hold on!" Fishbait threw a monkey wrench into the gears. "We send this to Intel, they'll know that what Rip said in that video is true."

Graves thought about it. "I don't know. It'd be the word of a shitbag terrorist against ours."

Ortiz also thought about it. "Maybe yes, maybe no. But it will take them forever to sort it out. And we'll be sidelined. Could take us months to get back out. If ever."

"This is bigger than Rip," Ghetto Chase put in. "Or the girls. Or us. That flag behind Rip on the video, it's the same flag as at the Tanzania embassy bombing."

Chase was right. He was on a roll. "This guy," he prognosticated, "wants to be the next Osama bin Laden."

Chapter Forty

Chad, Africa

Rip Taggart's ankle chain in his room-cell allowed him about six feet of freedom in any direction from the eyebolt to which he was tethered. Because of the location of the cells on the cement plant, away from direct sources of daylight, most illumination was supplied by generator electricity, and Taggart soon lost sense of day and night. He was pacing in circles the limits of his liberty, restless, his mind working on angles, when the door from the girls' quarters flew open and al-Muttaqi stalked in. His predatory eyes swept dismissively over the American.

"Meet your new cellmate," he announced and stepped to one side as Akmal and three Chechen guards hustled a new prisoner into the room.

Stunned, Taggart didn't know whether to celebrate the strange turn of events or burst into laughter. Working quickly with drills and hammers, the guards installed a separate eyebolt into the floor and chained Michael Nasry's ankle to it at a distance far enough removed from Rip that the two men could not get at each other.

Michael glared resentfully at al-Muttaqi. "My brother died for you," he accused, his voice raspy with anger and hurt.

"Your brother was more loyal than you," al-Muttaqi cautioned. He walked out of the room.

Akmal remained for another moment, looking uncertain, before he turned to follow the Emir.

"Akmal?" Michael called out to him, pleading. "All we worked for, don't waste it."

Akmal followed the winning side out of the room without a word and without a look back. Michael, disgraced and humiliated at being a prisoner in the very room with the man who murdered his brother, turned his back to the door in anguish and outrage. He kicked his tethered leg against the chain so violently that it almost jerked his feet out from underneath him. Resigned to his fate, at least temporarily, he lowered his head and walked the allowed length of his new restrained freedom, his ankle chain scraping across the floor with the sound of dry bones. He felt Taggart watching him in surprise and amusement. He peered up through his bushy eyebrows.

Taggart broke into a broad smile.

Chapter Forty-One

SEAL Command, Virginia Beach

Chase's flash drive of Afghan Police interrogating the captured Mujtahid, whoever he was, was enough to land Taggart in a federal prison if it were exposed, along with the rest of the team as accessories for covering up the crime. Having the tape and deciding how to use it to help free Rip posed a dilemma.

Following their morning PT run on the beach, sweating teammates gathered in tan shorts and white T-shirts next to the nibbling of the incoming tide to pursue further discussion on what they should do. In their background loomed the modern military building of DEVGRU Command, which controlled destinies and futures of SEAL Team Six.

Caulder had a contact through White Squadron and DEVGRU that seemed promising. Naturally, the contact was female, although not blonde.

"Let's be clear," Caulder was saying. "Once I ask this, there's no going back."

"You got a better idea?" Graves responded. He surveyed the others—Chase, Buddha, and Fishbait. "Anybody?"

They had been through all this before.

"How do we know she's going to say yes?" Ghetto wondered.

"They always say yes," Caulder replied flippantly. His woman killer smile, however, rang a bit false, and his Dennis the Menace self-assurance had gone almost dormant as tensions over Rip Taggart's fate grew.

"We have to try," Ortiz said. "No matter what happens to us, we have to try."

Bear's was the final decision. Nodding reflexively, burdened with concern, he clapped a hand on Buddha's shoulder and turned to the others. Chase and Fishbait each nodded his agreement. Caulder waited for the word.

"Okay," Bear said to him. "Agreed. We have to bring Rip home."

SEAL Team Six was a relatively small outfit, militarily speaking. Almost everyone knew everyone else, which made it difficult, if not impossible, to successfully sandbag in the hall that ran past the Command Briefing Room, the various squadron offices, and on to DEVGRU Command. Caulder attempted to appear inconspicuous as he waited in the busy hallway. Men called out to Caulder, made smartass remarks about his ancestry or love life, poked him on the shoulder, or whatever, but no one asked what he was doing. Teams kept their own secrets when it came to ops and team business with Command. Caulder's meeting with his contact must appear to be unplanned, a casual encounter without significance.

Lieutenant Camille Fung, the petite young officer who handled briefings and Intel functions for Commander Lee Atkins's White Squadron, emerged from her office, her shined boots clacking smartly on the hallway's polished floor. Caulder fell into step with her.

"Did you watch the video?" he asked.

"I watched it." She kept walking, noncommittal. She smiled at a passing junior grade officer.

"I have a translation," Caulder offered.

"I speak Pashtu, Caulder."

She stopped and started to say something. She broke off when two SEALs approached all geared up for training in the Kill House. When they passed on by, she said quietly, "He says Rip did it. Did he?"

"The dude's a terrorist. No one will believe him."

"But you do," Lieutenant Fung observed, "or you wouldn't be asking me . . . to do what exactly?"

"This is the guy who must be holding Rip. Maybe he has the Nigerian girls too. We need to get this to the Intelligence Community and find out who he is. So we can get them back."

"But, she surmised, "without our fingerprints on it?"

"I know. I know. It's a big favor."

She shook her head, unconvinced. They began walking again with Caulder still at her side.

"Do you realize how much trouble you guys could be in?" she asked rhetorically. "What I should do is give it to NCIS. Let them investigate and decide if it's true or not."

Caulder sprang his ace in the hole. "We think the guy in the video is American."

That stopped her in her shiny boots and starched uniform. Caulder pressed on. "What if he came back? What if he's not on the watch list? What if he kills more people?"

The lieutenant remained uncertain, even suspicious. "Who gave you the video?"

Caulder changed tactics. Charm and his prowess of persuasion had failed. That left forthrightness.

"Go to NCIS," he offered. "Do whatever you think is right. *After* we get Rip. *After* we get these girls back to their families."

Lieutenant Fung studied him with her dark, inscrutable eye. That ended the session and left the matter in limbo. She walked off, opened a door, and disappeared down another hallway. Caulder watched her go. Fuck. *Fuck!*

Chapter Forty-Two

Chad, Africa

For an hour, Michael Nasry sat chained on his side of the room opposite Taggart, looking morose and bitter, head lowered between his knees, unmoving. Taggart eyed him with a mixture of curiosity and disdain. This was the man responsible for seizing him and the girls from warlord Aabid and Boko Haram, only to take them into an even more threatening captivity. Too bad the Chechens and Boko Haram hadn't wiped each other out.

The door between Taggart's cell and the one occupied by Na'omi and her students had been left open, permitting the two sets of prisoners to see one another and communicate. Na'omi instructed Esther to take water to Rip. The girl poured water from a five-gallon gas can into a pitcher and took the pitcher and a cup into the next room. Smiling, she filled the cup and handed it to Rip.

"Thank you, Esther."

He drank and returned the cup, along with an affectionate pat on the child's head. Michael stirred for the first time since his hapless arrival and licked dry lips.

"Hey, I need some, too."

Esther eyes asked Rip what she should do. Taggart shot Michael a humorless smile. "Say please," he taunted.

Michael glared across the room with enough acid to have withered an acacia tree. He seemed to choke on the word, but he finally got it out. "Please?"

Esther took him water, but stayed as far away from him as she could. Michael drained the cup in one gulp and handed it back.

"Say 'thanks,'" Rip reminded him.

"This is all a misunderstanding," the skinny terrorist grated out from some deep, pained well. "I'll be out soon. You'd be better off keeping your mouth shut."

"I don't think so," Rip mocked. "Daddy looked disappointed in you."

That lit a nerve. "He's *not* my father."

Taggart shrugged. "He's the Butcher of Khost."

"*Isha'allah*, he'll kill one more before the day is out."

"Careful," Rip warned. "It might be you."

Michael withdrew into himself to stew over that possibility. Esther returned to the other room to join Na'omi, Abiye, and Kamka in watching through the door the strange and frightening clash between the two enemies.

After a few more minutes of silence, Taggart reinstated the conversation. "You're a long way from Detroit."

Michael dropped his head between his knees and flashed the finger at Rip. "Go to hell."

"Dearborn, right?" Rip persisted, nonplussed and curious about what prompted an American to join terrorists. "Most of the Muslims there don't betray their country."

Michael's body stiffened. His head lifted slowly to reveal a steady glare of hatred. "You want to talk about betrayal," he retorted bitterly. "My father was an engineer in Lebanon. He was respected. In America, he worked two jobs at minimum wage for forty years. Slave labor. He paid his taxes. He voted. And for what? If you don't have Bill Gates money in America, you're nobody. You're trash. America betrayed us."

"You and fifty million other Americans. But you think you're a special snowflake? That you're owned something?"

Na'omi in the other room had heard enough. She lashed out at Nasry, unable to control her anger. "How can you do what you do? The Koran doesn't include killing innocents."

"The Cross has been dipped in far more blood than the Crescent Moon," Michael replied stubbornly.

"You're worse than Boko Haram," Na'omi cried. "They're just thugs. You coach your murders in pretty words. You use God to justify your barbarity."

Michael glared at this . . . this impertinent *woman.* His voice lowered dangerously. "We all think God's on our side. We all fight the war we believe in."

He turned his back to her and dropped his head between his knees.

Chapter Forty-Three

SEAL Command, Virginia Beach

Waiting again. It was always the waiting. Waiting for the geeks and spook to come up with something. Waiting for . . . Just *waiting*. The team had heard nothing back from Caulder's request of Lieutenant Fung that she have Intel check out the flash drive obtained by Ghetto Chase. To a man, while they waited, they also had to consider the possibility that Lieutenant Fung would betray them and go to NCIS with the tape to initiate an investigation into the role Bear and the others might have played in covering up Taggart's execution of the Muj in Kunar.

While the members of Taggart's old team waited, they worked off their anxiety in frenetic activity and training—Bear Graves on the shooting range, burning off rounds; Buddha Ortiz jogging miles to exercise out the last kinks in the leg he injured during the team's takeover of the tanker *Nautilus II* in Lagos, Nigeria, to capture the Boko Haram courier; Ghetto Chase on the beach toting life-sized dummies and flipping truck tires in the Monster Mash obstacle course; Fishbait Khan sprawled on the ground, eye to his rifle scope, squeezing the trigger of his .308 sniper rifle; and Alex Caulder . . . doing Alex Caulder things.

Graves, Ortiz, Chase, and Fishbait emerged from the Atlantic framed by the red sun rising above the tide. They were in full dive gear from a night dive training in water insertion. Graves had sent Caulder ahead to either see if Lieutenant Fung had any news for them, or if she had left a message. Fung had an early bird reputation for coming in to work at sunrise.

In the shallow surf, the four men removed their fins and masks and ascended the beach in a pod. They paused by the water to quietly wait on Caulder. They soon spotted his angular form loping toward them. He wore his wet suit bottom and booties, but no shirt. Bear noticed that his naturally jaunty gait was missing. He moved out to meet him.

"Anything?"

"Fung hasn't gotten back to me. We're either going to find Rip—or the NCIS dickheads come knocking, and maybe we go to Leavenworth."

Leavenworth Prison was a hell of a way to end a SEAL career. But no one in the team was under the illusion that he might not end up there.

"So that's it," Ortiz said with some resignation.

"That's it," Caulder said.

Buddha gazed out to sea, tasted the salt on his lips, thought of all that he could lose. He shook his head as sarcasm bubbled in his soul. "Nice."

"And I just got here," Chase remarked. He felt like the guy who arrived after the last act of a play and only knew what he was told about it. He wondered if he could still be a lawyer when he got out of military prison.

He separated from the others and walked up the beach, disturbed at the prospect. Buddha and Fishbait joined him. Caulder and Graves lingered behind.

"So, that line you talked about between good and evil?" Caulder noted. "Remind me which side we're on."

"Things aren't that simple. You told me that."

Caulder shook his head in mock consternation. "Jesus, Bear. Rule Number One: Never take my advice."

Chapter Forty-Four

Chad, Africa

Boredom became a common enemy shared by Rip Taggart and Michael Nasry in their joint prison cell. With both men chained to the floor by their ankles and visits by Na'omi and the girls officially forbidden, they had only each other to while away the silent hours. Nasry proved to be poor company as he spent most of his time either staring off into space or up against the opposite wall with his head between his knees and his arms around his shins. Day and night blended together into a single continuum.

Rip attempted conversation both to relieve the monotony and satisfy his curiosity about this American jihadist.

"Where'd you go to school?" Rip asked him.

Nasry was having one of his staring-into-space sessions. "What do you care?"

"You're a college boy. I can tell."

Michael apparently decided humoring him was better than sitting chained to the floor like a dog and brooding over his fate. "I dropped out of Michigan after my father was beaten half to death for being Muslim," he said. "By men like you."

Rip ignored the cheap shot. "I bet you were on scholarship."

Nasry turned his head aside.

"What then? Medicine? Engineering?"

Michael remained silent, still, contemplating something uncomfortable from his memory.

Taggart surprised himself by beginning to talk about his own life, revealing details that he rarely shared even with those nearest him. Gloria once commented how after all the years she and Rip were together she knew little more about him than on the day they were married. In a rare moment of reflection, Rip considered the possibility that he was actually talking to Na'omi, who was sure to be listening from the other room, rather than to the terrorist.

"White trash like me don't go to college," he reminisced. "For us, it was either jail or the military."

Michael stirred. "It's your country."

"My father got drunk one night and went to town on me with a metal pipe," Rip continued. "Broke my arm, lacerated my kidney. So I chose number two, the military. I wanted to be the toughest so I became a SEAL."

That was a story he had never told Gloria. He wanted Na'omi to be listening. Perhaps it would help her understand why he was the way he was.

That was the end of conversation for today. Al-Muttaqi and Akmal interrupted, sliding into the cell through the outside door and across the larger room where Na'omi and the girls were confined. Both terrorists wore tribal robes. Until now, Taggart had only seen Akmal in his khaki like uniform. Rip also noticed how Akmal avoided looking in Michael's direction.

The Butcher of Khost's ruthless eyes settled on Taggart.

"I have begun my negotiations for you," he announced without preliminaries. "Twenty jihadists out of Guantanamo."

He switched his hard gaze to Michael. "Boko Haram doesn't want money," he said in the same monotone. "They want your head."

That created a reaction. "No! Emir!" Michael cried out.

"You wanted to sacrifice yourself for the cause," al-Muttaqi reminded him. "Your time has come."

A beaten man, Michael lowered his head between his knees. His body shook in spasms of fear.

Taggart spoke up. "The girls come with me," he demanded.

"No!" al-Muttaqi snapped. "Our Muslim brothers need wives."

To Michael, he said, "They will go back to Boko Haram with you."

Na'omi in the next room overheard his decree. She sprang to her feet, terrified all over again by the horrors of rape and abuse she and her girls had endured while in Boko Haram captivity. Only Esther, Abiye, and Kamka remained of the classroom of girls originally taken in the terrorist raid on Na'omi's schoolhouse. Boko Haram had sold the others off as "wives" and sex slaves. The thought of Esther, Abiye, and Kamka suffering the same fate was too dreadful to contemplate.

"No! *No!* Please?" the teacher begged, running from her room into the other and directly at al-Muttaqi. "You can't do that."

Akmal intercepted. He shoved her back from the Emir and slapped her hard across the face when she continued her protest.

"Enough!" al-Muttaqi barked.

"I won't go without them," Rip insisted.

Al-Muttaqi sneered. "You don't have a choice."

With that, he turned and walked out, his back stiff. Na'omi gathered her girls in her arms.

They looked confused, not quite comprehending how events unfolding around them might lay waste the rest of their lives.

Michael called out to Akmal in desperation as the Emir and his new disciple left. "Akmal! Don't let him do this to me."

Akmal hurried out without looking back.

"*Akmal!*"

Chapter Forty-Five

Virginia Beach

Lena Graves drove directly to the cemetery after school where her husband Joe promised to meet her so they could plant fresh clippings at Sarah's gravesite. She arrived early; Joe was still at Command training with his team. She stood next to the tiny earthen mound with its little marble tombstone, staring down at it, striving bravely to hold back tears. She wiped her eyes quickly when she heard Joe's GMC truck drive up outside the gate.

The truck bed was cluttered with bundles of carpentry wood and other items, including a new power table saw still inside its box. Joe got out of the truck prepared to work wearing jeans, boots, and a flannel logger's shirt. He sorted through gardening tools and pots of live baby roses and marigolds in his truck and carried them in his arms to where Lena waited for him at Sarah's grave. He paused for a moment inside the stone arches of the gate to look at her with her hair golden in the fresh morning sunshine raying through the lone oaks and maples. When she looked up at him, he saw in her also the terrible hurt and sadness that dimmed her blue eyes and had faded the pleasure and hope out of their marriage.

Without a word to each other, they got down on their knees, one on either side of the grave, and began digging to plant their offerings, working in the silence of the growing tension between them. Graves tamped fresh soil around the roots of one of the little rose bushes. Its blooms glowed pink, as delicate as the life of a child. He felt Lena's eyes on him.

"Joe . . . ?"

He ducked his head, unwilling to meet her eyes, wracked by guilt and regret and futility.

"All I know is death," he murmured in a voice so thin it sounded as though it might snap at any moment. "Everything I touch, everything I see . . . I destroy."

If sins had consequences, as Pastor Adams asserted, and God would punish a child for the sins of its parents, were not the parents likewise punished?

"Joe . . . ?" Lena tried again. She sounded numb. Hadn't she been punished enough? "Joe . . . ?"

It took her another try to get it out. "Joe . . . I don't think we should have a child together."

Graves was too stunned to respond. He bent forward over the grave and its newly planted blossoms, hands flat on the ground, head lowered until his forehead touched the tiny mound of earth.

His cell phone buzzed, the familiar summons to Command: *999999*. He didn't have to look at the screen. Slowly, feeling empty inside, he stood up, not knowing what to do with his hands or his eyes, almost afraid to look at the flowers for fear he would wilt them. Lena lifted her face.

"Go," she said softly.

They looked at each other a long interval, Sarah's grave between them, before he turned and made his way, head down, toward his pickup. Bitter tears of heartache shook Lena to her core after he was gone.

A storm out to sea in the Gulf Stream kicked up waves that broke against the white sand beaches of Virginia. Riding his surfboard through the breakers, Alex Caulder dropped to his knees on the board and guided it through the briny foam to the sand below his shack. He pulled it out of the water and sat on it to gaze thoughtfully out to sea. A sand crab legged up beside him and regarded him just as thoughtfully from its stilted, exclamation point eyes. He smiled at it just as he cell phone rang that all-too-familiar DEVGRU satellite buzz.

He took the cell from the pocket of his board shorts and removed its waterproof sleeve: *999999.*

He sighed. He looked back out to seas. He looked at the sand crab. Then he dialed a number.

"Hello?"

"Dharma?"

"How are you?"

"Listen, I was hoping to see you. Just to talk or maybe—"

Her live voice became a recording. She had cut him off and switched him to call waiting. "*How am I? I'm not really here. I'm in the air, in the ocean. I'm everywhere and nowhere. Don't bother to leave a message. I won't return your call.*"

The message ended with a beep. Caulder stared out to sea for another minute before he rose and dragged his surfboard up the sand toward his cabin.

The Ortiz family—Ricky, Jackie, Anabel, and Ricky Jr.—were having an outing on the beach at the Boardwalk. So were lots of other sun worshippers. Sun umbrellas sprouted on the sand like colorful mushrooms. Laughing children chased each other in and out of the surf. Near-naked bodies slathered in tanning oil glistened on beach towels. It was a perfectly normal day in a perfectly normal world far removed from the terror and violence of Buddha's alternative universe.

Wearing bathing suits and carrying towels around their necks, Ricky and his family tramped up from the beach as the sun cooled down in the west. He shifted the weight of the cooler from one shoulder to the other as he and Jackie chatted about Anabel's dance class and R.J.'s Little League. She stabbed a discarded paper cup off the sand with the point of her umbrella.

Fifteen-year-old Anabel walked distracted with a conch shell held to her ear. Ten-year-old R.J. noticed it was the shell he found while beachcombing and left on top of the cooler to be saved.

"Anabel, give it back to me!" he demanded, making a bluff run at her.

She menaced him with the prospect of a backhand. "Hold on."

That stopped him. "It's *mine*," he protested.

What mothers did best was arbitrate their children. "Anabel, give him his shell."

Triumphant and impatient, R.J. kicked sand at his sister and attempted to snatch back his prize. Anabel dropped the shell in the sand.

"Anabel! I hate you!"

"It's your fault."

"*You* did it."

Jackie sighed. Once more into the fray. "Both of you, that's enough."

Sunbathers strolling on the boardwalk stopped to look and laugh. Ricky set down the cooler and used it a rest to dry sand off his bare feet. If Jackie was the family arbitrator, he was its peacemaker.

"Ice—sorbet anyone? Anabel?"

His daughter shook her head. She still seemed distracted, apparently preoccupied with weighty thought. He gave her a long look.

"I should get back anyhow," Jackie declined. "I have that dinner tonight."

She had been bubbly with excitement all afternoon. Her new pharmaceutical sales job kept her running. "It's a big client, Ricky."

"You'll get it," Ortiz assured her. "Don't worry about us. We got this, right, guys?" he called out to the kids.

R.J. jumped up and down, smiling broadly and waving his arms. *Yea! Pizza!* Anabel seemed less excited. She walked up to her father like she had something to say, that pretty Latina face of hers set with determination that reminded him so much of Jackie. All afternoon at the beach she kept stealing off by herself to mope. Jackie attributed it to teenage angst.

"Princess? What's up?" Ortiz asked her.

"I . . . uh . . . Look, I'm just going to say it."

Uh-oh. Jackie alerted. This was serious. Anabel sounded just like her father did before he dropped some bomb—such as he wasn't going to quit the SEALs and take the GSS security position until after the team found Rip and brought him back.

"I don't want to go to dance school," Anabel declared.

Ricky's mouth dropped open in astonishment. "What are you talking about? It's been your dream."

Jackie lent reinforcement. "Anabel, you are going to that school."

Mother and daughter were so much alike, with identical stubborn cores of steel. "No, I'm not. It's not fun anymore. I want to be with my friends."

Disbelief swept Jackie's face. "Your father's leaving the service so you can go. I took the job to pay for it."

Jackie looked to Ricky for support. It occurred to both of them simultaneously that this matter over Jackie's new job and Rip Taggart's abduction—her being away from home so much while Ricky was frequently deployed—had disrupted family life.

Ortiz's cell phone buzzed. Both knew what the sound of that ring meant before Ricky looked at the screen: *999999.*

Anabel had her mind on rebellion. "I'm not going."

She stomped her foot and huffed off down the boardwalk toward the parking lot. Jackie called out after her.

"Anabel!"

Jackie sighed. The family had needed a nice day off together. Now, the day was falling apart.

"You have to be back for the kids before I leave for dinner," she reminded Ricky.

"I've been recalled, *Bonita* . . . I don't know when I'll be back."

"Ricky!"

His cell chimed—a text from Graves. All it said was: *Rip.*

"It's about Rip," Ortiz passed on to his wife.

Suddenly concerned, she asked, "Rip? On the video?"

"I don't know."

They locked eyes. A crack appeared in her tough girl exterior and tears welled in her eyes. She stepped away to the boardwalk and looked out over the sand and all the happy, normal people. Ricky walked up behind her.

"Come on. I'll take you home first."

He wrapped his arms around her from behind and kissed her on top of her head. Silently together, they stared out past the normal people to the restless undulating of the Atlantic. From nearby, R.J. watched them, worried.

Chapter Forty-Six

SEAL Command, Virginia Beach

Recall brought most of Commander Lee Atkins's White Squadron to the Command Briefing Room, including the team of Bear Graves, Caulder, Ortiz, Chase, and Fishbait. Some of the SEALs wore street clothing, having been rallied from off liberty, while others, like Graves, were in work uniform. Tension mounting in the room brought wedges of silence. Commander Atkins and Lieutenant Fung escorted in two suits from Washington, one a woman of about forty in a pants suit, the other a rawboned man, bald down the middle of gray hair. Caulder tried to catch Lieutenant Fung's eye, but she ignored him.

Bear's team exchanged worried looks. Were these strangers NCIS?

Commander Atkins walked to the front of the room. He and Lieutenant Fung, both wearing dress blues, added a touch of formality to the assembly.

"I think you all know Ms. Anna Houlding, National Security Advisor," he opened, dipping his chin in her direction. "This," he went on, indicating the rawboned man wearing a dark suit and red power tie, "is Jim Beauchamp, White House Counsel."

Caulder caught Graves's eye. There appeared to be some heavy shit coming down. The question was, on whom was it about to fall?

"Boys," Atkins announced, "we caught a break. We think we know who has Rip and the girls."

That welcome news swept a wave of relief through Bear's team. Bear even managed to smile.

Caulder released in an explosive rush the breath he had been holding.

Two blown-up photos appeared side-by-side on the big screen. One came from the Chase flash drive Caulder gave to Lieutenant Fung. The other was a passport photo. Both showed the same man, who appeared to be in his late twenties with a thin face, bushy eyebrows, and dark, narrow eyes. Lieutenant Fung had come through for them after all.

Commander Atkins identified the man. "Michael Nasry. Born in Dearborn, Michigan. Dropped out of University of Michigan. The same flag from the Tanzania and Dubai bombings is behind Rip in his so-called confession video. If this guy has Rip, apparently he's part of that organization."

"Are we any closer to a location?" Graves wanted to know.

Atkins hesitated, then nodded a *maybe.* "The intel you snatched in Panama puts the Chechen, Akmal Barayev, in an old cement plant Russia abandoned when it was still the Soviet Union. In southern Chad. There's a very good chance that Nasry is there too."

"This the same group that killed Buck?" Ghetto Chase asked.

"Looks like it."

Payback would be sweet. Atkins dipped his chin at the National Security Advisor. "Ma'am."

She strode briskly to the front of the room and assumed her part of the briefing. "The White House is quietly negotiating Rip's release," she disclosed. "The girls, too, if they're there. We're hoping to avoid another . . ." Here, she chose her words carefully in referring to the SEAL fight with the Chechens. ". . . *military adventure* in West Africa. But, if negotiations don't work, you go in and bring them back."

While ransom was never authorized, POW exchanges were reasonably legit.

Fishbait spoke up. "What about Nasry? We just gonna let him go if Rip's exchanged?"

A thin smile gleaned from the advisor's careful makeup. "The minute all the hostages are safe—" She paused to let that sink in. "—*we incinerate the bastards.*"

Caulder felt like jumping up to deliver her a standing ovation. Commander Atkins thrust out his palms for attention.

"White Squadron is wheels up in two hours," he said. "Tidy up your home life."

An hour later, a driver from Support chauffeured Bear's team onto the tarmac at Naval Air Station Oceana where a C-17 Globemaster set outside the hangar warming up. Team members were kitted out in combat gear and carried in packs what they could not load onto their persons. They unassed the Suburban in the midst of apparent confusion. The scene began to sort itself out as departure time drew near.

Gear littered the tarmac prepared for loading—camera cases, body bags, computers, gun cases, boxes of ammo, heavy weapons, and parachutes. Blue, white, or silver cargo vans and white box trucks unloaded even more equipment, while GMC Suburbans let out more SEAL operators. White Squadron was going to war.

Bear Graves offered Buckley's Texas Lone Star patch to Chase. "Take Buck's heater on the target, Chase."

Ghetto nodded. "Roger that." It was an honor.

Chapter Forty-Seven

Chad, Africa

Rip Taggart and Michael Nasry, each lost in thought, sat against opposite walls in their shared cell, their chains running across the floor to eyebolts that kept them separated. Na'omi had slipped into the room with them. Deep in melancholy, she sat on the floor nearest Rip just inside the doorway prepared to hustle back to her own side should the lock bolt rattle on the outside door. Abiye and Kamka were taking naps on their bedrolls. Esther quietly got up from her roll and, with baggy gray trousers and tunic several sizes too large for her, pants legs cuffed up to her knees, walked in and across to sit down close to Rip. She rested her head on his arms.

"Is it true?" she asked in a tiny voice. "Are we going back there? To those . . . men?"

Michael turned his back to them. Rip, who had always been awkward with children, encircled the child with his arms and drew her into its protective embrace. "You're going to come with me."

Na'omi overheard. Her voice flared at him from across the room. "Don't lie to her, Richard."

Esther looked up into Rip's face. She wanted with all her heart to believe. Seeing the truth in Rip's eyes, she puckered up to cry. Reluctantly, she broke free and scurried back into the girls' side of the prison. Na'omi pierced Rip with a disappointed look before she got up and followed the child to comfort her, leaving Taggart and Nasry alone.

Rip considered his cellmate, the seed of a feasible plan beginning to germinate. Cops used it all the time: turn the bad guys against each other, use them.

Dust motes illuminated by the single bulb hanging from the ceiling swirled in the stale air. A cockroach ran up Michael's pants leg. He ignored it. It eventually tumbled off his knee and fled for the nearest corner. Michael looked as though the Prophet Muhammed had personally told him that jihadists never really received seventy-two virgins in Paradise, or that a martyr who strapped a suicide bomb on himself and blew up a school bus full of children went to hell. In little bitty pieces.

Rip decided his scheme was worth a try. "You're the recruiter, right?" he ventured. "The golden tongue."

He paused a beat to let that introduction set in.

"So," he suggested, "recruit Akmal."

Michael scowled suspiciously. "To do what?"

"Kill the Emir."

Michael took in the thought before outright dismissing it. For Rip, that meant it was a start. It was also a good sign that Nasry seemed willing to discuss the hurt he felt over al-Muttaqi's betrayal of him.

"I met Muttaqi in a CIA Black Site," he revealed in a distant and painful voice. "They told me it was Romania, but they never let us outside. The Emir stopped the other prisoners from killing me for being an American."

"So he could have you killed by Boko Haram?"

Rip wondered what al-Muttaqi was doing as a CIA prisoner in Romania. Had he been captured under another name and then, with the CIA and US Intel unaware that he was actually the Butcher of Khost, released along with Nasry? Such things happened in a war as convoluted and confusing as this one. This counterterrorism business could be sort of like *Spy v Spy* in the old *Mad* comic books.

Rip kept up the pursuit. "Your brother died for Muttaqi," he pressed. "This is how he repays loyalty? You're going to just roll over and let him kill you?"

Michael's body jerked as though from a jolt of electricity. His eyes narrowed.

"I will never help you," he vowed.

Chapter Forty-Eight

Chad, Africa

Jockeying for position in far-flung corners of the globe in the ongoing War on Terror involved coordination, diplomacy, calibration of indigent assets, deceit, and treachery. In this kind of war, no one trusted anyone and everything was fair game. Since deceit and betrayal were expected tactics of people who beheaded journalists, hung children on crosses to die, and sold kids for sex slaves, most in the US SpecOps communities learned to play by the same rules. Negotiate? Yes. Negotiate some more? Yes. But never give the enemy a chance to have the last option—or he would take it. Anyone who trusted a jihadist terrorist was a fool—and soon a dead fool. You did to them what they would do to you—only you did it first.

As Commander Atkins stated during pre-mission briefings before the SpecOp airlift to Chad: "As soon as Rip is safe—either through the exchange or we go in and get him—we'll have our JTACs disappear the place with a couple of thousand pounders."

Negotiations to exchange hostage Rip Taggart for terrorist detainees at Guantanamo had proceeded through terrorist contacts within legitimate governments in the Middle East. It was all done undercover and in the dark, so that the US couldn't be really sure of exactly who in the underground hierarchy it was dealing with. US Intel knew that the same group that held Taggart—and possibly the Nigerian females—had previously blown up an American embassy in Tanzania, the Film

Festival in Dubai, and were apparently planning to wave the green-and-black flag on US soil for further actions.

Working through the US State Department and the government of Chad, the CIA acquired a small remote civilian airport to use as a forward operating base. The airport was located on a lightly forested savannah north of the old abandoned Soviet cement plant, which all evidence indicated had been taken over by terrorists and Chechen fighters as a training facility. The hostage-prisoner swap was to take place on the cement plant property.

C-17 Globemaster transport planes with a range of more than six thousand miles flew in the SEAL Six squadrons and their subordinate troop units as time drew down for the most critical part of the operation—the actual exchange of captives. A company of Seventy-Fifth Rangers brought in twenty high-value terrorists held at Guantanamo. Military Black Hawk helicopters set concealed inside a small hangar, along with their pilots and crews on standby.

"The hostage exchange is a day or so away," Commander Lee Atkins commented during a strategy session. "A Ranger element will provide cordon security, in case the exchange falls through and we have to go in. One SEAL troop will be the QRF . . ."

No one knew where these things would end up when they started, but they rarely ended as expected.

Commander Atkins and his subordinate troop leaders delivered final briefings to White Squadron Six as the countdown proceeded. Senior Chief Bear Graves's team and two other teams from White Squadron filed into the briefing area in the hangar's open bay facing the runway. Squadron Commander Atkins and a CIA spook waited for the SEALs to take seats in front of monitors and easels and screens with a variety of still shots and video clips showing the abandoned cement plant farther south.

Satellite stills revealed overall panoramas of the plant's dilapidated buildings. While ISR intel disclosed unusual activity at the plant, the place by all appearances was long abandoned. Acacia trees and thorn bushes had crept into fallen fences. The great main building consisted of a number of adjoining constructions to form a massive central unit with a myriad of connecting passageways. Many smaller outlying buildings had collapsed into rubble. Telephoto shots from ground assets provided close-up images of vital features. Blueprints of the entire plant had been acquired. Crucial rooms and areas had been encircled with marker pens.

"What about the girls?" Buddha Ortiz asked.

"ISR and our birds are blocked by the roof, so we don't have eyes on them," Atkins explained. "They're not part of Rip's exchange as far as we know."

"So they might not even be there?" Fishbait said.

The commander nodded. "That's what we have to find out."

The CIA agent took over. "They have food at the plant, but no water," he noted in pointing out weaknesses to the terrorist defenses. "Water is delivered every other day by a Nigerian, a local Baggara Arab who looks Libyan, and another local grunt . . ."

Graves noted a possible way to get an advance look inside the plant to counteract expected perfidy.

Chapter Forty-Nine

Chad, Africa

A dusty pickup truck with a three-hundred-gallon water tank in its bed chugged across a dry streambed and followed an even dustier road through scrub savannah forest toward an abandoned Soviet cement plant located on a stretch of high plains beyond. Three men occupied the truck. The driver was a lighter-skinned Buggara Arab, his passenger might have been Algerian or Libyan. The man in back with the water was a dark-skinned African wearing a bush hat and a red scarf around his neck.

The pickup kicked up a plume of dust as it swept around a blind curve. Shouting out in surprise, the driver hit his brakes hard to avoid crashing into an older model Fiat stalled in the road, blocking it. The truck slid to a dangerous halt, almost tossing the African in back across the cab. He managed to hook a hand into the passenger's open side window to save himself.

Two men out in the dust and hot sun repairing a flat tire jumped out of the way. One was a big black man, apparently an equatorial African. The other might have been from somewhere in northern Africa. Both wore nondescript baggy civilian cotton trousers and open shirts, normal attire for this part of the country.

Ghetto Chase shot Fishbait a glance as the truck came to a squalling halt on damaged brakes. *Ready?* Fishbait returned a casual nod. Nearby, Graves, Caulder, and Ortiz lurked in a corpse of trees with a CIA spook and SEALs from Two Troop's Quick Reaction Force, all of whom were prepared to take out the truck's present ownership should there be a dispute.

Fishbait approached the driver's side of the truck. He looked impatient as well might a traveler delayed by unforeseen circumstances. Chase ambled up to the passenger's door wearing a genial smile.

"Brother, can you help us?" Fishbait requested in Arabic.

The truck driver's agenda did not include being delayed. He scowled. "Get your car off the road," he barked, also in Arabic.

A Sig Sauer pistol seemed to magically appear in Fishbait's fist. He tapped its muzzle against the driver's temple. The guy's eyes almost popped out of his head. He froze behind the wheel.

The surprised front seat passenger found Chase's pistol jabbed against his temple. The African in back, who had recovered from nearly being tossed from the truck, whipped out a handgun, a move that turned out to be a fatal one for him. Ortiz's suppressed rifle *Thumped!* twice from the roadside trees. The man crumpled. The body wedged between the water tank and the back of the cab.

Graves covered the prisoners while, working quickly, Fishbait and Chase zip-tied the driver and passenger, jerked bags over their heads, and turned them over to other SEALs. Ortiz and Caulder pulled the dead African off the truck and dragged the body into the woods. Two support techies with bags of gear rushed out of the timber.

"You got five minutes," the CIA agent told them.

They accomplished their tasks in four. One planted a pin camera with a stub antenna out of sight inside the truck's front grill while the other crawled underneath the vehicle to install a flat-box repeater transmitter with an antenna. They gave thumbs up and stepped out of the way. Job completed.

Fishbait slid behind the truck's steering wheel, the swarthy-skinned CIA agent took shotgun, and Chase sprang into the truck bed to ride with the water tank. The spook spoke into a pack of Marlboro cigarettes.

"Radio check?"

A techie wearing earphones gave him another thumbs up. The agent placed the cigarette pack on the truck's dash in front of him; it contained a voice-activated microphone. Fishbait passed his pistol out the truck window to Graves.

"They might search us," he said.

Chase likewise relinquished his weapon.

"The QRF will launch if it goes sideways," Graves assured them.

"Yeah. To pick up the pieces," Fish snorted.

He gave the pinhole camera in his shirt button a last check and kicked over the engine. Graves looked up at Chase in the back of the truck.

"Chase? You good?"

"Check." Ghetto would have blended in almost anywhere in equatorial Africa.

As soon as other SEALs cleared the Fiat off the roadway, having quickly replaced its "flat" tire, Graves gave the truck fender a ringing slap with his open palm. Fishbait drove off down the road toward the cement plant with Chase and the CIA spook.

"I should be the one going in there," Graves remarked. A leader didn't *send* his men into danger. He *led* them.

"Yeah, you'd fit right in," Ortiz wisecracked. A big white guy who looked more American than Mr. Clean.

Graves smiled. The dust cloud left by the truck faded as it, his two SEALs, and the spook disappeared around a curve and into spindly forest in a lowland valley.

Chapter Fifty

Chad, Africa

The big-headed character with the big axe from Michael Nasry's video game typed a question in English on the screen: *Where are you, Nilofar?* Akmal pushed back with a sigh and waited, although he knew it was hopeless. Using social media as well as the Game, he had attempted to communicate with his sister in Panama for days. He had received no response. Scowling at the computer as though his lack of communication was the big-headed character's fault, worried about why Nilofar hadn't replied to his entreaties, he finally shut down the computer and rubbed his face wearily with both hands.

A Chechen guard entered his room without knocking, simply opening the door unannounced and walking in. Akmal looked up, annoyed at the intrusion.

"Akmal, the Emir wants to see you," the Chechen said in Arabic.

Akmal rose and obediently followed the guard into and down the hallway to the rows of offices where Michael had established his nerve center. It was now Emir al-Muttaqi's nerve center. Recruiters busily clacked away on their laptops and computers in other parts of the office. They were four men and two women in hijabs. One of the four male recruiters, Kashif, now perched nervously on the edge of a chair at the Emir's desk in the inner part of the office. An armed Chechen stood rigidly to either side of Kashif's hot seat. Akmal frowned, but only to himself, as he considered what crime the recruiter may have committed.

Emir al-Muttaqi was busily sorting through sheaves of documents at his desk. He looked up, frowning, when Akmal wended his way across the office.

"I have to make it right," al-Muttaqi fretted in Arabic, his black beard seeming to bristle with temper. "The SEAL wasn't worth it."

"But Boko Haram?" Akmal replied, also in Arabic. "They're animals."

Kashif's hands trembled lying in his lap. "The SEAL helped get our recruitment up," Kashif offered.

"*As-kol!*" al-Muttaqi snapped.

Kashif was too overwrought to let it go. His Arabic tumbled out in a frantic stream. "Fifty thousand hits in two days. In North America alone, we—"

His mouth froze open and his eyes bulged in terror as al-Muttaqi calmly produced a pistol from his robes. Akmal likewise simply stared in horror as al-Muttaqi, without a blink of his dark eyes, shot the terrified recruiter through the forehead. One of the two females cried out in alarm in reaction to the crack of the pistol shot. The other screamed when brains and blood slashed against the wall behind Kashif.

Tense silence fell over the room, but only for a second. The nerve center went back to clacking and humming, each worker afraid he might be next if he showed any interest, fear, or curiosity about the Emir's behavior.

While everyone pointedly refused to notice, Kashif's body slowly toppled out of the chair and sprawled face down on the floor where dark blood quickly pooled around his head. Al-Muttaqi gestured his pistol at the dead man.

"He said that Michael was the key to our future success," the Emir said, still in Arabic.

Saying *that* about Michael was Kashif's crime that called for capital punishment? Horrified by the unexpected murder, Akmal nonetheless struggled to control his reaction and maintain an impassive front. Anything less could cost him his own life.

"Do you think that is true, Akmal?"

Akmal got it out as quickly as he could, and hopefully in the right tone of sincerity. "No, Emir. I remain loyal," he pledged.

The Emir studied him as coldly as a poisonous snake posed to strike a crippled bird. "Michael said the same thing. There will be other talented men. More trustworthy. You may go."

That was it? That was why he was summoned—to witness Kashif's execution? Akmal nodded with expected subservience and walked out of the nerve center after a final quick look at the dead recruiter. Al-Muttaqi watched him go, then ordered the Chechen guards to clean up the mess.

Akmal's innards remained twisted in turmoil when he entered the room-cells where the hostages were held. He passed briskly through the outer room where Na'omi and the three schoolgirls were held and on into the next room where Taggart and Michael remained chained by their ankles to the floor.

Despondent but still curious, seeking some clues as to what might be intended for the prisoners, Na'omi quietly moved to the doorway and flattened herself to one side where she could eavesdrop on the quiet conversation between Akmal and Michael.

"*Al-ameeer katal Kashif*," Akmal burst out in Arabic. "*The Emir killed Kashif*."

Michael drew a deep breath, shocked by the news but not surprised. He started to reply in Arabic, but immediately switched to his native language. "The others will—they will obey him now."

Michael remained sitting with his back to the wall. Akmal squatted on his haunches next to him. In a quiet voice, looking concerned, he said, "I can't reach Nilofar. On the Game."

"Don't tell Muttaqi that you tried," Michael warned. "He'll kill you, too."

"My sister should know her husband is dead," Akmal said in Arabic again.

Nilofar's husband, Akmal's brother-in-law, had been the dead Chechen commander left behind when Michael and Akmal fled the Boko Haram village with the hostages during the SEAL raid on it. He had also been Akmal's contact to provide Chechen fighters for the operation, and for the training facility in Chad.

"I can't help you," Michael said. "I'm being turned over to Boko Haram."

Akmal looked away, clearly troubled. Michael scooted on his butt closer to his former recruiter co-commander.

"Akmal, you think Muttaqi would have thought of making the video?" He indicated Taggart with a gesture. "You have to convince him to free me."

Taggart was listening carefully and recognized an opening to fertilize the seed he had planted in Michael's mind.

"Hey, Akmal," he called out.

"Shut up!"

"Akmal, you have to kill Mutaqqi."

Akmal walked grimly toward Rip and backhanded him hard across the face.

"Akmal!" Michael exclaimed. "Leave him alone."

Astonished at Michael's response, Akmal slowly returned to Michael's side. Out of sight beyond the doorway, Na'omi continued to make herself a part of the wall.

"We are a new path to Jihad," Michael reasoned. He sounded desperate to convince Akmal that they had to work together if either of them hoped to survive al-Muttaqi. "You and I. I saw your face when you realized everything we worked for was coming true. Muttaqi is stuck in the past. We're the future. All you are to Muttaqi is a strong back. Be a slave like the Zanju who rebelled against the Abasid Caliphate. Be like Ali ibn Muhammed."

He paused to check how well he might be getting through to Akmal.

"Akmal, you killed your Russian commander once for the sake of Allah," he continued more desperately. "You can do it again. For our cause, Akmal."

Akmal stared at Michael, but was not looking at him. Instead, he saw Kashif's brains being blow out and splattered on the wall. His demeanor, his sense of survival, hardened.

"The Emir is right about you," he said. "You have no loyalty."

He spat contemptuously on the floor at Michael's feet, turned and walked out of the room and on past Na'omi without noticing her.

Chapter Fifty-One

Chad, Africa

Michael Nasry prayed quietly on his knees, his head on the floor facing Mecca. Na'omi slipped into the room and approached Taggart where he stood against the far wall watching Michael.

"Richard . . . I understood a little of what they said," she whispered. She had been closer to the two men than had Taggart and therefore had a better vantage point. "Somebody got shot . . . Something about his sister, not being able to reach her. On a game."

Michael ceased praying. Rip saw that he was listening. He raised his voice, speaking directly to his fellow inmate. "Akmal has a sister? She a terrorist, too?"

Michael ignored him and continued to pray quietly. Or at least he pretended to pray. Rip sensed Akmal may have provided him even more fertile ground to continue Michael's cultivation.

"This game?" Rip pursued. "It's a video game?"

Michael remained on his knees, forehead against the floor, butt raised.

"That's how you communicate," Rip deduced. "A private chat room. A bunch of terrorists join the game and create their own little message board lobby . . ."

Michael stopped pretending. He lifted his head and looked across the room at Rip and Na'omi.

"You think it's untraceable . . ." Rip said.

"I know it is."

"Unless one of the computers gets snatched."

That caught Michael's attention. He rose to his feet.

"Maybe Akmal's sister isn't talking because she's been compromised," Rip suggested slyly, playing it for everything he could wring out of it.

"You don't know that!" Michael flared.

Rip shrugged. "Akmal's worried about it. I bet Muttaqi would worry about it, too. If . . ."

He paused suggestively with the implied threat. "If . . . he was to find out."

The expression that grabbed Michael's face was like he was trying to swallow something too large to digest all at once. "You're playing a dangerous game," he warned.

Again, Rip shrugged. "We have nothing to lose."

Michael rose to his feet, prayer over, and considered the situation. Al-Muttaqi was serious about turning him over to Boko Haram, who would undoubtedly behead him. So what did he have to lose by playing along with the American SEAL, if, in doing so, he increased his chances only by a slight margin? What if he *could* gain control?

"What do you want?" he asked Taggart.

"Let the girls go. They . . . Na'omi deserves to live."

"What do I get?"

"Me."

Michael's eyes continued to bore into the SEAL's as he considered all angles and possible outcomes. Na'omi looked troubled, worried at Rip once more attempting to offer himself as a sacrifice for her and her students.

Chapter Fifty-Two

Chad, Africa

The abandoned cement plant loomed just ahead, gray wreckage sprawled over a knoll and down a shallow draw surrounded by plains and, in the distance, woodlands of acacia and native hardwoods. Fishbait at the wheel of the dusty commandeered water truck nodded at his CIA counterpart to get ready. The spook was a rather large man of about forty with a northern African appearance and a sweeping mustache. He stuck his head out his open window and called back to Ghetto Chase riding with the water tank.

"Remember," he cautioned. "Don't speak. Limit your eye contact. Think meek."

"Got it." *Don't speak, think meek.*

A dedicated satellite tracked the truck as it approached the massive main wreck of a building. The eye in the sky clicked in close until the truck filled the frame of the generator-powered HDTV screen marked *SAT* at the SEAL FOB located on the small civilian airport. Graves, Caulder, and Ortiz returned from assisting in hijacking the water truck and joined Squadron Commander Lee Atkins, other SEALs, spooks, and techies gathered around several screens, each marked in white tape according to camera source: *SAT, Chase, Fish, Truck.*

The *Truck* camera concealed in the vehicle's grill displayed the plant's open double loading doors. The road leading up to them appeared well-traveled enough to indicate this to be the plant's main entrance. As the truck pulled up to the doors, the camera image on *Truck* flickered and the screen turned black.

"What the hell!" Caulder muttered, alarmed.

"Jesus . . ." one of the Intel support guys exclaimed. "The truck camera is out."

This unexpected occurrence sharpened the suspense.

Unaware of the camera outage, Fishbait pulled up and braked the truck outside the loading dock entrance that led into the big open area of the cement plant. Fishbait sat at the wheel all cool and casual by outward appearances and waited for the approach of a man with a long, full face and a tight crop of curly black hair. He wore an unforgiving expression, a white Arab robe, and an AK-47 slung across his back. Chase riding with the water tank adjusted his clothing to make sure the tiny camera concealed behind the button of his shirt framed the guy in the robe and two armed, uniformed guards accompanying him. Chase had seen soldiers like this during the fight at the Boko Haram village where Buck died.

The man in the Osama bin Laden robe hesitated when he saw strangers manning the water truck, In Arabic, he demanded of the driver, "Where's Farouk?"

Fishbait affected a tired yawn, like he had been working all night bringing water to the desert. "Sick," he said.

"Who are you?"

"Malouf."

The atmosphere at the airport FOB tensed as Commander Atkins and other SEALs, spooks, and techies watched with bated breath the three remaining HDTVs marked *SAT, Chase*, and *Fish*. The *Truck* screen remained blank. A mic from the truck's undercarriage comm package relayed sound and voice from the cement plant. An Intel support tech translated the conversation from Arabic to English.

"He's asking who Fishbait is."

His suspicions not allayed, the man in the robe scrutinized the two men in the truck's cab, both of whom appeared to have had a late night or something. The shotgun passenger looked as bored and as ready to end his work day as the driver did. He scratched his nose and then his balls and gazed out across the sunlit plains with little interest.

White Robe stalked completely around the truck, looking. He even dropped on all fours to look underneath it. He examined the fittings on the water truck, dipped out a palm full of water and sniffed it. He stopped at the passenger's window and turned his attention to Chase, who was leaning on his elbows across the cab of the truck, pretending to nap.

"*Me ismak*?" White Robe questioned him in Arabic. "I don't recognize you either. What's your name?"

Chase stared uncomprehendingly. He shook his head, shrugged, and lifted his palms in the universal *I don't understand* sign.

At the FOB on the screen marked *Chase*, Ghetto's pin camera framed the Arab, who, still suspicious, laid his hand on the pistol holstered at his belt. Both the sound and the image had been degraded through relay to satellite and then back to the FOB's HDTV. The screen flickered.

"What's he saying?" Ortiz asked.

The language guru shrugged. "It's too far away."

"Come on . . . Come on . . ." Caulder fretted.

Graves shared a look with Ortiz, his impatience as marked as Buddha's.

White Robe gesticulated at Chase in a further effort to make the ignorant African understand. "Get down off the truck."

Fishbait leaned out his open window, saying nonchalantly in Arabic. "He doesn't speak Arabic. He's a Christian from Cameroon."

White Robe slithered around to the driver's side. "*Eya b'tal-fen la'Abdul*?" he asked. "If I call Abdul, he'll vouch for you?"

Fish's mind went into momentary freeze-lock. His pinhole camera relayed the Arab's full face to the FOB. The audio feed cleared up in the close range between Fish's camera and his subject, allowing the conversation to reach the FOB.

"*Meen' Abdul?*" Fish replied innocently, back on script. "Never heard of him."

The Intel tech at the FOB sounded the alarm. "They could be compromised."

Commander Atkins called out for comm support. "Get the QRF ready. Now!"

Comm cued his mic and reached for the toggle switch. Graves stopped him.

"Commander, sir. Look!"

The *SAT* screen showed White Robe waving the truck forward into the cement plant.

"Belay my last," Atkins ordered as the men inside the hangar room breathed a collective sigh of relief.

Chapter Fifty-Three

Chad, Africa

White Robe sniped in Arabic at Fishbait as he drove the truck through the loading dock doors into the cement plant. "You shouldn't work for an infidel."

Fishbait shrugged.

SEALs at the FOB continued to watch HDTV screens as the truck disappeared off the *SAT* screen. HDTV images on *Fish* and *Chase* degraded somewhat inside the plant with flickering and brief blackouts. The Intel support asset bending over his computer made progress on identifying the nasty Arab in the white robe.

"Facial Recon has a match on that guy," he reported to Commander Atkins. "Akmal Barayev, former Russian Spetsnaz. Nilofar's brother."

Caulder performed a face shrug. "Guess we knocked on the right door," he said.

A uniformed Chechen inside the plant's large, enclosed loading area motioned the truck to park near a row of five-gallon gas cans waiting to be filled with water. The CIA agent remained inside the truck while Fishbait got out. Fish's gaze swept the large area, taking in everything for future reference while also capturing it on his pinhole camera. To his left, a row of doors appeared to be partially rejuvenated offices with a hallway leading off them beyond into the interior. Infantry packs, web gear, comm equipment, weapons, and other kit were stacked in one corner along with cots where men apparently slept. A large tarp to one side of the open bay doors covered what appeared to be a heavy weapon on a truck, either an antiaircraft gun or a mortar. The entire area resembled a messier version of a SEAL staging base.

Fish counted ten Chechen soldiers in BDU cammies rustling about, but they paid little attention to the water crew. Fish suspected there were more soldiers either further inside or on perimeter picket. He shifted about casually to allow his camera to catch as much as he could without arousing suspicion. The camera forward it to HDTV at the SEAL FOB.

"Look on as many faces as you can," the Intel supervisor requested of his video techies.

"Check out their rifles," Caulder observed.

Fishbait had turned so that his buttonhole camera focused on a Chechen standing with a rifle across his body at port arms. The rifle was equipped with laser sights.

"Definitely from the same bunch of guys we dumped at the BH village," Graves noted.

A facial recognition square appeared over the screen face of the Chechen with the laser sights. The Intel guy declared a match. A name appeared on the computer next to the HDTV—Achmed Khasanov—along with his date of birth and other vitals.

In the meantime, Chase was busy playing the part of unskilled African laborer. He hopped off the back of the truck, opened the tailgate, and attached a hose to the tank. Four Chechens with slung rifles brought up more five-gallon cans to be filled. They were a mean, sour-looking bunch, as judged by HDTV close-ups of them at the FOB. They approached Chase and went on by with no more than a glance.

Chase nonchalantly turned in a three-sixty to give the FOB a panoramic view through his camera. Men at the airport FOB watched the feed. The image stopped on the gear in the corner. Chase zoomed in with his camera to reveal rifles and ammunition boxes.

"Correlate this image with the blueprints," the Intel support super requested. Another tech with a large blueprint of the cement plant was busy marking out vital locations.

"And get a head count of the enemy," Commander Atkins added.

Things were about to get even more interesting. As Chase used a hose running from the water tank to fill up the line of five-gallon cans, he casually leaned up against the side of the truck so that his camera recorded the row of offices across from him. A strange-looking man in Arab garb—white robe and a checkered *kaffiyeh*—emerged from one of the offices. He wore a beard like most ISIS and al-Qaeda terrorist leaders. He was dark skinned with the expressionless face of a corpse. He eyed Chase for a moment before ambling toward him. SEALs at the FOB regarded him curiously on HDTV feed.

"Zoom in," the Intel chief requested.

The Arab's jackal face filled the screen. A square appeared over it as the facial recognition app kicked in. Caulder's brow creased in concentration. He leaned toward the screen for a better look.

"Holy shit!" he exclaimed.

Graves and Buddha recognized the man at the same time.

"The Butcher," Graves said.

"Muttaqi," Ortiz echoed. "He's with this Michael Nasry guy?"

Excitement buzzed throughout the FOB. "Lock it up," Atkins ordered.

The Intel computer beeped. Al-Muttaqi's picture and vitals appeared on the screen.

"We have a confirmation," the Intel man said. "It's Muttaqi."

Graves couldn't believe it. The last time he butted heads with the terrorist chief was in Afghanistan. "Jesus Christ. Muttaqi. Here."

He was another reason for disintegrating the cement plant off the face of the earth once the hostages were secured.

"Push that to the Joint Chiefs," Commander Atkins ordered his Intel staff.

Back on the floor of the cement plant, Chase hosed water into one can after another. White Robe, now identified at the FOB as Akmal Barayev, approached one of the Chechen guards waiting for water.

"Bring a can to the prisoners," he ordered in Arabic.

Fishbait overheard. *The hostages?* On a sudden impulse, he approached Akmal with a request. *"Badoe shekh,"* he said.

Akmal scowled, but he ordered another guard to escort the water truck driver to the toilet. By luck or by coincidence, Fishbait and his guard fell in behind the Chechen taking water to the "prisoners." The trio filed past the row of offices and down the hallway at the end toward the interior. Fish's escort directed him toward a door on the right of the hall.

Fish nodded, but as he turned to go into the bathroom he noticed yet another Chechen accompanying a small African girl down the hallway from where she had apparently used the toilet herself. She wore baggy gray linen trousers rolled up to her knees and a loose tunic. The two headed toward another door at the end of the dimly-lit hallway before which stood an armed guard.

Keeping a neutral face, Fishbait rotated slightly to scratch his butt and allow his camera to take in the girl and her escort before his guard shoved him into the overpowering stench of the bathroom. He didn't have to go, but he made himself perform anyhow under the Chechen's scrutiny.

The HDTV marked *Fish* at the FOB picked up only the Chechen disappearing through the guarded doorway and not the girl ahead of him.

"Where is he going?" Ortiz wondered about Fishbait.

Then it became apparent when his camera showed open holes in the cement floor which served as toilets. Caulder shrugged. *When you gotta go, you gotta go.*

Chase filled up the last empty can and turned off the hose spigot. Akmal approached and stared at him, his suspicions not yet abated.

"*Donc, tu parles Francais*?" he asked unexpectedly.

Chase hesitated, caught by surprise. Akmal took a threatening step toward him, his hand reaching for his holstered pistol. Caulder, Graves, and Buddha at the FOB stiffened when they saw the new threat.

"*Bien sur*," Chase responded coolly in French. "Of course I speak French. I'm from Camaroon."

Akmal eyeballed him, then turned and walked away. At the FOB, Commander Atkins gave Chase's teammates an inquiring look. "Chase speaks French?"

"Thank God for Harvard," Caulder said.

Akmal disappeared into the interior of the cement plant while Chase coiled the hose and placed it inside the truck bed next to the now-empty water tank. Sweat beaded Fishbait's face as he hurried back from his excursion to the toilet. Chase nodded at him. *Let's go.* Fish climbed into the cab with the CIA guy, started the engine, and, with Chase in the truck bed, drove out of the cement plant and onto the dusty road leading away from it. Chase finally drew in his first long breath since their adventure began.

Fishbait plucked the comm package—the Marlboro cigarette pack—off the dash and spoke into it as calmly as he could in light of his discovery. "*All stations, Delta Four. We are egressing the target. Break. Confirmed eyes on at least one female hostage . . . I say again: one female hostage is confirmed.*"

Holy shit! That was the general FOB reaction.

"I knew it!" Buddha exclaimed.

Graves sighed with some disappointment. "No Rip," he said.

Ortiz put a different take on it. "Probably keeping them separate."

Commander Atkins grabbed onto one of his comm support techs. "Push this to the Joint Chiefs immediately," he said.

Chapter Fifty-Four

Chad, Africa

Michael Nasry, even when he slept, maintained the same position of arms wrapped around his legs, head lowered between his knees. For hours he sat like that against the wall opposite Taggart, staring into space, his eyes slitted, his thin face slack. Sometimes he stirred long enough to take out a picture and look at it. Taggart watched his agony across from him.

A Chechen brought in a five-gallon can of water and left it with Na'omi for distribution. Another returned Esther from the bathroom. After that, the cells lapsed into a silence broken only by muted sounds of activity from other parts of the cement plant. The three schoolgirls in the other room took a nap gathered around Na'omi so she could look after them.

Rip rose and dragged his ankle chain as near to Nasry as it would reach. He sat on the floor cross-legged, his leanness even more marked from his near starvation captivity by Boko Haram. Michael turned his head and closed his eyes to avoid looking at the SEAL.

"Tell me about your brother," Rip requested.

Michael's eyes remained closed. "What do you care?"

"I shot him. I'd like to know."

Michael opened his eyes, but he still refused to look at Taggart. "Do you have a brother?" he asked.

"Half."

"Younger?"

"Eight years older."

"Did you want to be him?"

After a painful pause, Rip nodded. He remembered all too well. "He made it out from under my old man's thumb."

Michael stared past Rip and spoke in a quiet, nostalgic tone. "Omar wanted to be me. Same school. Same major. Same sports. Same blonde girls . . . Same . . ."

He hesitated before he added, "The Cause. . ."

"You recruited him?" Rip guessed.

A kind of regret entered the terrorist's voice. "He was braver than me. Smarter. He picked up Pashtu and Arabic faster than me. He insisted on the most dangerous missions. Muttaqi would send him into your bases to get intel. Your people never suspected him."

"Show me his picture," Rip said.

Michael scooted across the floor toward Rip until his chain stopped him. Rip did likewise. Michael took out a snapshot and slid it across the cement floor. Rip looked at it. The face looked vaguely familiar, but he would never have connected it to the kid he shot in Kunar if he hadn't already known who the kid was. He slid the photo back to Michael. Michael picked it up and looked at it.

"If I hadn't contacted him," he said—and this time there was no doubt about his regret, "he wouldn't have come to Afghanistan. Omar might still be alive."

"Is that your only regret?"

Instead of answering, Michael looked directly at Taggart and asked a question of his own. "What about you?"

"We have a saying in my world: You can't feed a lion lettuce." He took a deep sigh of breath and looked away. "It's what I am."

Rip looked at the floor for another long moment before adding in a voice almost too soft for Michael to hear, "I'm sorry."

Michael responded in the same soft, fatalistic manner. "It's what we are."

The two men, each imprisoned for different reasons, each having lived and fought on opposite sides of a curse that ravaged the globe in blood and destruction, looked long into each other's eyes. An understanding passed between them—that their only hope for survival depended upon each other. Rip searched for confirmation in Nasry's expression that he was prepared to go along with whatever Rip had in mind. Michael understood and nodded back.

Rip fortified himself with a deep breath before he seemed to go mad, jumping about rattling his chain and shouting from the depths of his lungs. The racket he made carried throughout the cement plant.

"Hey, hey! Muttaqi! I wanna see you! I got something to say!"

Michael waited quietly for whatever the SEAL had in mind to play out. By now he knew he had nothing to lose. It was Na'omi whom Rip's sudden bizarre behavior attracted. She rushed to the doorway with Esther and watched in surprise and confusion.

"Hey, hey!" Rip yelled. "I wanna talk to the Butcher! Hey!"

The outer door unlocked and Akmal strode in swiftly. He glanced at Rip. "Shut up! What do you want?"

"Your boss," Rip proclaimed, and lifted his voice even louder. "Muttaqi!"

Al-Muttaqi walked in behind Akmal. Osama bin Laden in his flowing white robe had been much taller than this toad.

"*Ma yu-reed hatha al-Farang*?" Al Muttaqi demanded of Akmal.

Akmal looked blank and shrugged. Al-Muttaqi strode over to the SEAL and glared hot coals into his eyes. Rip glared back.

"What?" al-Muttaqi demanded.

Rip knew this was his last hand. It was his to fold, raise, or hold. Everything depended on this one last pot.

"Akmal's sister's been taken," he blurted out

That caught the terrorist leader by surprise. "What did you say?"

Akmal looked about to choke. Rip gestured at him. "I overheard him. He tried to contact her on some game."

"Shut up!" Akmal shouted back like a cornered animal who saw no way to escape.

Rage threw him across the floor at the SEAL. He flurried punches that smeared blood on Rip's battered face that was only now beginning to heal from Boko Haram abuse. By acting quickly the guy was playing right into Rip's hands.

Rip repaid Akmal with a crafty smile and a right hook that sent him reeling back. Akmal circled his chained foe and prepared to charge in for another round. Deadly intention shown through his eyes: *Kill! Kill! Shut him up!*

"*Keef*!" al-Muttaqi barked.

That single command by his master seemed to take everything out of Akmal. He backed off, a creature now more to be pitied than feared.

"Is that true?" al-Muttaqi demanded of his underdog.

Akmal lips fluttered. "Emir . . ."

Rip sensed he still held the advantage and moved back in to stir the pot some more. "She's not answering. Right, Akmal?"

Akmal shot an accusing look at Michael, who squatted on the floor and pretended noninvolvement.

"Your communications have been compromised," Taggart pointed out, not knowing it but nonetheless letting his bluff run the table. "My people smell you, Muttaqi. They are coming for me."

The Emir's fists clenched at his sides as he fought not to panic. "Don't think I don't know what you're doing," he said to Rip. "Sowing dissent in my men."

Taggart chin nodded at Akmal. "I hate that fucker."

Al-Muttaqi's hard gaze switched to Akmal. Akmal's eyes darted about as though seeking some way out of the trap laid by the American, and by Michael.

"*Hatha sahheehh*?" al-Muittaqi asked in Arabic. "Is it true? You used the game to reach her?"

Akmal nodded in meek acceptance of his fate.

"And she doesn't answer?"

Akmal nodded again. Blood drained from his swarthy face.

"How long?"

"Days . . ." Akmal stammered. "Four days."

White with rage, the Emir slapped Akmal hard across the face. "Pack up immediately," he barked, still in Arabic. "We're leaving."

He stalked over to Michael, who remained disrespectfully seated on the floor. "Trucks will come for you faster than I thought," he pledged.

He poked a finger at Akmal. "You. Go with me."

He stalked out of the room. Akmal glared thorns at Rip and Michael and followed the Emir. Left to themselves, the prisoners exchanged a long look of complete understanding. One way or another, they were in this together to any foreseeable end.

Chapter Fifty-Five

Chad, Africa

Darkness crept over the Sahelian belt of southern Chad, but the FOB at the isolated civilian airport continued to hum with activity. Pilots, drivers, and crews of Black Hawk helicopters and fast transport American vehicles hauled in by C-17s and stored out of sight in hangars or other buildings worked deep into the night making sure their machines were serviced and ready and the crews rehearsed. The Command Center and briefing area at one end of the main hangar served as the apex for much of the activity as elements tweaked plans for eventualities should the hostage exchange not go down as planned.

Clusters of light illuminated key areas inside the hangar. Bear Graves, Ortiz, and Caulder were brief backing their key roles in the upcoming operation while they waited for the other two members of the team, Chase and Fishbait, to return from their water truck hasty recon inside the cement plant. Their most recent comm reported they were less than an hour out.

White Squadron Commander Lee Atkins stole up behind the three team SEALs while they huddled in the screen glow of a HDTV that displayed a grid reference graphic of the cement plant. Bear was pointing out key features on the grid.

"*Based on what Fish and Chase gave us*," he said, "*we believe the girls are in the northwest sector. We're still unsure of Rip's position, but we'll punch through and compress the target until we find him. Delta, we air land on the X . . . here.*" His finger slid across the screen. "*And move to our primary entry point . . . here. Chalk Three with Bravo will move on the south side and breach . . . here.*"

"What about the Cordon Elements?" Caulder asked.

"Rangers will tighten the noose when we're on-target. No one in or out."

Ortiz expressed reservations. "I hope these negotiations play out. Otherwise, this is going to be one shit show."

Either way, the bad guys lost. The trick was to get the good guys out first before J-Dams started crashing down from the heavens. In a moment of dark reflection, Bear wondered when it was that they became as sneaky and underhanded and dishonorable as the enemy. Everyone knew you couldn't trust the word of a jihadist during negotiations . . . Now, neither could the enemy trust the Americans. Either side worked what they could to their advantage and then blew up whatever was left. Like Caulder said, it was a hell of a way to run a war—but it was the only war they had.

"Okay, get your kits together," Bear said to wind up the briefing rehash "Keep studying the imagery and know our deconfliction points."

Commander Atkins had remained silent in the background until now. He gestured at Graves, "Bear, come take a look at this."

A sleepy E-6 radioman and an Intel asset sat with laptops in front of the HDTV thermal drone feed relay from the Predator. It displayed four white thermal heat signatures, one at each corner of the cement plant's main building.

"Those four men just came on-station," Commander Atkins explained, indicating the heat signatures. "They're new."

A small AV cart next to the E-6 was piled with radio sets and other electronic and comm gear. Graves tapped the radioman to request his headset. He punched the talk button to raise one of the SEALs on surveillance at the plant. He whispered into the mic.

"*Delta Eight, this is Delta One . . . Do you have eyes on that hostile on the south side of the complex?*"

"*Delta One, Roger that,*" came the immediate response from Petty Officer Pearce. "*He just came out. Bastard has NVGs. Looks like our old ones.*"

Pearce and his partner, both partially clad in ragged-looking sniper camouflage ghillie suits, crouched in the shadows of a large eucalyptus in a copse of acacia several hundred meters from the edge of the run-down cement plant. Presently, Pearce's attention was drawn to an enemy soldier outside the southern walls of the building, the source of the one white thermal shown on the Predator's screen. This guy swept the surrounding terrain through NVGs of a previous generation. These older ones revealed the night world in a liquid greenish glow. Pearce's NVGs, on the other hand, turned the world a strange gray-white with a much sharper resolution than the older ones.

Pearce continued to study the sentry, who lay low and still. "He stays very still," he radioed to Bear.

"Roger that. Sit tight. Over."

Pearce hunkered in the grass and snapped photos with a digital camera equipped with a high-powered night vision telephoto lens. Next to him, the other SEAL lay sprawled on his belly with a small parabolic microphone on a tripod next to him. Feed from Pearce's camera appeared on the FOB's HDTV screen superimposed over one sector of the drone's thermal imagery of the plant. The Intel asset wearing a headset listened to sounds picked up in and around the plant through the on-site SEAL's parabolic microphone.

Ortiz and Caulder joined Graves and Commander Atkins at the HDTV bank.

"What the hell!" Buddha marveled when he saw one of Pearce's relay frames showing the Chechen wearing a pair of NVGs. "They got NVGs now?"

"Somebody's been on Amazon," Caulder cracked.

"They see us on insert," Buddha fretted, "they kill Rip and the girls before we even get close."

The Intel man with the headset waved at Graves to attract his attention. "A lot of noise inside," he reported.

"What do you mean?"

"Metal on metal. Voices. I heard a truck start up. Then stop."

"What do you make of it?" Caulder asked him.

"Something's rattled them."

"The water truck?" Commander Atkins guessed.

The Intel man shook his head. "I don't think so."

An unsettling thought struck Buddha. "They're getting ready to move," he said.

Bear's head snapped toward Ortiz. *Damn! He was right!* Negotiations were off. These guys were moving.

Chapter Fifty-Six

Chad, Africa

Within the inner office, Hatim al-Muttaqi and Akmal watched a guard repeatedly smash his rifle butt into Akmal's computer. Pieces of it flew about the office. Al-Muttaqi eyed Akmal without expression.

"Ghessan says you broke off negotiations for the SEAL?" Akmal ventured in Arabic, still uncertain about where he stood with his boss.

"Until we're safe," the Emir said.

"And Michael? You'll go through with it?"

"Yes," al-Muttaqi confirmed. "The trucks are on the way."

Michael faced the same fate whether al-Muttaqi executed him or turned him over to Boko Haram for beheading. Akmal's heart pounded in his chest from anxiety, knowing as he did that his own fate may well lie in the balance.

"I'm sorry, Emir," he said in a plea. "About the game. I was upset about Bashir dying."

He was even more upset at his inability to contact his sister Nilofar to inform her of her husband's death in the Boko Haram village. Al-Muttaqi's expression softened, if only slightly. He stepped up to Akmal and gripped his shoulders with both hands.

"*Okmal, kul-lona nekh-toa* . . . We all make mistakes. But I know you will remain loyal."

Al-Muttaqi kissed him three times in rapid succession on the cheeks. Then he hoisted a duffel and walked out of the office. Akmal stared at Kashif's splattered blood drying on the wall and. Unsettled now more than ever, he heard his own heart pounding through his ears.

Emir al-Muttaqi proceeded on to the loading bay and dumped his duffel on the floor next to a stack of gun cases. All around him, men with a palpable sense of urgency were hurriedly loading gear and supplies into the backs of two military-style deuce-and-a-half trucks parked side by side. Dawn was already beginning to seep darkness out of the eastern sky.

Al-Muttaqi's burner phone beeped a text message. He glanced at the screen. Boko Haram: *Meet at rendezvous. Two hours.*

He dropped the disposable phone on the concrete and stomped it to ensure the information it contained not be recovered.

"We leave in one hour for the meeting," he called out in Arabic.

Chapter Fifty-Seven

Chad, Africa

Prepped and ready to go, Graves and his team paced at the starting line. Together, they ambled from the airport hangar into the African night. They were impressed with the muted blue-gray-white vision of their new NVGs as compared to the liquid green field of previous generations.

"Holy shit!" Caulder exclaimed. "These babies are crisp."

Bear removed his helmet and NVGs and walked off a ways underneath a sky so full of stars that some celestial giant must have dumped his basket of jewels across the heavens. Ortiz let out a deep audible breath and followed. There was something he had needed to say for a long time.

"Bear . . ." he began. "Bear, you need to know why Rip wanted *you* to lead Delta One."

Graves held up a palm to shush him. "Ricky—"

"No, I need to . . . Bear, Rip knew I had a family. He knew they were just as important to me as the team. That they . . . they, uh, might weigh on me, you know?"

Graves nodded. He understood. He might have been like that himself had Sarah lived.

"Bear, I'll never forget the quote he burned into me." He could still recite it word for word after all this time. "He said, 'Out of every one hundred men, ten shouldn't be in combat. Eighty are just targets. Nine are real fighters. Oh, but the *one*. One is a warrior, and he will bring the others back."

"Heraclitus," came Caulder's voice from out of the night, sourcing the original quote.

Commander Atkins accompanied Caulder, trailed by Fishbait and Chase.

"Just got word from JSOC," the commander announced in a grim voice. "Negotiations for Rip broke down. SIGINT picked up some Boko Haram chatter. A group based north of Benin City is sending a truck to rendezvous near a cement factory in Chad. Apparently for the female hostages."

"Our cement factory?" Graves said.

"There's only one in Chad. A Predator drone is tracking the truck. They're two hours away. The President pulled the trigger. H-hour is zero six hundred, local time."

"It'll be light," Ortiz pointed out.

Atkins looked at him. His eyes scanned the others. "You want to get Rip? Those girls?"

That was all he said. It was enough. He turned and walked back to the hangar with Fishbait and Chase. Ortiz turned to Bear and placed a hand on his shoulder.

"You're the one," he said. "You'll bring us home. You'll bring Rip and those girls back. Bear, that's why *you're* the team leader."

Moved, Bear gripped Buddha's forearm. Caulder joined them. Together, underneath the magnificent canopy of African stars, they walked side by side by side across the airfield surrounded by scattered forest and plains. Somewhere a night bird called out. It sounded like a woman's scream.

Chapter Fifty-Eight

Chad, Africa

Whereas battle itself was a group effort, preparing for battle was a personal thing. It had been so since the days of the Greek gods. A man entering the violence and maelstrom of combat could never be certain he would exit again. As with all combat outfits, each man of Bear Graves's team had his personal ritual in preparing for it physically, emotionally, and mentally. In the hours and minutes before battle, a ritual calmed and settled and helped provide perspective in confronting that most terrible of all life's milestones—death.

Silence prevailed in the hour before dawn at the FOB as Graves and his men prepared, each intently involved in his own process. Bear Graves methodically loaded bullets into magazines and stacked the clips in rows of eight mags each. Closing his eyes, he traced his finger lightly over his weapon and gear, checking by rote memory.

Buddha Ortiz, the team's demolitioneer, laid out his breaching primers and charges to pack carefully where he knew exactly where he could lay hands on them immediately during a shit storm.

Ghetto Chase disassembled his MK-48 heavy machine gun, cleared and oiled all the parts, and then reassembled it. He carefully layered belts of extra 7.62 ammo into the top of his pack as Buckley had showed him. Lastly, he took out Brad's Texas patch and Velcro'd it onto the sleeve of his cammies.

Fishbait adjusted and readjusted his battle armor before praying to Allah for bravery in battle and Paradise if he should fall.

Caulder isolated himself in a Zen-like state to commune with his inner self. Afterward, he slowly pulled on thin leather gloves, flexing his fingers. Then he was ready.

When all was prepared to go, Graves administered final equipment check. He passed from man to man, checked his gear and ended with a pat on the shoulder, back or helmet. That bit of human contact from a respected leader was what mattered. To a man, teammates responded to Bear with a knuckle bump, a slap on the helmet, a fake punch to his armored belly, little things that exhibited closeness and that brotherhood of men who went together to war.

Caulder was last in line to be equipment-checked. Bear adjusted Caulder's armor, not because it was necessary but instead in order to prolong the moment. They shared a long look, differences between them forgotten or forgiven in this last hour and minutes of truce and truth. Caulder grinned his reckless Dennis the Menace grin and the two men shook hands.

"Time to load the birds," Graves announced.

The team filed out of the hangar into the red glow of the rising sun. Bear drew in the fresh, fecund odors of equatorial Africa. God, how he loved this time of day. Buddha grinned at him.

Turbines were whining up on a trio of Black Hawks preparing to insert Bear's team and the other SEAL elements of the assault force. Their main rotors thumped the air and produced wind geysers that tugged at anything loose on the battle dress of the approaching SEAL teams.

Commander Atkins walked with Graves to the chopper flight line. Bear wore a small emergency combat pack on his back and carried an H&K 416 in his hand. He was helmeted and armored and prepared mentally and physically to go to war.

"Get those girls out," Atkins said to him. "Find Rip. Then, we'll sink some J-Dams into that structure and wipe it off the map."

Graves nodded. He looked determined. Atkins quietly pulled Graves aside as the team drew near the choppers and began to onload.

"I don't care what really happened in Afghanistan," he said confidentially, eyeing Graves for a reaction. It was the first time the commander had brought up Rip's "confession" video since the investigation went on hold. He clasped Bear's shoulder. "Just bring Rip home."

Graves suspected all along that Commander Atkins hadn't been fooled by the team's rather amateurish cover-up. After all, Atkins had come up in the teams and knew that brotherhood.

"Yes, sir," Graves said.

Commander Atkins stepped back as his White Squadron SEALs loaded quickly aboard the three Black Hawks. Rotors whirred and wheels grew light on the tarmac in anticipation of flight.

Chapter Fifty-Nine

Chad, Africa

African dawn broke over the cement plant. Abiye and Kamka slept fitfully on their mats in the shared portion of the twin holding cells. Esther lay between them with her eyes open and staring upward into the diminishing darkness. Next door, Michael Nasry was a beaten man. He seemed frozen into his customary sitting posture, legs drawn up to his chin, sleeping even more fitfully than his neighbors.

Like Esther, Rip Taggart remained awake on his side of the room. He sat with his back against the wall. Na'omi lay face down next to him on his sleeping mat. His hand rested protectively on her back. She stirred. He thought she was sleeping. Her eyes were merely closed to forestall the coming reality of another day in captivity.

"What do I tell the girls? Esther?" she worried in a quiet, resigned voice. Learning that they were to be returned to Boko Haram had plagued her waking and sleeping hours alike.

"If you get a chance to run, take it," Rip advised in a quiet tone to match hers. "If you can save just one of them, do it."

He felt her small body trembling underneath his hand. She sat up, turned to him, and folded herself into his arms. He held her tightly while she buried her face in the hollow of his throat and he stared over her curly black hair into space.

Michael across the room lifted his head. He looked numb as he gazed hopelessly into space.

The outer door opened, causing them all to startle. Nobody entered the prison this early in the morning. Opening the door allowed in more light and brought in Akmal, several Chechen guards, and two of Michael's three remaining male recruiters, further confirming Rip's assumption that something big was about to happen. Their heavy footfalls abruptly awoke Abiye and Kamka and made them and Esther cry out in alarm as the men stormed on through to the inner doorway. Akmal stood spread-legged in front of Michael.

"It's time," he announced, his voice flat.

"Where's Muttaqi?"

"You're dead to him already."

From the other room came muffled wailing as guards yanked Esther and her classmates off their floor beds and began zip-tying their hands.

"Teacher! Richard!" Esther cried out.

Na'omi sprang to her feet to rush to the aid of her students. One of the Chechens in the room intercepted and shoved her face against the wall while he zip-tied her hands behind her back. Another guard trained his rifle on Taggart as a warning for him not to interfere. Tears streamed down Na'omi's cheeks as the Chechen bum-rushed her out of the room. She managed to keep her eyes on Rip as long as she could.

A single word wrenched itself from Rip's gut. "Na'omi . . . !"

"Allah will watch over you," Michael called out to her.

And then she was gone, hustled on through the outer room and out the door into the plant. The three girls were too exhausted and terrified to even cry as they were likewise rushed out. Esther cast a last look at Rip through the interconnecting door. Rip reached a hand toward her.

"Esther . . . !"

The sounds of their swift exodus receded outside.

"Stand up," Akmal ordered Michael.

He zip-tied Michael's hands while one of the recruiters ordered Rip to his feet and bound his hands at the waist. Akmal unlocked Michael's ankle chain. He stepped to one side and flapped a hand at the door.

"Let's go," he said. His eyes avoided contact with either Michael or Taggart.

Michael faced Taggart for what he assumed to be the last time they met. "You should have shot me, too," he said before Akmal and two guards hustled him away.

Alone now in captivity, Na'omi and the girls gone forever, Rip paced like a caged cat, his ankle chain dragging and rattling on the concrete floor. Overcome with despair, he threw himself against the end of his chain in an attempt to wrench free. All he accomplished was to jerk his foot out from underneath him and deposit him hard on the floor, bruising his forehead and knocking the wind from his lungs.

He sat up when he caught his breath again and bellowed in rage. Howling in anguish and frustration, he scrambled to his feet and resumed pacing, pausing only long enough to smash his bound fists against the wall again and again until his knuckles were raw and bleeding.

Chapter Sixty

Chad, Africa

Michael's recruiters and the Chechens herded Na'omi and the schoolgirls from the cell, along a dimly lighted hallway, and then in front of offices with windows overlooking the large open loading bay that formed the center of the cement plant. Once again composed and stoic for the sake of her girls, Na'omi glimpsed Hatim al-Muttaqi's jackal mask of a face peering out one of the office windows. Her eyes flashed intense hatred as her guards drove her on past and onto the loading bay. Al-Muttaqi turned back into the office to finish packing his bags.

Several military trucks and a Land Cruiser sat parked in the bay, their drivers waiting nearby to receive evacuation orders. The loading dock doors thrown open allowed the first rays of the rising sun to stab yellow shafts across the wide floor. Guards shoved the African females into a fearful huddle at the edge of the floor, out of the way of other activities.

Akmal pushing Michael ahead of him soon appeared. "Don't do this," Michael beseeched his former comrade.

Akmal said nothing.

As the pair crossed in front of al-Muttaqi's nerve center, the Emir called out, "Akmal!"

Akmal pulled up short and waited until the office door opened. Michael and his surrogate father locked eyes.

"You will serve Allah now, Michael," the Emir promised.

That was it? The Emir stopped them to say only that, a farewell taunt before sending Michael to Boko Haram to be killed?

The Emir returned to more important business, saying to a nearby Chechen soldier, "*Kul lol-rejaal aan . . .* Have the men load the SEAL into the Land Cruiser. We're leaving now."

Akmal eagerly volunteered to take care of the "*ana b'ameloo.*"

"No. Take Michael to the loading bay and come back. I have something more important for you to do."

A stab of apprehension twisted cold steel into Akmal's gut, but he nodded obediently as he jerked Michael along toward the loading bay. The Emir returned into the office, leaving the door open.

"He's going to kill you now," Michael warned.

"Shut up! Just shut up!"

A cattle truck backed halfway into the bay and stopped with its diesel engine running. The driver stuck his head out his window and yelled for a nearby Chechen soldier to lower the tailgate. Guards rustled the African teacher and her students to their feet in preparation for loading.

Chapter Sixty-One

Chad, Africa

Sunshine rayed across a clear African sky, silhouetting three Black Hawk helicopters flying low above a mixture of forest and open plains. They streaked purposefully toward the nearby cement plant. The swift-passing choppers swayed grass, startled a flock of birds into flight, and stampeded a rare lone rhino. Bear Graves and his team were buckled into the webbing of the lead chopper. They sat in silence, weapons loaded and charged between their knees, faces grim encased in combat helmets. Terrain swept swiftly past doors left open for a quick "hop and pop"—helicopters in to the LZ, unass, and the back out again before the bad guys knew what the hell was going on. Raiders were hopeful that, *this time*, they would arrive in time to rescue their former team leader.

At the plant, Rip Taggart alone in his room-cell hunkered with his head lowered between his knees, his forehead bruised and his knuckles bleeding from taking out his rage on the cell. He looked up, puzzled, when Akmal retuned alone after disposing of Michael somewhere. A long look passed between the two enemies in which nothing was settled. Their expressions remained inscrutable, as unreadable as stone. Without a word, the terrorist bent and freed Rip's ankle from its chain. Rip took note of the long-bladed scimitar in Akmal's belt. He also noticed that Akmal's hands trembled slightly.

Still without speaking, Akmal escorted the prisoner from his cell, down the dusty hallway and across in front of the office spaces. The open loading bay had become a hub of frenetic activity with soldiers rushing about, gear being piled for loading, truck engines rumbling . . . Again, Rip had the impression that something big and unexpected was about to disrupt the training facility.

Rip finally located Na'omi and the girls on the far side of the bay nearest the loading dock doors. Guards seemed to be preparing them for loading into the bed of a cattle truck. He had no way of attracting Na'omi attention without chancing retribution against himself and, worse, against Na'omi and her students.

Akmal stopped Rip in front of al-Muttaqi's open office door. Inside, back to the door, the Emir appeared busy bent over packing a duffel.

"Emir?" Akmal said.

Al-Muttaqi turned, expressing momentary surprise at seeing the SEAL in Akmal's custody when he had expressly ordered other men to take charge of him. Akmal spoke up quickly before the Emir had a chance to recover and assess the situation.

"The SEAL has asked to speak to you."

Huh? Rip stared at the Emir, heard al-Muttaqi take in a ragged breath of confusion. Akmal quickly turned away. As he did, his body masked Taggart's bound hands from the Emir's view. In a final swift movement, Akmal sliced Rip's hands free with his knife, shoved him forward into the office, and closed the door on his way out.

Chapter Sixty-Two

Chad, Africa

Rapidly approaching Black Hawk helicopters like mirages in the rising sun barreled toward the cement plant now visible ahead on the distant horizon. Inside the plant, in al-Muttaqi's office spaces, a core of fear flickered across the Emir's face as he realized the SEAL's hands were free.

"Akmal!" he squalled in the acknowledgment that he had been betrayed

Now alone together, Rip Taggart and the Butcher of Khost were face-to-face after all the times they had played cat-and-mouse against each other in Afghanistan's Hindu Kush. Rip's head lowered and his eyes narrowed dangerously as he deliberately turned to the door and bolted it.

Outside the office, Akmal heard the bolt slide home. With pistol in hand and held alongside his thigh to conceal it, he waited with nerves jangling like bells in his ears for the SEAL to kill the Emir. Two unsuspecting Chechens rushed past him toward the hallway. Out on the bay men continued frantically rushing about to clear out and make the plant abandoned again before US SpecOps arrived.

Taggart advanced on al-Muttaqi across the room, wending his way through the debris of desks, chairs, and other discarded office equipment. The terrorist leader realized that he faced an extremely dangerous man and that, barring intervention, only one of them would walk out of this room alive. He backed away from Taggart's approach, one slow step at a time. His right hand reflexively reached behind toward his desk and the drawer where he kept the pistol he used to splatter Kashif's blood and brains on the wall. Black flies feasting on the bloody wall rose in a buzzing swarm and circled the room before returning.

"You won't get out alive!" al-Muttaqi vowed.

Rip kept coming, head low, staring, predatory. This man was something unique for al-Muttaqi. Terrorists targeted those who were helpless to fight back. Leaders of terrorists recruited others to do their work for them while they posted on Facebook and issued more threats through the international social media.

Al-Muttaqi's cadaverous face turned hollow in the eyes and jowls. His eyes bounced around in his head an instant before he lunged desperately for the pistol in his desk drawer. Rip was only a step behind him. Al-Muttaqi managed to grip the weapon, but not hold on to it. Taggart slammed the drawer on the Emir's wrist, cracking bones. Al-Muttaqi roared with pain.

Rip got in a punch that knocked off the Emir's *kaiffiyeh* and released his long gray-black hair in a spray. The shorter, hairier man charged to grapple with the SEAL. Locked together, they rolled across the desktop and fell to the concrete floor with Rip on top. Grunting and cursing, the two men pounded each other with fists, elbows, and knees while each tried to avoid becoming enmeshed in the Emir's long white robe.

Al-Muttaqi possessed the physical advantage. Although shorter than Taggart, he was heavily muscled and ruthless. On the other hand, Rip had been losing weight and strength during weeks of captivity, poor food, and torture. Only rage and raw hatred would likely bring him out of this encounter alive.

Outside the locked door, Akmal listened to the banging and crashing of the fight inside the office. His nervous eyes scanned the area to make sure no one realized what was going on until after it was over and he and Michael took control.

Out on the floor he saw the kidnapped schoolgirls already aboard the cattle truck and huddled together, terror-stricken. A guard lifted Na'omi bodily and hurled her into the truck on top of her students.

Michael was attempting to stall joining them as Chechen guards rushed him across the bay toward the cattle truck.

"Wait! Wait!" he cried out in Arabic. "I have something to say to the Emir."

"There's no time," a big Chechen named Ghessan responded. "Get in the truck."

Ghessan, in charge of the detail, chin-dipped at the other guards, who promptly grabbed Michael by the arms and bodily manhandled him onto the truck, depositing him unceremoniously at the feet of Na'omi and her girls. He rose to his elbows, glaring hate and defiance out at his former subordinates.

The fight inside the nerve center was brutal and ugly and not going well for Taggart as he wrestled on the floor with the heavier man, gouging and biting and thumbing and punching. Al-Muttaqi broke free and again dived for the pistol in his desk drawer.

This time he succeeded in reaching it. Pistol gripped in his hand, he whirled around to fire. But Rip was right on his ass and swiped his gun hand to one side just as the gun discharged. The sharp crack of the gunshot echoed throughout the plant. Akmal outside the door winced in alarm, feeling Rip might be dead. That wasn't the way it was supposed to work out. The way he planned it was for Taggart to "escape" and kill the Emir, after which Akmal became the hero by slaying the infidel killer. Michael would have called it a win-win situation.

After sweeping the Emir's gun aside, Taggart drove the web of his left hand viciously into al-Muttaqi's throat. The Emir dropped the weapon and, choking and coughing for air, clutched his throat with both hands.

Rip dived for the loose pistol. Al-Muttaqi was still dangerous. Although still hacking for breath, he tackled the SEAL before he laid hands on the gun. Entangled with each other, the mortal enemies crashed over a sleeping cot, breaking it into jagged pieces. They rolled on the floor, each seeking the upper hand to end the brawl.

Ghessan in the loading bay startled at the sound of the gunshot. He banged on the side of the cattle truck. "*Dawir el shaheena*!" he yelped.

The truck engine roared to life but remained stationary for the moment. Ghessan sprinted toward al-Muttaqi's office where the Emir had once again seized the advantage and had Rip pinned to the floor and was strangling him with both hands, his face and his fierce eyes only inches from Rip's, the foul odor of his breath blasting into Rip's nostrils with the toxicity of paint thinner.

Rip's vision blurred from air deprivation. He felt himself weakening as he approached the verge of lapsing into unconsciousness.

Ghessan shouted at Akmal as he sprinted toward the door. "*Wayne el amir* . . . ? Where's the Emir? What was that shot?"

"He's with the SEAL," Akmal responded quickly. "I can't open the door."Ghessan tried it himself. The bolt was solid. "Emir!" he called out.

The big Chechen hopped back a step and began desperately kicking the door with his size-twelve boot.

"Akmal, get help!" he shouted.

Akmal hesitated. The Emir would surely kill him if he survived the SEAL. In resigned desperation, his hand snaked toward his pistol. Good sense took over and his resolve faltered. There were too many witnesses who would rather shoot first and talk later.

Ghessan looked back from the door and saw the indecision on Akmal's face. He whipped out his own weapon and pointed it at Akmal.

"Get help *now!*"

Akmal nodded spastically and started toward the hallway where Chechens were clearing out rooms. Behind him, he heard another gunshot as Ghessan attempted to blast open the lock. He glanced back and saw the door remained intact. Out in the bay, soldiers and guards had stopped whatever they were doing to gawk in confusion, not knowing what was going on and without orders to guide them.

As Rip quickly weakened and ran out of breath, his hand scrabbled around on the floor seeking anything he might use for a weapon. He encountered an unknown object, an old rotary telephone base that had probably been here since the Soviets left. In a last attempt to save his life, he smashed the telephone against al-Muttaqi's head. Stunned, the terrorist rolled off the SEAL and next to the pistol Rip had knocked from his hand. Al-Muttaqi grabbed for it.

Before he could bring up the weapon and fire, Rip spotted a jagged wooden leg from the sleeping cot they had smashed into kindling. Up on his knees, he lunged forward at al-Muttaqi and with his remaining strength stabbed the splintered point of the leg down and deep into al-Muttaqi's throat.

Black gouts of blood spurted. Al-Muttaqi's eyes rolled back in his head, and the Butcher of Khost died as he had lived—violently.

Ghessan had found something with which to smash the window to the office. He reached through the shattered glass to unbolt the door and charged inside shouting, "Emir! Emir!"

Taggart dived for the gun still in the Emir's hand. Ghessan gaped at his fallen leader in his death throes and hesitated a moment too long. In one fast, fluid movement, Rip combat-rolled on the floor and brought the pistol up for a snapshot. The slug drilled the Chechen through his chest and sent him reeling back out the door.

Akmal had almost reached the entrance to the hallway when he heard more gunfire. He looked back in time to see Ghessan stagger out backward through the office doorway and collapse. Taggart appeared fierce and bloody with a gun in his hand and spotted Akmal, who had obviously planned to betray both him and al-Muttaqi. Maybe the Emir had been right; it was difficult to find loyalty among terrorists.

Taggart snapped off a quick shot at Akmal, who jumped back and fled down the hallway. During these few minutes of confusion before a general reaction set in, Rip stalked deliberately toward the hallway into which Akmal had ducked for cover.

Akmal made it to the other end of the hallway where it opened into other rooms. He poked his head around the corner as soon as the shooting ceased.

Taggart was gone.

Chapter Sixty-Three

Chad, Africa

Gunfire on top of the urgency to evacuate the cement plant and the Emir's unexplained failure to take charge left the Chechens running about in a state of disorganization with everyone shouting at everyone and vehicles kicking over their engines in anticipation of getting out while the getting was good. A couple of soldiers, who apparently observed Akmal under fire by the escaped SEAL, ran to his aid. The SEAL slipped away into the plant's interior.

Michael Nasry was as disoriented as everyone else by the sudden outbreak of confusion. In the back of the cattle truck he struggled in vain against the zip-ties that bound his hands.

"Akmal! Akmal!" he shouted as the truck jolted into gear and slowly exited the plant through the loading doors into crisp morning sunlight.

Events were now unfolding at warp speed all over the area of operations. At the airport FOB, White Squadron Commander Lee Atkins and other planners and leaders, including spooks, techies, and Intel dweebs congregated in the Command Center before the bank of HDTVs to monitor events. Satellite feeds showed the cattle truck emerging from the plant. Guards in the back of the truck kept watch over what appeared to be female hostages huddled together.

"We've got movement," an Intel asset droned. "Four men. And . . . And four female hostages. No visual on Taggart . . ."

After a moment, he added, "Looks like Nasry's in the back of the truck."

"Put it on the box," Commander Atkins requested tersely.

The squawk box on a table immediately began broadcasting back-and-forth chatter among the assault force.

"How far out is the assault force?" Atkins asked.

"Five minutes!" Bear Graves shouted in the lead Black Hawk above the throbbing of rotor blades and the roar of wind past the open door. He thrust out a hand to his team, fingers splayed.

Ortiz slapped Caulder on the helmet and showed him five fingers. Caulder passed it on to Fish and Chase, who relayed it to the other SEALs inside the chopper. Chase reached a hand up to rest on Buckley's Texas patch Velcro'd to his sleeve. Caulder turned back in his canvas seating to face out the open door and the terrain passing by beneath at fast speed. One of the helmeted SEALs in another Black Hawk flying parallel in formation above the treeline flashed a big cavalier grin and shot Caulder the middle-finger salute. Caulder laughed and returned it.

With Emir Hatim al-Muttaqi confirmed dead and no one to dispute Akmal's account of how it happened at the hands of the escaped SEAL, Akmal felt safe in taking charge to straighten out the confusion. He sprinted across the loading bay waving his arms frantically as the cattle truck exited the plant through the loading dock doors.

"*Woakef el shaheena*! Stop the truck!"

A Chechen in back guarding Michael and the female hostages pounded the top of the cab to attract the driver's attention. The truck braked to a slow stop. Michael sprang though the back opening in the tall sideboards. He spread the alarm as he cut Michael free.

"The Emir is dead! The SEAL killed him!"

The Chechen stared in disbelief. "Muttaqi is dead?"

"*Katelabou el SEAL . . .*" Akmal shouted back in Arabic. "The SEAL killed him. Michael is in command now."

Michael sprang to his feet. He was both surprised and confounded by his sudden turn of fortune. One minute he was a prisoner to be exchanged to Boko Haram forces, while al-Muttaqi was ordering evacuation of the plant. Now, the Emir was dead and Akmal had declared Michael in overall command.

"We must hurry, Michael," Akmal urged. "Let's take the truck and go."

"Where's Taggart?"

"Forget him. Let's go."

Michael's bushy eyebrows lowered. His eyes turned to vengeful slits. He saw everything clearly now. Taggart had somehow orchestrated this entire mess by turning Michael and Akmal against each other and al-Muttaqi against both of them. The Americans may or may not be coming, but that didn't mean Taggart would be allowed to escape with immunity. He would still pay for Omar's death with his own.

"I can't leave without the SEAL," Michael said with no compromise. "Akmal, you know that better than anyone."

The four Chechens in the truck were watching him. Now leaderless, they shuffled about uneasily, uncertain about what they should do. Michael raked his eyes across them one by one, making his assessment. At least one of the four was loyal to him. Two were neutral. The third probably leaned toward al-Muttaqi. Except al-Muttaqi was dead—and good riddance.

Michael snatched the AK-47 from the hands of the nearest guard, one of the neutrals. He stood with his legs solidly and defiantly planted and challenged "I am the Emir now."

He threw out both arms with the rifle clutched in one hand and lifted his head so that his voice rang back through the open door to the Chechens and recruiters inside the cement plant.

"*I am the Emir now!*"

Chapter Sixty-Four

Chad, Africa

Excitement and tension continued to build at the FOB. Satellite imagery on the *SAT* HDTV screen displayed the back of the cattle truck after it exited the cement plant. Michael Nasry stood legs apart with his arms spread, rifle in hand, while he shouted triumphantly.

"What the hell is happening?" the CIA agent puzzled. He looked at Commander Atkins. "Do we abort?"

Stern-faced, Atkins shook his head. "We need to get in there *now*. This is the only shot we're going to get."

He turned to the radio operator. "Update the assault force."

Bear Graves in the lead chopper listened to new instructions and intel coming through his comm headset. "Roger that," he acknowledged.

He quickly printed the message on a whiteboard to disseminate it to the rest of the team and the other SEALs in the Black Hawk. "Hey!" he shouted to get their attention.

He held the board above his head for everyone to see. On it he had sketched a rough outline of the main plant building, north side. An arrow pointed to the loading bay exit, with a terse notation underneath it: *Girls/Nasry.* Below this appeared a second note: *Hostage rescue.* With his marker, Bear underlined that one twice for emphasis.

He provided more detail through the team intercom. "Teacher and girls are by the door with Nasry. No visual on Rip. Remember, hostage rescue. Watch your shot placement."

The SEALs responded with nods of understanding or thumbs up.

Michael at the north door of the cement plant snapped his head toward the distant *Whump! Whump! Whump!* of approaching helicopters. Stunned Chechen soldiers stared transfixed at the sight of three gnat-like specks low in the sky that rapidly grew into the distinctive shape of Black Hawks. How had al-Muttaqi known? A calm descended over Michael as he regained his footing.

"Everyone inside!" he ordered in Arabic.

"You heard him," Akmal chorused. "Go, go."

Guards leaped overboard from the truck and hustled inside. The truck with Na'omi and the girls in it reversed through the loading doors and back into the cement plant.

Elsewhere, deep inside the rambling complex of structures, Rip Taggart on the run slipped out of sight into what appeared in the poor light to be a closed storage area. He removed his bloody tunic and tossed it aside. Standing there lean and unshaved, his hair dark and grown over his ears, barefooted and bare chested, wearing only loose shepherd trousers, he resembled some primitive savage on a blood quest against an enemy. He checked for ammo in the handguns he had commandeered from al-Muttaqi and the Chechen giant after he killed them. Only three cartridges had been fired from al-Muttaqi's gun. The other pistol was loaded with a full clip.

He looked up when he heard the thumping of approaching Black Hawks. A grim smile touched his thin, bruised lips.

Chapter Sixty-Five

Chad, Africa

Confusion had turned to controlled chaos as Chechen soldiers hurriedly geared up and took positions for the upcoming fight. Akmal, a Chechen himself who had been training his countrymen in Special Warfare tactics since he arrived at the plant, assumed control authority as he took his place in the open bay and waved and shouted men into action. Michael's three surviving male recruiters, who had been so full of courage when plotting the remote bombing of innocent people, looked terrified and completely out of their element when Akmal issued them weapons with which to join in the defense. The two female recruiters were dispatched to round up bandages and any available medical supplies.

"Get the heavy gun into position!" Akmal barked. "Hurry!"

Two soldiers popped into the bed of a three-quarter-ton utility truck and stripped the tarp off a DShK 12.7mm Russian-manufactured heavy machine gun, the rough equivalent of an American 50-cal.

Michael had his own priority mission. He strapped on a combat vest and grabbed an AK rifle and a pouch containing NVGs, a radio, and spare ammo.

"I'm going to get the SEAL. We can't have him at our backs," he informed Akmal.

His eyes fell on Na'omi and the three girls, Esther, Abiye, and Kamka, who had been thrown out of the cattle truck and now huddled together on the concrete floor.

"Watch them!" Michael ordered a Chechen named Zakir, pointing at the females.

"They're coming," Akmal yelled anxiously. "We need you here, Michael."

Michael acknowledged that with a nod, but nonetheless turned away and called out, "Farooq, Aziz!"

Two Chechens double-timed up to him.

"Michael—"Akmal protested.

Michael clasped his arm. "You've trained the men well, brother," he said. "Kill as many Americans as you can."

His gaze switched to Na'omi and her terrified young students. "This will be over soon," he assured them. In an afterthought, he added, "One way or another."

With that, he led the two soldiers deeper into the compound, disappearing. Akmal rushed to the loading doors with the rest of his defenders and looked out. It was at this door that the main battle for the cement plant would develop. Slanted rays of sunshine from the east flashed off the whirling blades of approaching helicopters. They were a few miles away at most.

Na'omi and her students held hands and looked up in fearful supplication as the sound of helicopters came to their ears.

The door gunner in the lead chopper slapped Graves on his helmet and held up two pinched fingers. Graves passed the signal along. "Thirty seconds!"

The countdown began. Calm and determined, the SEALs waited to get out the doors for the assault, weapons ready. Green canopy below turned to scattered trees and then to a wide brown plain with a dust trail of a road running out of the forest and across the cement plant compound and its main door. Graves and Caulder nodded at one another. *Here we go.*

At the FOB, an image of two enemy soldiers running out of the compound appeared on the *SAT* screen. The Intel tech alerted.

"Sir," he called out to Commander Atkins. "That's an RPG team."

"Push that to the birds. Now!"

Chapter Sixty-Six

Chad, Africa

Deep within the cement plant and its dank and dim cave-like atmosphere, Michael Nasry and his two soldiers, Aziz and Farooq, were on the hunt for Rip Taggart. But while they were on the hunt for *him,* he was on the hunt for *them.* Michael split up his men in a large darkened space cluttered with rusted and discarded machinery as they maneuvered to close in on the disappeared SEAL. Rip merged into the shadows among the machinery and, through eyes, ears, and honed senses, clocked the whereabouts of each of the three.

Gripping al-Muttaqi's pistol, he crouched motionless as a BDU-uniformed soldier crept from shadows into dim light and back into shadows, his head swiveling, eyes darting, AK-47 ready for action. Like a predator stalking prey at a water hole, Rip slipped soundlessly on bare feet from one concealment to another, keeping pace with the soldier as he angled to cut him off before he rejoined Michael and his comrades.

The soldier was wary. He halted every few steps to scan his environment. His breath quickened. Every instinct warned him he wasn't alone.

He ventured forward a few steps and froze. Rip moved with him, ranged out ahead on the man's projected trajectory. He crouched behind what appeared to be some sort of huge grinding stone. He heard the man's excited breathing, the steady shuffle of rubber soles on concrete. Fear could be smelled. It smelled like soured sweat. This man was afraid.

The soldier crept forward. Suddenly, an arm snaked out of the shadows and closed like an iron band around the man's neck, choking off his breathing and any attempt to shout for help. Rip rode him to the floor, holding on until the man's struggles ceased and he collapsed into Paradise—or wherever baby killers went when they died. It was done within seconds.

Rip kept low for another minute to cautiously check out his surroundings to make sure he hadn't been seen or heard. Satisfied, he rose, slung the deceased's AK-47 over his shoulder and frisked the body to claim a frag grenade, an extra full magazine for the AK, and a combat knife.

The *Thump! Thump! Thump!* of arriving helicopters resonated throughout the plant, counterpointed by the sounds of a number of enemy soldiers running up a far set of steel stairs toward the roof to fend off what might be an imminent infiltration. Rip waited until they passed out of earshot before he decided to give up on stalking Nasry and head back toward the loading bay where he knew he could find Na'omi and the girls. Arriving there took precedence over killing Nasry.

Almost as soon as Rip evacuated, Michael and the other soldier swept through the machinery and discovered Aziz lying face down in old grease and rat shit. Farooq rolled him over. Aziz's eyes had frozen open in a sightless bulge.

"*Ikhtasat* . . . His rifle's gone!" Farooq determined.

Michael suddenly knew where the SEAL was headed. He had witnessed the growing bond between Taggart and the teacher since the first day he stole them from Aabid. He shouted for Farooq to follow him as he doubled back through the machinery toward the loading bay.

"Akmal!" Michael barked into his radio, his voice strained and hoarse with foreboding. "Akmal. He's coming to you. He's coming for the girls."

Chapter Sixty-Seven

Chad, Africa

Black Hawks swarmed the cement plant like giant hornets. Crew chiefs in army matte-cammies and heavy goggled helmets leaned far out the doors into the wind over their mini-guns, secured to the bird by umbilical-like safety straps as they scanned for targets. Some suicidal fool on the ground hiding in a weed-overgrown washout outside the walls initiated the fight when he jumped up with an RPG and launched a rocket grenade at the lead ship.

The missile flew wide, not enough lead. Its contrail hissed a streak of smoke through the air that led back to the shooter. Mini-guns from all three choppers opened up with the screaming ratchet blasting of 20mm shells that furrowed across the ground and through the gunner, exploding him in a pink mist of flesh, guts and blood.

A truck technical with a DShK anti-aircraft machine gun mounted in the bed and manned by a driver and two gunners sped out from the plant's open loading doors and onto the outside road in an effort to obtain a clear field of fire on the helicopters and bring them and their troops down. The gun apparently malfunctioned. The two gunners struggled desperately to rack the jammed charging handle while at the same time maintaining their balance in the bed of the moving truck.

Finally, they got it working. The gunner squeezed off a green tracer that arced through the sky before the gun jammed a second time. Again, the gunners worked frantically to clear it, succeeding in unleashing another barrage of tracers at the fast flying targets before one of the Black Hawk crew chiefs lit up the enemy gun and truck and chewed it from front to back. Exploded pieces and chunks of metal and flesh splattered all over the countryside.

That took care of the enemy's heavy weapons. The Black Hawks split up and broke for their respective infil sites, harassed now only by pinging of small arms fire striking the choppers' metal skin. Akmal and his men at positions on and about the heavily-defended north doors sprayed the sky with AKs.

"*Jayeen*!" Akmal cheered. "Here they come. Glory and honor is ours!"

The SEAL tactical plan called for fighters to infiltrate the cement plant at three key points. Bravo Team's chopper banked steeply at full RPM to discharge its chalk on the south backside of the compound. Echo Team bounced toward the flat roof of the main facility. Delta's chopper with Bear Graves's team and supplements charged in low and fast straight ahead toward the field that lay north of the plant. This was the Chechens' most heavily-defended sector and the site where SAT had located hostages in the cattle truck, which had now retreated inside.

Bravo men attempted to blow their way through the south walls. The breaching charge produced a burst of smoke with no effect on the steel door. Bravo's team leader came up on comm: "*Bravo has a foiled breach. Move to secondary breach point.*"

Echo troops discharged on the roof and immediately engaged a group of Chechens. The brief firefight disintegrated into a running gunfight-retreat as the enemy scurried back inside for better cover and defenses.

The Black Hawk transporting Bear Graves and his team confronted a wall of lead and steel from the north door. They made a hot touchdown on a landing zone under fire. Men scrambled out onto the ground, leaping from the chopper even before its landing wheels kissed the earth. The bird leapt back into the air and reverted from transport to gun ship. Its red tracers pounded into the north building and its defensive points at and near the loading bay doors.

"Go! Move!" Graves urged his SEALs as Akmal and the enemy poured heavy fire at them.

Intel, spooks, techies, and Commander Atkins at the FOB stressed themselves in an effort to maintain cool as the AO ignited into action. Ironic that of all the technologies in the world, combat still came down to relying on boots on the ground.

Bear Graves split his Delta team into two mutually-supporting elements. Caulder led one with Ortiz, Fishbait, and a couple of other White Squadron SEALs. Graves took Chase with him, along with a PJ medic and two SEALs called Wes and Pee Dee.

"Break right!" Graves commanded.

Chase opened up with his heavy machine gun, laying cover fire for Caulder's element as it hustled in bounding overwatch toward the plant's loading doors, firing as it charged. He continued firing cover for Bear's men as they broke for a small circular structure of stone and concrete located a couple of hundred meters short of their objective at the north doors.

A Chechen sniper on the plant's roof armed with a 7.62 sniper rifle methodically took aimed shots at running, dodging targets on the open ground below. A round smacked through the calf of Pee Dee's right leg. He cried out and staggered to his knees. Almost immediately, he regained his feet and gamely in a strong limping gait made his way to the rock structure where he took cover with the rest of the team.

Off to Chase's left flank, Fishbait hurled a smoke grenade out ahead of his element. "Smoke out!"

White-gray smoke fizzed from the canister and billowed out clouds that quickly spread in the morning breeze across the flats, obscuring team positions and concealing men from barrages of bullets that whipped and snapped across the battlefield.

"Moving!" Caulder shouted to his element.

His men, who had gone temporarily to ground, sprang up and renewed their sprinting assault through the smoke for the walls. The Chechen sniper on the roof changed positions to get a better angle. Chase was waiting for him. He delivered a burst of 7.62 from his machine gun that chewed through the lip of the roof and tore the sniper into bloody hamburger. Threat eliminated.

SAT and thermal imagery of the three on-ground SEAL teams, along with radio chatter and gunfire, provided the SEAL FOB with a picture of what was going on. Commander Atkins watched Graves's two Delta elements, one with Caulder leading toward the bay doors, the other with Graves in command laying down cover fire from the circular structure.

"*Delta has one wounded, non-urgent,*" Bear reported via comm. "*Pushing to primary entry.*"

The Chechens were presenting a good accounting of themselves with a chattering thunder of rifle fire. Flat on his belly in the slag piles, Akmal fired bursts from his AK. One of his soldiers went down screaming with pain. Akmal directed another to drag him back into the relative safety of the plant.

His radio hissed. He could tell it was Michael, but he was barely coherent through all the static.

"Michael, you're broken," he responded. "Repeat again."

He broke off to shout encouragement in Arabic. "Maintain your rate of fire! Make your shots count."

A bullet thudded into the ground near his head and skipped in ricochet to smack into the plant's metal walls, erupting a shower of sparks. Akmal tried again to react to Michael on the radio. All he received was more static.

Inside the loading bay while the fight raged outside the cement plant's north doors, Na'omi, Esther, Abiye, and Kamka cowered on the floor while the Chechen Zakir kept herd over them. Abiye and Kamka buried their faces against Na'omi's breast, but Esther kept watching as men darted about firing guns.

Akmal suddenly appeared out of the turmoil and paused in the bay to shout at Zakir, "Zakir! Bring the girls here."

Zakir complied immediately by prodding the females to their feet with his rifle and driving them like cattle toward Akmal and the battle. The girls burst into visceral terror when they realized they were to be used as living shields.

"No!" Na'omi balked.

"Move!"

"No!"

Zakir yanked the smallest of the girls, nine-year-old Abiye, away from the others and thrust the muzzle of his rifle against her temple. She froze in terror, her eyes wide and pleading for teacher to save her.

"Move!"

Chapter Sixty-Eight

Chad, Africa

The enemy turned out to be more formidable than expected, exhibiting some tactics that mirrored those of US SpecOps. Bear Graves and his element kept low and under cover at the circular concrete structure and returned fire as Caulder and his SEALs maneuvered against the plant's outer wall. Breathing heavily, they occupied the corner of the building east of the loading door where most of the terrorist force were concentrated. Akmal's men had taken up defensive positions at a series of thick exterior supporting pillars and were laying down heavy fire against the American attackers.

Caulder dropped to his knees to peek around the corner of the building toward the door. Drawing no fire, he pulled and tossed a smoke grenade. It popped and hissed white billowing smoke in the midst of the defenders.

"Grenade out!" Buddha Ortiz signaled.

His frag looped high and exploded among the terrorists with a blasting burst of white light and fire that threw shrapnel in all directions, eliciting cries of pain and surprise from defenders.

Inside the plant, Rip Taggart was busy with his own maneuvering. He crept down a hallway that led from the machinery area where he had strangled the Chechen and relieved him of his rifle. He emerged at the mouth of the hall that opened at the back side of the landing bay, to the rear of defenders at the doors. Smoke and the flash-bang of exploding grenades obscured the terrorists from clear view. They flittered in and out of sight like ghosts in fog as they continued their desperate fight to hold off the SEAL assault.

Closer to him, he spotted Na'omi and the girls. They were clear of most of the smoke and action, but one of the Chechens was prodding and kicking them forward toward the doors. It was obvious what was happening. The terrorists were about to employ an old trick of hiding behind women and children to compel a ceasefire.

Taggart gripped his commandeered AK and crept closer, leaving the hall and darting into the shadows of supporting pillars and other objects along the walls. The Chechen was too busy trying to herd the reluctant females to pay attention to what was going on at his rear and on his flanks. His ears rang from grenade explosions and his eyes and lungs burned from smoke inhalation. The girls kept trying to elude him and run. They wept and sniffled from the acrid eddying of smoke and threw themselves on the floor. Losing patience, the Chechen shouted and cursed and kicked the children until they got up. The maddening noise of battle—explosions, rifle fire, shouting, screaming—added to his frustration and distraction.

A single rifle shot from inside the building and to the rear went unnoticed in the bedlam. Surprise and pain flicked across the guard's face before he plunged forward onto the concrete floor, a bullet through the back of his head. Na'omi endeavored to control the girls' mixed cries of horror and delight at witnessing simultaneously the terrorist's violent death and Rip's appearance among them. Rip had to pry himself free; all three girls wanted to hug him at the same time. He caught Na'omi's eye.

"We're going," he said, pointing to the rear.

He pulled vigil at the back edge of the smoke while Na'omi gathered the girls and fled with them into the plant's interior. Rip closed in behind as Na'omi and the students stampeded down the long hallway that led deeper into the cement plant's bowels.

Akmal was so occupied with the fight and blinded by smoke that he failed to notice that Zakir had not obeyed his order and brought up the hostages. By now, it was becoming clear that his only hope in getting out alive was to use the females. The bodies of dead terrorists lay strewn all over the loading bay. The pitiful cries of the wounded filled the plant like a scene from Dante's *Inferno*. American SpecOps forces were closing in from all sides and would soon power through the open north door.

"*Eerjaa*!" Akmal bellowed. "Fall back! Fall back!"

As Taggart and the rescued girls retreated from the one hallway into an intersecting one, they caught sight of Michael Nasry and his soldier Farooq returning on the run from the interior.

"*Stop them!*" Michael shouted furiously to no one in particular, since his soldiers were already occupied with surviving.

Before he or Farooq had a chance to open fire, Rip and the females disappeared down the adjacent hallway. Michael and Farooq experienced a moment of indecision on whether to chase Taggart or join the fight at the door. In the moment or so they mentally debated their next course of action, SEALs launched their final assault.

On the field outside at the low circular structure that Bear and his element used as cover, the PJ had finished bandaging the wounded SEAL's leg.

"Stay with him," Graves ordered.

Whereupon he, Chase, and Wes hurtled the concrete basin and plunged forward to where Caulder's attackers were slipping along the plant's outer wall toward the north doors. All at once, to the surprise of both SEAL elements, resistance suddenly ceased. The defenders were apparently withdrawing deeper into the plant to form a secondary defensive line, leaving behind bodies, smoke canisters hissing, and the receding pounding of fleeing boots. The concrete was slippery with blood.

SEALs seized weapons from the wounded to prevent suicidal attacks as they swept through the landing bay and into the plant's interior. An eerie silence replaced the thunder and roar of battle. Even the most innocuous sound—the scuffle of a boot, the click of a rifle bolt, a whimper—produced a hollow echo. By all indications, Nasry, Akmal, al-Muttaqi, and the few surviving soldiers were gone.

So were the hostages.

Chapter Sixty-Nine

Chad, Africa

Having discovered the loading bay abandoned except for the dead and seriously wounded, Bear Graves radioed a SitRep to Commander Atkins at the FOB. "*Fox Two Two, Delta One. We are internal at Alpha Zero One Zero.*"

A quick search of the area turned up no sign of Rip or the other hostages.

"They must be deeper in," Ortiz suggested.

Graves nodded. "*Fox Two Two,*" he radioed. "*No joy in Alpha. Moving south to Charlie One Zero.*"

"*Roger, Delta. Be advised Bravo has pushed to secondary entry post on east side.*"

Apparently, Bravo had not yet busted into the plant to enter the fray.

Caulder quickly and quietly took point to lead the team deeper into the massive complex, a rat warren of passageways, catwalks, rooms, pillars, and discarded equipment. A line of what had previously been office spaces when the cement plant flourished fronted the open loading bay. Caulder shot up a hand when he came across a dead soldier lying on his back outside an open door. The window in the door had been busted out.

Weapons up and ready, Graves, Caulder, and Buddha pushed into the poorly lit office to check it out while the rest of the team pulled security. A busted sleeping cot, papers, an old telephone, and other items scattered about on the floor seemed to indicate a brawl having occurred, a real donnybrook complete with fresh blood on the floor and dried blood on the wall.

A second corpse lay on the floor face up surrounded by a thick pool of fresh blood. This one was a sturdy man with a mullah beard and a white robe stained red. The end of a wooden stake, apparently a leg from the broken cot, protruded from his throat. The scene reminded Caulder of old vampire movies in which Count Dracula is staked through the heart in the final scene.

Ortiz knelt to check the face. "It's Muttaqi," he discovered.

"Holy shit!" Caulder reacted.

Ortiz snapped photos for debriefing and After Action Reports—and to prove the bastard was really dead. To Graves and Caulder, scene evidence indicated that al-Muttaqi was not collateral damage from combat, nor that he was the victim of some internal leadership dispute that would have left him either beheaded or with a bullet through the skull. Graves and Caulder nodded agreement at each other. A terrific fight ending in a stake through the vampire . . . It seemed the work of a skilled fighter like Rip Taggart. Did this mean Taggart was alive and here somewhere in the cement plant?

SEAL Team Six did in Osama bin Laden. It appeared Six may have been instrumental in killing Emir Hatim al-Muttaqi, the Butcher of Khost.

"*Muttaqi is dead*," Graves reported to Commander Atkins. "*Delta moving into Sector Bravo One One.*"

The team headed out tactically while Atkins and the CIA agent at the FOB exchanged startled looks. This was big news, but they had no time now to appreciate it. The mission was not over.

Bravo Team reported it had successfully entered the plant from the southeast quadrant. "*Fox Two Two, Bravo One. Good breach at secondary.*"

Echo Team on the roof had initially suppressed resistance. It was now encountering renewed opposition. Rifle fire cracked in the background of Echo's comm to Atkins: "*Echo has two wounded. Holding position.*"

Atkins immediately issued a new order. "*Ready the QRF.*"

Chapter Seventy

Chad, Africa

Michael, Akmal, and a number of their surviving soldiers in various locations pushed deeper into the dingy depths of the cement plant searching for the escaped SEAL and the female hostages. Akmal attempted to radio Lieutenant Abdul to go to the roof with some men to take on the onslaught of US SpecOps.

"Abdul! Hold them on the roof!"

He received no response, not even static. Extreme urgency infected his transmission. "Abdul, come in. *Abdul!*"

He turned off the mic. No use. He drew only one conclusion. "We're about to be overrun."

Michael was more optimistic. He still held a card to provide one last desperate chance. "We get to the hostages before the Americans do. It's the only card we have left."

Chechens spread out into another of several immense rooms encompassed within the main building. Here, laborers had once mixed lime and other ingredients in vats set among a series of grand cement pillars that extended from the ground floor upward through an open second floor to the ceiling. The concrete mixture was then transferred to kiln chambers on the main floor for drying and heating. Catwalks ran around the entire second floor of the building and intersected others extending above and across from side to side. Little light penetrated into the gloomy depths, which made for pockets of shadow and darkness. The smaller kiln chambers were without any light at all except for that which entered in strangled form through the small entrances.

Concealed with Na'omi and the girls inside the black of one of the kiln chambers, Rip cut the zip-ties that bound the hands of Na'omi and her students. He suddenly sensed movement in the outer pillar room. He cautioned the girls to silence by quietly placing his fingertip across their lips one girl after the other. A shadow blocked out what little light entered the kiln. A soldier stuck his head into the chamber for a quick look. A breathless moment passed while the fugitives clustered together behind the heater itself. One whimper, a gasp from the children, and it was all over. If forced to shoot, Taggart knew some of them would die in the exchange. Na'omi clutched his one arm in a fierce grip while Esther clung to the other.

The soldier soon moved on with the others. Their footfalls quickly receded. Rip emitted a reserved sigh of relief. He touched Na'omi's lips as a signal to keep the children quiet and hidden while he crept to the chamber's open back exit and peered out into the gloom.

The first thing that caught his attention was a square of sunlight that outlined the edges of a door high above them at the far corner of the catwalk. Obviously the door opened to the outside. He signaled to Na'omi, who made her way to his side. He pointed up.

"We get to that door," he whispered, "we get outside. The good guys will see us"

A nearby steel ladder beyond a darkened section of the pillar room climbed up to the catwalk. However, Akmal halted his group's exploration between the kiln chamber and the ladder, blocking access to it. His suspicious eyes scanned the huge room and penetrated shadows and the dark entrances to the smaller kiln chambers. He sensed too many places in here where people could hide and not be discovered without a more thorough search.

"Check back behind us," he instructed one of his soldiers, a rawboned man named Tarik.

Rip spotted Tarik returning across the pillar room, pausing to enter each kiln chamber. Rip motioned Na'omi and the children to hide the best they could. Like frightened mice at the appearance of the cat, they scurried into the darkest corner of the chamber. No way would they not be discovered.

Cautiously, leading with the muzzle of his AK, Tarik passed on by the chamber where the escaped hostages crouched in hiding. Talk about luck. But before they had a chance to catch their collective breath, Tarik spotted something on the floor. He squatted to pick up the severed end of a zip-tie. His eyes widened in sudden recognition of what this meant. He sprang to his feet and charged directly into the kiln chamber where he came face-to-face with Rip Taggart and the girls.

Rip was ready for him and beat him to the trigger. He squeezed off two quick rounds from his purloined AK-47. The concussion from the 7.62 bullets slammed the man backwards and dropped him to the concrete. The twin reports reverberated throughout the plant. Rip heard shouting and the drumming of footsteps.

"Come on!" he urged his little entourage.

Bear Graves and his team of SEALs blowing through hallways, pushing hard, also heard the shots from the unsuppressed AK. Caulder on point motioned them down a hallway toward the source of the gunfire. That put Americans at one end of the football stadium-sized room and terrorists at the opposite end, each element unaware of the other's presence, each charging blindly on a collision course toward a single objective. Which force reached them first was a matter of life and death for Rip and the girls.

Rip led the way with Na'omi and the girls running as hard as they could across the pillar room toward the steel ladder that led up to the catwalk and the sunshine-outlined door. All they had to do was reach the door first. *Freedom.*

Chapter Seventy-One

Chad, Africa

A round zipped past Taggart's head. Another sparked off the ladder railing near the fleeing girls. Rip dropped to one knee on a lower ladder rung and returned fire at Chechens running across the pillar room. The Chechens dived for cover.

"Na'omi, get the girls down! Now!" Rip shouted.

He lay out more cover fire as she and her students crawled behind a stack of steel plating left on the catwalk above. The door to freedom could have been a thousand miles away for all their chances of reaching it alive.

Rushing to the sound of gunfire, Graves's SEALs pushed on down a dark corridor that paralleled the pillar room, unaware of the existence of the inner room only a wall or so away where Michael, Akmal, and a Chechen soldier had linked up and were maneuvering to cut off the hostages from reaching the sun-outlined door. They stormed up a ladder that intersected the top catwalk to place anyone who tried to reach the door at a disadvantage. Michael called out to Taggart as the initial exchange of fire tapered off.

"Give yourself up! Save the girls!"

Rip succeeded in reaching the steel plating where he crouched down with Na'omi and her students. Na'omi shook her head as a warning for him not to negotiate with these people. They were ruthless liars.

"He'll kill us before he lets us go," she cautioned.

Akmal's plaintive wail of despair penetrated the sudden quiet. "We're not getting out, Michael. The time for talking is over. This is the day we die."

"Remember your village," Michael reminded him in a lower tone. "Remember Layla."

"I am."

But remembering seemed to help little.

Repossession of the SEAL and the girls provided Michael with negotiable assets for his and Akmal's freedom, their only assets under present circumstances. He had used the SEAL, the SEAL had tried to use him. That didn't mean he intended to compromise years of scheming a revenge for the death of his brother Omar. Sooner or later the SEAL would have to die.

"That's the deal," Michael bargained, calling out to Taggart. "Save the girls. That's what you want."

Taggart sized up his surroundings, taking in the escape door at the end of the long catwalk they were on. The only way they could reach it was to make a run through the open. He nodded to himself, working on a decision. He retrieved the commandeered grenade from his trouser pocket.

"Richard—" Na'omi cried out in alarm, afraid of what he might be planning.

"I'll just be a few steps behind," he promised.

"We're not leaving without you."

He squeezed her hand. "Lady, you're giving me a headache."

She realized that whatever he planned might not end well for him. His priority was to save her and her students, no matter what sacrifice it required of him.

"Right behind us. You hear me, Richard?"

"You're the boss."

Rip's eyes narrowed dangerously. He pulled the grenade pin but kept a grip on the spring-loaded handle.

"I'm coming out," he yelled for Michael's benefit. To Na'omi in a lowered voice, he said, "When I throw this, you get to the door. The good guys are out there."

"Richard—?" But she and the three girls nodded bravely.

Ready? Rip nodded encouragement and hurled the grenade. Not at Michael and Akmal, who were out of throwing range, but down from the catwalk to where the other Chechen soldiers had sought cover behind scrap machinery, pillars, and anything else big enough to hide behind.

"*Kounboula yadaweeya*!" Akmal warned with a frantic yelp.

As the grenade plummeted through the air, Chechens scrambled for the safety of the kiln chambers. Na'omi and the girls seized the diversion to make a break along the catwalk for the door. Esther brought up the rear, wringing her hands in terror and crying out with each step.

The grenade exploded with a clap of doomsday thunder in enclosed spaces. Chechens screamed as shrapnel tore into flesh. Rip immediately opened fire on Michael and Akmal and the other man on the intersecting catwalk to keep them out of action until Na'omi and the girls reached safety.

He dropped a soldier down below with a round and spanged other shots off the walls and railing near Michel and Akmal. The two terrorist leaders and the Chechen flattened themselves on the catwalk and returned fire.

Na'omi, Abiye, and Kamka reached the door. Bullets sparked in front of Esther, panicking her so that she fled back toward the steel sheets of plating. She tripped and fell on the catwalk where she lay curled into a paralyzed ball of fear Rip plunged to her rescue.

He was almost to her side when a round struck him low in the left side of the torso, stopping him in his tracks. His body went numb from shock. He staggered back, rapidly losing consciousness. He dropped the AK-47. It bounced off the catwalk and clattered to the concrete floor two stories below.

With his consciousness fading, he saw Akmal charging along the intersecting catwalks as though prepared to finish him off. Michael ran right behind him.

"No!" Michel shouted and knocked Akmal's weapon aside before he could fire it.

Akmal stopped to stare defiance at his fellow terrorist. That was as far as it went. Akmal's eyes bulged as he spotted a helmeted SEAL running along a side catwalk. He threw up his rifle and fired past Michael.

Bear Graves and his team down below unleashed precise fire that killed one Chechen. The others broke for cover in a firefight that raged only briefly before the terrorist soldiers fled from the field of battle, leaving Michael, Akmal, and a Chechen isolated up on the catwalk.

Na'omi hustled Abiye and Kamka out the doorway into the sunshine. That was when she missed Esther.

"Esther!"

She turned back onto the catwalk, eyes darting for the girl. She spotted her cowering where she had been caught in a crossfire between Bear Graves's team and the terrorists. Bear motioned for Na'omi to keep going and stay with the other girls.

At the same time, he saw Nasry and another soldier dragging Rip's body down a side passageway—and he saw the girl hiding. That gave him a split second to solve a moral dilemma. He either rescued the child and brought her out to sunshine—or he went after his former team leader. What would Rip have done?

There was only one answer. Bear went after Esther. He sprinted along the catwalk while Caulder and the others covered him with withering automatic rifle fire. He scooped up the child as he ran. Akmal leaned out from a doorway and popped a round at Graves's backside that caught him in his upper armor plate. Stunned by the impact, he stumbled and fell. Esther cried out as she tumbled from his arms.

Gasping for air, Bear crawled to Esther and used his own body as a shield. Bullets sparked and skipped off the steel catwalk. Akmal, overcome with martyr's passion, charged from the doorway directly at the SEAL and the child.

"*Allahu Akbar*!"

Fishbait caught the fanatical asshole dead to rights. His first bullet struck Akmal's chest plate and bounced off. It would have stopped an ordinary man, but at the moment Akmal had gone mad with fury and devotion. Fishbait tipped the muzzle of his carbine and tapped off two quick rounds that pierced the maniac's neck and throat and brought him down permanently.

Allahu Akbar that, asshole!

Graves was still struggling for breath. He managed to call out to Caulder. "Get Rip. We'll get the girls."

Caulder fell to immediately. "Buddha, Chase. On me."

The three teammates took off in the direction Taggart was last seen being dragged off the catwalk. Fishbait and Wes headed toward the door through which Na'omi, Abiye, and Kamka had disappeared. Esther, shaking with fright, clung to Graves.

"Shhhh! Shhhh!" he comforted her. "I got you. You're safe now."

Gaining his feet, he picked her up like a father would a child. Holding her tight, speaking softly, he carried her outside where Na'omi and the two other children stood blinking in the sunshine. SEALs from the QRF and from Echo Team ran toward them.

In the meantime, Caulder, Ortiz, and Chase closed on Nasry and the other soldier as they dragged Rip's comatose body into a dark tunnel that opened at the base of the cement plant.

"Get on your NVGs," Caulder directed as the three dived into the tunnel on the trail of Rip and his abductors.

Chapter Seventy-Two

Chad, Africa

Michael Nasry and the Chechen soldier with him dragged Rip Taggart through the entrance to the large black tunnel that skirted down off the floor of the cement plant near a set of concrete stairs going up to the next floor. Perhaps at some point in time, the tunnel had been a conduit for waste water, a secret passageway, or an escape route, which would have made sense considering the paranoia of the old Soviet Union that built it. Whatever it was, the two terrorists hustled Taggart into the black bowels of the plant.

Having regained consciousness, Rip was still weak and groggy and suffering excruciating pain from the bullet wound to his torso. Completely blinded by the tunnel's absence of light, he stumbled along, pushed from behind by Nasry and the unseen Chechen. The two of them were undoubtedly equipped with NVGs, judging from the speed and confidence with which they negotiated the tunnel.

Taggart knew his SEALs would follow no matter if the tunnel led to hell. Somewhere in the dark behind them, Rip heard the scuffling of feet, the occasional surreptitious footfall, the clank of a weapon or gear as SEALs entered the tunnel in pursuit.

Before taking to the tunnel, Chase combat slung his machine gun over one shoulder, barrel forward and ready for action. Ortiz slapped a fresh clip into his carbine. Caulder led his teammates cautiously into a black hole made manageable by space-age NVGs that provided white-gray illumination of a steep decline ahead.

Caulder's helmet tapped the low ceiling. He stooped slightly to accommodate it. The tunnel emitted the dank odor of a cave filled with bat guano. Dripping water *plop-plopp*ed from the ceiling and ran shallow rivulets down the floor. Caulder signaled his teammates that he heard splashing footsteps ahead. He picked up the pace. So did their prey.

The tunnel bottomed out and ran level for the length of a football field before it turned upward and soon opened into a room filled with more unusual machinery. It was as dark as before, but Rip realized it was a room and not a continuation of the tunnel when he stumbled into large vats connected to various machines and engines. Annoyed, Nasry jerked him back and shoved him in another direction.

Rip couldn't let his SEALs walk into an ambush. "Hey!" he yelled. "I'm in here!"

The darkness of the tunnel seemed to absorb the sound. He couldn't be sure if he had been heard or not.

"Shut up!" Michael threatened.

For further emphasis, the soldier with Nasry smashed his rifle butt against Rip's back between his bare shoulder blades. Rip staggered forward and fell to his knees. Michael jerked him to his feet and handed the wounded and dazed prisoner off to the guard while he led the way to a grated stairwell leading up out of the darkness.

Not far behind, the three SEALs in pursuit reached the bottom of the decline and crossed over the level area where the tunnel opened into the room of dead machines. Caulder peered around the corner through his NVGs and glimpsed the Chechen skulking across the foot of a moldy concrete staircase leading up and out. He snapped off a quick shot that slapped the man's arm and caused it to flop uselessly like that of a rag doll. The wounded soldier yelped in pain and took cover behind a steel box-like contraption.

Michael retook control of the prisoner. "Hold them off," he whispered to his soldier as he pushed Rip staggering up the stairs. The guard moaned but held his position; he was too badly injured to continue anyhow.

Caulder signaled for Chase to cover with his machine gun while he and Ortiz maneuvered through the jungle of jagged steel and discarded machines to flank the guard. Through his NVGs, Chase spotted the Chechen peek out his head from hiding. He unleashed a three-round burst of 7.62 that flickered and sparked with the impact of bullets on steel and concrete. The enemy soldier ducked for cover.

"Chase, cease fire," Ortiz whispered through his helmet comm.

He and Caulder crept through the graveyard of rusted stock and found the wounded soldier leaning against the wall by the stairs, his eyes closed from pain. He never knew what hit him. Ortiz's round blasted through his head like an axe through a pumpkin. Caulder bounded ahead and up the stairs with Chase and Ortiz on his heels.

The stairs led into another large area jumbled with even more detritus from when the cement plant was a thriving manufacturer. Daylight flooded in from a passageway on the other side of the room and silhouetted a huge cement mixer with a concrete stalagmite stuck to its lips. Michael tossed his NVGs aside and directed Rip ahead of him toward the light.

Even in his weakened condition, Rip attempted to slow down Michael's escape by snagging onto anything he could reach and pretending to fall. Michael knew what Rip was doing and had no patience for it. He manhandled Rip toward the lighted passageway. Keeping Rip alive for negotiation purposes offered his only hope of escape.

Caulder, Ortiz, and Chase lifted their NVGs when welcomed by light at the top of the stairs. Nasry had already anticipated their blundering into his trap. He opened up with his AK-47, but prematurely as it turned out. The SEALs had already pinpointed his location from a tapping sound on the floor transmitted by Rip.

Nasry's preoccupation in fending off SEALs closing in on him provided Taggart the chance he had been seeking. He lunged for Michael's rifle and succeeded in laying both hands on it. They struggled for control of the weapon, both men grunting with effort.

Rip had lost too much blood and strength. His bare torso was stained with red from his neck into his saturated shepherd trousers. With a desperate burst of strength, Michael cast him to the floor and obtained control of the rifle. He brought it to bear, the muzzle looking like the tunnel itself before Rip's eyes.

The two men glared at each other in a moment of truth. Rip knew he was about to die and that Michael would finally achieve revenge for his brother Omar. Michael started to say something, but nothing passed his lips. The two men formed an unmoving tableau for all of ten seconds before a rifle shot rang out. The bullet smacked into Michael's chest above his armored vest, dropping him to the floor next to Taggart.

Bleary eyed and dazed from effort and loss of blood, Rip saw Caulder rush forward, his carbine trained on the fallen terrorist. Michael was on the verge of shock. He raised his hands in supplication.

Chapter Seventy-Three

Chad, Africa

Although drifting in and out of consciousness, Michael Nasry still managed a long look at Alex Caulder bending over him. Suddenly, he remembered that face from a night in Kunar.

"You were . . . there," he stammered. "That night."

Caulder nodded.

"My . . . my brother begged for his life," Nasry said, his voice going weak. "I won't."

Dark eyes in his thin face burned with defiance. "Do it," he said. "*Do it*!"

Caulder's carbine remained trained on Nasry's forehead above the bushy brows. His emotions warred within the depths of his soul. This man was directly responsible for the brutal terrorist deaths of hundreds, perhaps thousands, of innocent people. He had gone through his savage life creating havoc and misery in the name of Allah, had in some twisted way lashed out in retaliation against his own native country that he blamed for having rejected him when in fact he had rejected it. Caulder wanted to kill the terrorist because of all these reasons, *wanted* to do it so badly that he began to tremble with resisting the almost-uncontrollable urge to just do it. It must have been that way for Taggart in Afghanistan when he executed the man's jihadist brother.

"Shoot him!" Chase urged, his blood still heated from battle.

That was what brought Caulder back from the bend, that blood lust in the voice of a refined and educated man from Harvard who could discuss Keats and Beethoven while at the same time harboring a devil in his soul. If such inclinations dwelt in a man like Chase, could they not infect anyone under the right circumstances? For the first time Caulder truly understood what happened to Taggart that night in Kunar.

He lowered his carbine, and, with a sigh, replied to Chase's exhortation to kill the prisoner. "I already shot him," he said simply.

He backed off as Michael closed his eyes and lapsed into shock. Rip lying on the floor next to Nasry looked up at Caulder, watching him, taking in what he did and, more significantly, what he did not do.

"Is that Nasry?" Ortiz asked.

Caulder nodded. "Yeah."

Buddha dropped on his knees next to Rip and tore open a pressure bandage.

"Where are the girls?" Rip asked.

"Bear has them. They're safe."

Safe. Enormous relief swept through Rip. *Safe.* That word circled in and out of his thoughts. He saw in his mind Na'omi's face. Esther's. Abiye's and Kamaka's. *Safe.* There had been times during these past weeks in captivity when he feared none of them would survive, that they would never be safe again.

"Can you move?" Chase asked him. "We got to get you moving."

Ortiz and Chase helped him to his feet. More SEALs from the assault force appeared at the top of the stairwell, calling out to avoid friendly fire. "Blue! Blue!"

"Over here!" Caulder summoned. He nodded toward Nasry as the SEALs approached. "Get that piece of shit in the helo," he said.

Bear Graves and Fishbait were outside the plant with Na'omi and the girls and a congregation of SEALs and Rangers when they heard the relayed news that Rip Taggart had been recovered.

"*Delta One copies*," Bear responded. He drew in a deep breath. The long journey to save Rip was ended. He turned to Na'omi.

"We have Rip," he told her.

It took her a moment to accept that it was true. She collapsed to the ground, covered her face with her hands, and wept with relief. Esther rushed to her side, stretched her little arms around teacher, and began to cry with her. Graves stared down at them.

It had been an eventful and tension-filled morning at the FOB for Commander Atkins and the rest of the Command team. Emir al-Muttaqi, one of the most sought-after HVTs in the terrorist theater, was dead. Other HVTs, like the American Michael Nasry and the Chechen Akmal Barayev were either dead or in custody. Boko Haram and Chechen terrorists in Africa had suffered important losses and setbacks. Today, the War on Terror had made progress.

HDTV screens at the FOB were tuned in to show SEALs leading female hostages to safety. One of the screens displayed Rip Taggart in a joyful reunion with his old teammates who had never given up on him. Confronted with this, it was all Atkins could do to control his own emotions and present a command face. He smiled and toggled his radio.

"*Fox Two Two, Team One actual*," he broadcast to the field. "*Good work, boys. Let's get them home.*"

Chapter Seventy-Four

Chad, Africa

"We're flying you to a base outside Lagos," Commander Lee Atkins informed Na'omi as he escorted her and her three students to a Black Hawk helicopter waiting on the hangar flight line.

Graves and Fishbait followed. Esther held on to Bear's hand. Fishbait brought the other two girls, carrying the youngest of them, Abiye, in his arms. All had been fed and showered and issued new clothing—short skirts, red blouses, and new black shoes for the children, a longer, more modest dress for Na'omi. She had scrubbed her hair into a black luster. She looked fresh and lovely in the afternoon sunshine.

"Your families will be waiting for you there," Commander Atkins further stated, smiling at Na'omi.

Na'omi had only one question. "Is Richard all right?"

"Yeah," Graves said.

"He told me about you," Na'omi said.

Bear wasn't sure how to respond, so he smiled and said nothing. He watched another Black Hawk preparing to land at the hangar.

Commander Atkins touched Na'omi's arm. "It's time to go, ma'am."

Na'omi had so many things she wanted to say to Richard. She lingered with Bear. "Can you . . . ?" She faltered. "Please, tell him . . . tell him thank you . . . For everything."

Bear nodded.

"God bless you."

She hugged the big man impulsively and kissed him soundly on his cheek before she gathered her students and ushered them toward the helicopter's open door where the crew chief waited.

Esther reluctantly released Bear's hand. SEALs were her new heroes, especially Mr. Richard and now Mr. Bear. She and the other girls continued waving vigorously out the Black Hawk's open door as the chopper's rotors began to spin up.

A Black Hawk arriving from the cement plant hovered and set down behind the one that would be transporting Na'omi and her students to Lagos. Rip Taggart lay inside the cabin on a stretcher with an IV hookup and a padded dressing around his middle. A pararescueman sat with him. Caulder, Ortiz, and Chase alighted from the bird and waited alongside it. Graves and Fishbait joined them.

"They got to fly him out for surgery, Bear," Caulder explained.

Bear nodded. He boosted himself into the cabin and knelt at Rip's stretcher. They had so much to say to one another, but no easy way to say it for such men and their guarded emotions. Bear merely gripped Rip's hand, saying nothing.

"Had to be you guys, huh?" Rip noted.

Bear grinned. "Had to be. We did it."

Rip grinned back. They did it. He pulled Graves closer. "How's that daughter of yours? You named her Sarah—"

Bear took a second to recover. Rip wouldn't have known about Sarah. "Yeah, Rip, we did," he said, burying the hurt deep inside as he always did.

Rip was back. The team was complete again. The five rough men crowded into the chopper with Taggart. Caulder flung his arms wide and embraced Bear with his Dennis the Menace exuberance. They shook hands, pounded one another on the back, and embraced in the heads back way of macho men.

Rip's eyes happened to shift outside the helicopter to the other Black Hawk where Commander Atkins had just handed Na'omi inside. She looked back at him and smiled with warmth and deep affection. Emotion suffused Rip's face. His free hand reached for her. Hers reached back.

The door to the chopper closed. In the next moment the helicopter lifted off the flight line, and Na'omi was gone. Rip watched the bird until it disappeared from view.

Na'omi with her face pressed to the glass of a porthole gazed back at the airport until it and Rip's helicopter merged into the African terrain. She settled back in the canvas seating and held Esther in her arms.

Chapter Seventy-Five

Virginia Beach

The C-17s went wheels down at NAS Oceana at dawn. Robert Chase and Fishbait headed to Robert Sr.'s home for breakfast. Ortiz, Graves, and Caulder underwent their regular decompression ritual at the Gulfstream Diner. It would be a few days yet before Rip recovered and returned stateside. After debriefings, the team had a few days off to readjust into their "normal lives."

Ortiz eased his Fusion along the familiar streets of the Cedar Crest subdivision—a tree-lined suburban neighborhood with mostly normal folks, dogs in the backyards, kids on the sidewalks with skateboards, two-car garages, and PTA meetings on Mondays . . . Ricky bubbled with barely contained joy at being home again after all that had happened to him and the team since they left on deployment. Nothing made a man appreciate peace more than having returned from war.

He had called Jackie from the diner to let her know he was coming home. She was waiting for him seated on their front porch stoop. She rose smiling and waving when Ricky drove up. She wore her go-to-work clothes—a stylish above-the-knees skirt and a white, ruffled blouse complimented by a red scarf. He jumped out of the car and ran to her.

"We got them, baby!" he enthused. "Rip. The girls. We brought them home."

He dropped his duffle and whisked her off her feet in his arms as they kissed.

"I'm so proud of you," Jackie said.

"I told you I'd take care of it, didn't I? Because that's what I do."

They exchanged a confidential moment before he scooped her up in his arms and, both of them laughing, carried her up the porch steps to the front door.

"Ricky, wait!"

He wasn't listening. He managed to get her through the front door, although not very gracefully. Still, they made it inside with her in his arms and not on the floor.

"My mother!" Jackie gasped through her giggles

"What about her?"

He had the bedroom on his mind. A small fierce-looking woman put that out of the question when she barged down the hallway toward them, her complaints trailing her like exhaust smoke from a worn-out Cadillac.

"You need to change the mattress in the spare room," Carlotta, Jackie's mother, nagged. "It's lumpy. I don't know how you think anyone can sleep in there."

Surprised, Ortiz set Jackie back on her feet. Carlotta barely acknowledged his presence as she proceeded to the kitchen to bang pots and pans on the stove.

Jackie shrugged apologetically. "I needed help," she explained.

Things had obviously changed while he was away. He began trying to reorganize things in his mind, to find perspective. "Okay. Your mom's visiting. That's good. I was gone. But, we got Rip. That means I can get out of the SEALs now, take that contracting job. And Anabel, she's not going to dance school anymore. So you can quit your job. Things can get back to normal."

Jackie let her first high heel shoe drop. "I'm not quitting my job, Ricky."

He had barely caught his breath from that one before Carlotta rushed back through like a winter breeze to drop the other high heel. "And I'm not visiting," she clarified. "I'm moving in."

Ricky's eyes switched back and forth between the two women. He felt cornered.

"I like what I'm doing," Jackie said. "I like that part of me."

"I-I don't understand," Ricky stammered.

"Yes, you do, Ricky. I know you do."

She let him catch his breath before hitting him with another high heel. "I don't think you should leave the team," she said.

That one caught him really cold. He stared at her, not knowing what to say. She kissed him quickly on the cheek and picked up her briefcase on the way out the door. "I have to get back to work," she cast back over her shoulder with a happy smile. "Let's do a party for Rip, okay?"

Jackie bounced out the door, leaving Ortiz alone with his fierce little mother-in-law.

"Close your mouth," Carlotta said. "Bugs will fly in."

Bear Graves drove home from mission, through his neighborhood not far from the Ortizes with its own nearly identical subdivision houses, trees lining sidewalks, and kids playing in their front yards. A red rose lay on the front passenger's seat of his GMC truck. He parked at his house and got out with his rose and his go-bag slung over one shoulder.

Eager to see Lena, expectant, he rushed inside and dropped his bag by the front door.

"Lena?"

Puzzled by the lack of a response, he walked deeper into the house. Everything was clean, orderly, cold and empty. She wasn't home. Something uncomfortable squirmed in the hollow of his stomach. He climbed the stairs to the second floor.

"Lena?"

His steps began to drag as he walked the hallway to the bedroom they shared. The bed had been neatly made, unslept in. He stared at her closet, feeling like a kid afraid to open the door because of the bogeyman inside. Finally, he did. Her clothes were gone. A note lay on the dresser. He read it, his face turning gray with dismay.

Walking much slower, his shoulders slumped and his head down, his heart wracked with suppressed emotion, he descended the stairs and stood at the bottom in the hallway for a few minutes, feeling the emptiness, feeling . . . *deserted, abandoned.* Like the cement plant in Chad or the Boko Haram village in Nigeria where everybody got up one day, moved, and left what remained to scavengers, rodents, and terrorists.

He placed the rose on the dining room counter where Lena would find it when she returned. *If* she returned, knowing she wouldn't. Without Sarah, the big house had been empty too long.

Alex Caulder's daughter, Dharma, strolled along the beach behind her dad's beachfront shack. It was difficult for a girl to maintain gothic while wearing board shorts and a blue tank top. Even her black lipstick was missing. The only thing remaining of her dark identity today being the white skunk stripe through her dark hair—and even that seemed to be gradually disappearing.

She was barefooted and splashing in the hiss and crash of the Atlantic surf. She saw her dad farther down the beach waiting for her on the sand and gazing out to sea. Two matching surfboards rested on the dune next to him. He nodded out at the ocean and the sun on it when she approached.

"What do you see?" he asked from his best Zen tone.

Dharma threw her hands wide. "Water?"

Duh.

He gestured for her to sit with him. She did, side by side. He had promised to teach her to surf today.

"Lesson one," he said, pointing, "You wait to look where the wave breaks. How it moves. Does it crash or does it crumble."

She had a question about something else. "I heard what you did. It's all over the news. That was you guys, right?"

"Maybe," he replied, and left it at that.

"Well, it's pretty cool."

He looked at her. "Oh, yeah?"

"Those girls? Back with their families. Yeah."

Caulder nodded.

"What going to happen to Rip?" she asked.

Caulder shook his head. "I don't think he ever thought he'd come home."

Dharma ruminated on that while she and her dad looked out to sea together. "The crash and the crumble," she said. "That's complicated, Alex."

"Yeah," he agreed.

A half-smile played on his lips. There was something like pride in it when he looked at her and saw an identical sardonic smile cross her face. Waves hissed at the sand. A seagull skimmed by low on the beach and squawked at them. Dharma laughed.

"So now what?" she wondered.

Good question, no easy answer. Go with the wave. He stood up in board shorts like hers and offered his hand. She took it and he pulled her to her feet.

"We paddle out," he said, and that was enough.

That was life. The two of them balancing boards on their shoulders walked down to the water, father and daughter together and the entire world before them.

Chapter Seventy-Six

SEAL Command, Virginia Beach

Morning light from the Atlantic slanted onto the several buildings controlled and utilized by SEAL Team Six. Inside Six Command, White Squadron Commander Lee Atkins pushed back from his cluttered desk and regarded Rip Taggart across from him with a mixture of approbation and genuine concern. Two weeks had passed since Taggart was evacuated from Chad. Now out of the hospital and recovering with bandages still wrapped around his ribs, he was clean-shaved and his hair neatly trimmed. In jeans and an open-necked untucked shirt, he appeared to have regained a few pounds from those he had lost during his long ordeal as a hostage.

"Just starting to look at my options," Taggart was explaining to his former commander.

Atkins burned a moment before responding, nodding to himself as he sought the right approach to the delicate matter of Taggart's legal status when it came to his shooting of the terrorist in Kunar Province over two years ago.

"We all feel for you, Rip," Commander Atkins said. "And I don't even know the half of what they did to you. But the hard truth is, now that you're back, there's going to be some tough questions about what went down that night in Kunar."

"There are no questions," Rip replied. "I did it. My guys weren't involved. End of story."

Atkins dropped his hands in his lap and leaned back in his chair.

"I need that to be clear," Rip continued. "Is it clear?"

The commander studied him for a long thoughtful moment. "It's clear."

"Good."

He rose from his chair to go. Atkins stopped him.

"Rip, I don't know what the White House is going to do. They could bury you for this . . .We can't protect you."

Taggart had already accepted that he would be going this alone, without the team. He nodded his understanding and started for the door. He paused and look back.

"Sir, take care of the team and the Command."

Chapter Seventy-Seven

SEAL Command, Virginia Beach

From the commander's office, Taggart headed out the back way to the parking lot in order to avoid running into the men he had known. It was too painful his being here and not being a part of it like in the old days. He reached his Ford truck in the parking lot before he caught himself. He sat at the wheel, engine running, looking out across the Atlantic in the direction of Africa, thinking about Na'omi and Esther and how his team, his SEALs, had not given up until they were all free again.

He couldn't just leave and disappear, he scolded himself. He owed the team that much anyhow—at least a last word, a good-bye, an explanation, *something*. He started the Ford's engine and skirted around the big building to the entrance that all the teams used through the Team Room.

As he approached down the hall, he overheard his guys in their cages laughing and joking and grabassing. Just like old times. He girded himself and stopped in front of the team leader's cage that had once been his, but now belonged to the team's new senior chief, Bear Graves. Graves saw him first.

"Rip! Hey!" he greeted.

Bear, Buddha Ortiz, Fishbait Khan, and Ghetto Chase were gearing up for a day's training in the Kill House, and, afterwards, perhaps a few runs through Monster Mash. The four SEALs mobbed Taggart, adlibbing a variety of rough greetings and some man hugs. They hadn't seen Rip since his return from Africa and his stay at Walter Reed.

"Easy, boys," Rip cautioned good-naturedly, wincing form his unhealed wound and a solid *embrazo* from Ortiz.

Bear spread his arms wide, displaying the cage. "What do you think? Like you remember?"

"Well. Still smells the same."

"There you go," Ortiz approved. "Like you remember."

Chase came up to shake Rip's hand. "I'm Chase, by the way."

"Sure you are," Rip said. "The hard charger with the MK-48."

"Everybody else's at the Kill House," Graves said, meaning Caulder and guys from the squadron. "Let me call them back."

Rip's palm went out to stop him. "No, no. You guys got to train."

"Forget it," Graves said. Rip was home; it was time for a celebration. "Beer lamp's coming on."

"Still got a mug with your name on it," Ortiz noted.

"Fellas, I'm good. Really," Rip protested. "Just came to poke my head in."

Ortiz rolled his eyes. Same ol' Senior Chief. Training always came first. "You coming to the party this weekend?" he asked.

Rip smiled. "Jackie making that guacamole?"

"You know she is."

"Then I'm in."

They group-smiled. Then it was back to business. "I'll get them started, Bear," Ortiz volunteered as he rounded up Fishbait and Chase and they headed out with weapons, helmets and other training gear for the Kill House.

"Rip—welcome back, man," Fishbait called back.

"Yeah," Chase agreed. "Good to finally meet you."

Graves lingered while the others went scuttlebutting down the hall. "How's the side?" he asked.

"Straight shot, went right through."

"Good, good."

Bear scratched his nose, shuffled his feet.

Rip noticed his discomfort. "You can say it, whatever it is," he invited.

Bear obviously didn't want to bring it up. But it was something he had to know.

"That video," he said, looking even more uncomfortable now that he had brought it into the open. "What you said. To us . . . Did you mean it?"

Rip was wishing he had never showed up today. What could he say—that he had let himself be used as a propaganda puppet for terrorists against his own people, his own country? That by betraying himself, his SEALs, was the only way he could have saved the other hostages? It was a decision he made; he would have to live with it. But he didn't want to discuss it.

Alex Caulder saved both Bear and Rip from further embarrassment when he came loping into the Cage Room. "Bear, you got that new holo-sight . . . ?"

He caught up in surprise and delight upon seeing Rip. He broke into that wide Dennis the Menace smile that said mischief lurked beneath the surface. But the smile faded when the expressions on the faces of his friends warned him that he had interrupted something serious.

"I'll give you guys a minute—" he offered and started to withdraw.

"Caulder, hold up," Rip said. He turned to Bear. "We'll talk about it another time."

Graves hadn't taken his eyes off Rip. But now he smiled and squeezed Rip's shoulder. "I'm glad you're home."

"Me, too."

Bear left the cage to Rip and Caulder.

"You look good," Caulder decided. "Moving like an old man, but good."

They grinned at one another. Rip sobered. He had something he needed to bring up. "Caulder," he said after a beat, "you were right. In Afghanistan."

"I don't know that anymore," Caulder admitted. Not after how badly he had wanted to shoot Nasry when he had him down.

"You were right," Rip insisted.

Do you remember what you said to me, Rip? About killing. That the hardest lesson to learn is when not to pull the trigger. And you said, "Watch out for the dudes who can't tell the difference . . ." If you can't control your emotions, Rip, you can't lead us.

Rip had left the team soon afterward.

"You were right," Rip repeated. "Every word."

Caulder felt as though Rip had just given him absolution. The air in the cage suddenly seemed stifling. "Well," he said, "I better get out there."

"That's the job."

"Uh, Rip. When you're up for it, why don't you come by the house, get a little beach time in."

"I'd like that."

Caulder smiled and left Rip alone in the familiar cage that had previously been his. He stood for long minutes letting his eyes trace every corner of the cage, every piece of equipment, every memory, as though this would be his last time. Then, quietly, he left the cage and exited Command by a door where he wouldn't have to run into any of the other guys.

Chapter Seventy-Eight

Virginia Beach

The blonde waitress at the Gulfstream Diner, with whom Alex Caulder was having his on-again, off-again fling, remembered Rip Taggart as the SEAL who came back from a mission and had his ritual breakfast of "three eggs over medium and crisp bacon." This time, he had breakfast alone in front of the plate glass window that overlooked the wide expanse of the beach and the Atlantic Ocean. Farther down, with summer in full swing, vacationers massed the long stretch of the Boardwalk and its beaches. American flags whipped and snapped in the wind. The SEALs' rescue of Taggart and the African teacher and her girls had dominated the media cycle since news of it leaked out.

Breakfast without the guys didn't taste as it should. Rip picked at his plate, then asked for the check. The blonde waitress brought it to him. He nodded his thanks. She started to rush off to her next table, but suddenly stopped and took a second look. She started to return to his table, but he looked so sad and withdrawn that she had second thoughts and kept going.

From his shirt pocket, Rip withdrew the colored drawing Esther sketched for him while they were held captive at the cement plant. Esther had drawn Na'omi and him in the middle with herself, Abiye, and Kamka on either side. They were all smiling and holding hands.

He was still musing over the picture when an older customer accompanied by a younger couple and their son of about eight or so—the All-American family—approached his table.

The man of about sixty wore thick eyeglasses and a cuffed shirt tight across the belly. "Mister Taggart," he said, "I hope you don't mind, but I'd like to shake your hand."

"Sure." Rip folded the drawing back into his shirt pocket.

"I don't care what anybody says about you, I would've killed that raghead too."

Rip folded into himself as he had folded Esther's drawing into his pocket. He looked at the older man, at the man's grandson, who seemed impressed and eager to shake Rip's hand and ask childish questions about what it was like to kill somebody. He sighed and took out his wallet to pay the check.

The man stopped him. "It's taken care of. If it were up to me, you'd never pay for another meal the rest of your life."

Rip made a point of leaving money on the table as he left.

"Come back, hon," the blonde waitress invited.

The TV at the breakfast counter was turned up full-bore as he walked out the door accompanied by the dramatic voice of a talking head with another "news flash."

"*. . . New details have emerged about the daring daytime rescue of former Navy SEAL Richard Taggart . . .*"

Was simply being left alone too much to ask for?

Chapter Seventy-Nine

Virginia Beach

Jackie Ortiz, her daughter, Anabel, and her mother, Carlotta, were bustling all over the house decorating for today's party to celebrate the team's safe return from Africa and the success of their rescue mission. The TV played another "News Flash" as Ricky, under his wife's tutelage, hung an enormous *Welcome Home* banner across the backyard among an array of American flags draped off the back deck and the privacy fence. The outdoor grill, picnic table, foldout tables, and chairs were scattered about the yard.

"*—and the kidnapped girls of Benin City, which brought an end to just under a month of captivity—*"

The front doorbell rang. Jackie, wearing her most colorful party dress whisked through the kitchen on her way to answer it. Mama Carlotta was busy preparing and arranging dishes of food on the counter as the small TV in the corner continued to blast.

"*—the President called the operation a clear message to America's enemies and lauded the courage and skill of the rescuers, calling them the very best of what America has to offer—*"

Jackie turned it off.

"The President was talking about Ricardo," Mama said, properly impressed.

"If he had something nice to say, maybe you can too," Jackie proposed as she headed on down the hallway to answer the doorbell.

Joe Graves stood on the porch with Ricky Jr., who had appeared from playing next door with a neighborhood buddy. Graves affectionately mussed the kid's hair. "There he is, man of the house," he teased.

R.J. grinned and playfully tapped Bear in the belly with his fist. "Uncle Joe's here," he announced enthusiastically to his mother when she opened the door. Laughing with the excitement of this special day, R.J. promptly disappeared again, waving down-street at buddies waiting for him.

Jackie took in Graves's appearance—slacks, white shirt, shined shoes . . . All done up and decked out to go a'courting.

"Lena's coming," Jackie informed him. "You'll get one shot. Don't blow it."

"Uh, okay. I mean, I won't."

Chapter Eighty

Virginia Beach

Rip Taggart was on his way to the Welcome Home party being thrown by Ricky Ortiz and Jackie at their home. Alone in his old Ford two-seater truck, he drove through a suburban American world he never thought he would see again—strip malls, gas stations, and neat little subdivisions tucked behind full-scale malls. Americans were busy going about their usual affairs, wonderfully oblivious of the violence and terror that marked much of the rest of the world.

Other team members, as well as SEALs, friends, and family members, had already filled the Ortiz backyard. There was a party going on with plenty of cold beer, snacks, music playing, and giggling children running about. Graves, Caulder, and Buddha Ortiz were grilling hamburgers over charcoal when Fishbait and Chase walked up.

"Beermeister has arrived," Fish announced dramatically.

Chase brandished two bottles of Jose Cuervo Especial. "And," he acknowledged, "he brought the Cuervo."

Fishbait promptly passed out clear plastic party cups, which Chase began filling from one of his bottles.

"Rip here yet?" Fishbait asked, looking around.

"Not yet," Ortiz said.

Caulder was busy providing lovelorn advice to Bear Graves. "Like I was saying, Bear, you need to get down on your knees, beg, crawl on your belly, whatever it takes."

"So," Bear replied skeptically, considering the irony of Caulder's tattered and stained love life, "*you're* giving *me* marriage advice now."

"Why?" Fish wanted to know. "Lena still at her sister's?"

"It's temporary," Graves said hopefully.

Leave it to Caulder to take away any sting by employing diversion and wit. "You guys met Buddha's new roommate?" he asked with an impish wink. "Instead of one Jackie, now he's got two."

He nodded attention to Jackie's fierce-looking little *mamacita,* who had ensconced herself on a lawn chair in the shade of the oak tree. She reached out and snagged R.J. as he ran past chasing a little girl with a red bow in her hair. She licked her fingertips and pressed down R.J.'s cowlick, doting on the kid.

"Go ahead and laugh, Caulder," Ortiz challenged. "But you're not careful, Dharma's gonna starting calling you 'Dad.'"

"Never happen." But he didn't seem that sure of it. Nor did he sound as though he might disapprove.

"Uh-huh," Ortiz badgered. "Man the grill, *padre*. You are *papa* now."

Ortiz headed inside to pick up another platter of hamburgers for grilling. Jackie, Anabel, and Dharma were kicked back in chairs on the deck in the middle of light conversation. Jackie smiled happily at Ricky and he kissed her on top of her head as he flew past. Anabel and Dharma were getting better acquainted by discussing their respective high schools. Dharma had gone gothic again, but in a more subdued version.

"So you're at Oceanside?" Anabel said to Dharma.

"Go Raiders!"

"How are you classes?" Jackie asked Dharma.

"Better question," Anabel cut in, laughing, "how are the boys?"

"They're *boys*," Dharma answered, dismissing them. "I date college guys."

Jackie looked at her in surprised disapproval. "You *what*?"

Dharma hedged. "I mean, not *date* date. Not technically."

From the corner of her eye, Jackie spotted Lena Graves arriving. Lena appeared to have dressed special for the occasion—and, perhaps, for a reunion of sorts with her husband. They had not seen each other since the team returned from Africa.

Lena's long blonde hair was done up in a coiffeur. A sleek black dress clung to her lithe figure. As Jackie got up to go greet her, she overheard Dharma say to Anabel, "Hey, you want an e-cig?"

Jackie stopped dead in her tracks to blister her daughter with *that* look before she caught up with Lena. The two women hugged and strolled together across the backyard among the other guests, avoiding the grill where Graves and his teammates were gathered laughing and grabassing, but in a more acceptable manner in a public venue with womenfolk around.

"You okay, honey?" Jackie inquired of Lena. "I'm glad you came."

Lena avoided discussing it. "Looks like a good party."

Graves had been waiting for his wife, hoping she would show up. He left the grabassing at the grill to wend his way across the yard to intercept her. Jackie gave him a pointed look. *Don't screw it up.* The big clodhopper didn't seem to know what to do with his hands and feet. But his eyes . . . They were on Lena.

Jackie discreetly dismissed herself. "I'll get some ice."

"I . . . uh . . ." Graves stammered when he and his wife were alone. "I left some messages, but, uh . . ."

There was little subtly about him. Like most SpecOp warriors, the only way he knew was straight ahead with all guns blazing. He took one of those deep breaths that helped him think.

"When are you coming home?" he asked bluntly.

Lena sighed and shook her head in exasperation. "Joe, not now. I'm here to see my friends."

She turned to walk away. He stopped her with a touch on her shoulder. "I'm ready to try again, Lena."

She studied him, eyes meeting his for a long, searching moment. "I need some time."

That left him in a dry hole. He didn't know where to go from there. Maybe he should listen to Caulder after all—drop down on his knees and weep and beg. Instead, he said, "Well, can I get you a beer?"

She almost smiled before she nodded acceptance and walked away to rejoin Jackie. Bear hurried inside to the fridge where Ortiz was getting out more cheese for the burgers.

"How'd it go?" he asked Bear

"I'm getting her a beer."

"It's a start," Buddha acknowledged.

"Yeah."

The kitchen opened into the straight hallway that led to the front door and the full-length windows on either side. Graves extracted two bottles of beer from the fridge. As he started to return to the back deck, his eyes strayed down the hallway. Through the door windows, he caught sight of an old Ford pickup parked across the street, Rip Taggart behind the wheel.

He drew Ortiz's attention to it. "He's just sitting there," he said.

It was, Bear thought, the saddest thing he had ever seen. A party going on and Rip out there by himself. He started down the hallway to the front door. Ortiz stopped him.

"I'll do it," he offered. "Get your wife that beer."

Chapter Eighty-One

Virginia Beach

"Amigo," Rip greeted Ortiz as Buddha walked across the street and up to where Taggart sat unmoving in his old Ford truck.

"You coming in or what?" Buddha asked him.

"Atkins said you might be getting out. Going to some fancy contractor."

"I don't know. Maybe."

"You in a suit. I'd pay to see that."

Ortiz smiled. "Come on in. Everybody's here for you. It'll do you good."

Rip hesitated, then resumed staring out the windshield. "Thought I'd drive back to Idaho. See my old man."

It suddenly dawned on Ortiz. This was good-bye. Rip wouldn't be coming back.

"You're gonna miss the guacamole."

"Best I ever had," Rip said. "How they doing?"

"Bear and Caulder?

Rip nodded.

"They're getting there," Buddha said.

"They are, aren't they?"

He looked across the street at the house. A banner stretched across the front porch read: WELCOME HOME, RIP! He looked down at his hands gripping the steering wheel.

"You keep an eye on them, amigo," he said.

Buddha nodded. There was so much he wanted to say, but there were no words for it.

"Kiss that beautiful family for me, okay?" Rip said.

He cranked up the truck and drove to the concrete pier behind the Beachcomber Bar & Grill, once owned by his ex-wife Gloria. Rip had heard after he came home that she had a son and was starting a new life with a *normal* guy who stayed close to hearth and home. She deserved that for all she had put up with him and his SEALs.

Rip quietly and slowly walked the length of the pier to where it extended out past the surf into deeper water. He stood at its very edge and for a long, melancholy time watched the Pacific undulate toward him and crash and hiss against sand. The sun hung low at his back in the west and stretched his shadow out over the water where bait fish skittered. A sand crab poked up its stilted eyes and looked him over. A black-and-white tern *scree*'d disapproval when he lit a cigarette, a habit he'd taken up after leaving the SEALs.

This pier was where Gloria mentally and emotionally divorced him shortly after the failed Kunar mission, where Rip shot Michael Nasry's brother. There had been a team drinking party. The others left about midnight. Gloria closed her bar and found Rip at the end of the pier tipping empty beer bottles off the railing and staring into the outer blackness, mumbling to himself. "What does anything matter . . . ?" He had already left the SEALs and resigned from the Navy.

Gloria quietly watched him. Tears glistened on her cheeks. Then she turned and walked away, leaving him staring into the inner darkness of his soul.

That was nearly three years ago.

Now, standing at the end of the pier, thinking, remembering, looking out over the sunset-tinged Pacific, he smiled to himself and unfolded from his shirt pocket the sketch Esther made for him at the cement plant. It depicted in crayon him, Na'omi, Esther, Abiye, and Kamka all together, like a family.

His gaze lifted to the Pacific's watery horizon. It was almost like, with a little imagination, he could see all the way across to the other side of the world. He was so absorbed in his reveries that he failed to note the approach of a slender young form wearing blue jeans and a hoodie with the hood down to reveal the face and head of a teenage girl with buck teeth, acne, and stingy straw-colored hair.

She retrieved her cell phone and hit *record* before she approached Rip, still looking out to sea with his back to her. The tide crashed against the sand and the pillars of the pier, masking the sound of her light footsteps.

"Excuse me."

Startled, Rip turned to confront a young woman holding a cell phone close to her breast. Her hand shook uncontrollably. Her other hand hid inside the pocket of her hoodie.

"Are you Richard Taggart?" she asked.

"Who are you?"

"Marissa. From Oregon."

The name meant nothing to him. Before he could inquire further, the pocket of her hoodie exploded. The bullet caught Rip in the belly and staggered him. Blood spewed between bare fingers clutching the wound.

"Michael told me about you," Marissa said.

She extended the revolver from the tattered remnants of her scorched pocket, her hands no longer trembling. She took aim and shot Rip again, the report echoing out over the ocean and back into the sunset.

Rip dropped to the concrete pier, on his back, motionless, eyes wide and staring into the pink-tinged sky. Marissa videotaped the body with her phone, then calmly turned and walked to a Honda Civic parked in a corner of the lot at the head of the pier. She slid into the driver's side and placed the pistol on the passenger's seat.

Now that it was done, Marissa Wyatt's hands began trembling again. For months now, Michael Nasry had been grooming her for just such an operation. The friendless teen asthmatic from the Pacific Northwest living with her grandmother had just proved herself one of Nasry's prize recruits. All it took was to make her a member of a team, provide camaraderie and purpose and a soccer jersey.

She took a deep breath to collect herself before she dialed a number on her cell phone.

"It's done," she reported.

She paused for the brief congratulatory response.

"Who's next?" she asked.

She listened. A fresh-faced smile lit up the otherwise homely face of a teen who might have been the girl next door in any American neighborhood.

Also Available

$14.99 paperback original
ISBN 978-1-5107-2208-8
Ebook ISBN 978-1-5107-2209-5